She's here again,

Drew McCasslin thought as he slammed his racket against the tennis ball. For the third time that week she was sitting at the same table. She hadn't been there when he'd started playing, but he'd known the minute she'd walked out onto the patio.

She was tapping a pencil against a tablet in a manner he now associated with her. Could she be another reporter? Yet she seemed impervious to everything going on around her.

Unaccountably he resented her indifference, which was irrational, since all he wanted was to be left alone.

He made up his mind. If she were still there when he came out of the locker room, he'd speak to her.

Dear Reader,

Two of your favorite authors are appearing in Silhouette Classics this month, and these early books should please those of you who have only recently become fans as well as those who are looking for a trip down memory lane.

Ever since her first book, Erin St. Claire has figured at the top of many of your lists of favorite authors, and with novels like *A Secret Splendor* to her credit, it's no wonder. That was her first Silhouette Intimate Moments, and it was in many ways a book ahead of its time. The issues it deals with, adoption and the feelings—and rights—of a child's natural mother, have been recent headline makers, but Erin's deeply emotional approach lets you know right away that this is not only a romance but one of the most affecting novels you may ever read.

But since Silhouette Classics brings you not one but two top-notch authors every month, there's more to come. Our second book this month is *Finders Keepers*, by Dixie Browning. With the warm, down-home touch that never fails to bring a smile to readers' faces, Dixie presents the story of Hallie Parrish, Trenton Northcutt and the truth about what families are really made of.

We hope you'll love these books just as much this time as you did when they were first published, and we hope you'll keep reading our Silhouette Classics every month. After all, a love this good just has to be better the second time around.

Leslie J. Wainger
Senior Editor

Erin St. Claire

A Secret Splendor

Silhouette Classics

Published by Silhouette Books New York

America's Publisher of Contemporary Romance

SILHOUETTE BOOKS
300 East 42nd St., New York, N.Y. 10017

Silhouette Classics edition published April 1988

Silhouette Intimate Moments edition published December 1983

ISBN 0-373-04611-1

America's Publisher of Contemporary Romance

Printed in the U.S.A.

Chapter 1

SHE'S HERE AGAIN, DREW MCCASSLIN THOUGHT AS HE slammed his racket against the tennis ball. For the third time that week she was sitting at the same table, the one nearest the ledge overlooking the tennis courts. The table's brightly striped umbrella partially shaded her face.

She hadn't been there when he and Gary started playing, but he'd known the moment she walked out onto the patio, which was an extension of the club's outdoor snack and cocktail bar. He had missed a ball when he let his attention wander to the graceful way she smoothed her skirt beneath her hips and thighs as she sat down.

"Better every day," Gary said to him as they met at the net to catch their breath, take a swig of Gatorade and towel mop rivers of sweat that saturated sweatbands couldn't absorb.

"Not good enough," Drew replied before taking a long pull at the bottle of lemon drink. Over the bottle's length, he eyed the woman sitting on the patio above them. Ever since the first day he had seen her there, she had inspired his curiosity.

She was bent over the table tapping a pencil against a tablet in a manner that he now associated with her. What the devil was she always writing down?

Slowly, he lowered the bottle from his mouth, and his blue eyes narrowed with suspicion. Could she be another blood-sucking reporter? God forbid. But it wouldn't be unlike an enterprising tabloid publication to send bait like that to trap him into an interview.

"Drew? Did you hear me?"

"Huh?" He swung his eyes back to his tennis opponent. A friendly opponent for once. "I'm sorry. What did you say?"

"I said your stamina has improved since last week. You're running my ass all over the court, and you're barely winded."

Drew's eyes crinkled at the corners as he smiled, obscuring the tiny white lines in his bronzed face. It was a smile reminiscent of the days before he had learned the definition of tragedy. "You're good, but you're not Gerulaitis *or* Borg *or* McEnroe *or* Tanner. Sorry, chum, but I have to be a helluva lot better than you before I'm ready again for the big fellows. And I'm not there by a long shot. No pun intended." The once-famous grin flashed again in the Hawaiian sunlight.

"Thanks," Gary said dryly. "I can't wait for the day I'm stumbling over my tongue and you've still got enough energy to jump the net when the match is over."

Drew slapped him on the shoulder. "That's the spirit," he gibed goadingly. He picked up his racket and twirled it with the absent-minded finesse that had come from years of thinking of it as an extension of his hand.

A cheer and hearty applause erupted from a group of female spectators. They were clustered on the other side of the fence surrounding the courts. Their vocal approval increased as Drew walked back to the base line.

"Your fans are out in full force today," Gary said with a taunting inflection.

"Damn groupies," Drew grumbled as he turned around and glared at the women who clung to the fence like hungry zoo animals at mealtime. And he was the feast. He scowled at them angrily, but that only seemed to stir them rather than to repel them. They called outrageous endearments to him and flirted shamelessly. One, wearing a brief halter top, peeled the side back to flaunt a heavy breast with his name, decorated with flowers and hearts and lovebirds, tattooed on it. Another had a bandanna, the kind he wore as a trade-mark sweatband around his forehead every time he played, tied high around the top of her thigh. He looked away in disgust.

He forced himself to concentrate on the ball as he bounced it idly, planning his serve, plotting to fire the ball across the net to bounce in the back corner of the serve box and spin out to the left, Gary's weak backhand side. One of Drew's "fans" called out a lewd invitation, and he gritted his teeth. Didn't they know that the last thing he was interested in was a woman? My God, Ellie had only been dead . . .

Dammit, McCasslin, don't think about Ellie, he warned himself. He couldn't think about Ellie when he tried to play or his game went straight to hell. . . .

"Mr. McCasslin?"

"You've got him," he had said cheerfully into the telephone receiver that sunny day in paradise when the last thing a man would expect was for his wife to die in the tangle of metal and glass of a car crash.

"Are you alone?"

Drew had pulled the receiver from his ear and looked at it in puzzled amusement. He laughed out loud. "Yes, I'm alone except for my son. Is this going to be an obscene phone call?" He'd meant it as a joke. He'd had no idea how obscene the call would actually be.

"Mr. McCasslin, I'm Lieutenant Scott with Honolulu P.D. There's been an accident."

He didn't remember much after that. . . .

Now he took up the ball and bounced it in his hand as though weighing it. Actually, he was trying to erase his mind, to wipe it clean of memories that made his insides churn. His eyes gravitated to the woman still sitting at the patio table. Her cheek was resting on her palm as she stared vacantly into space. She seemed impervious to everything going on around her. Didn't she hear all the commotion from the women at the fence? Wasn't she the least bit curious about him?

Apparently not. She hadn't so much as glanced at the tennis court. Unaccountably, he resented her indifference, which was irrational, since all he'd wanted for the year since Ellie's death was to be left alone.

"Hey, Drew," called out a singsong voice from the gathered fans, "when you're through playing with your balls, you can play with something of mine."

The *double entendre* was so blatant and so crudely bold that Drew's blood boiled, and when his serve sliced through the air, it was but a blur. For the rest of the set, he kept up that kind of anger-inspired play. When it was over, he'd granted Gary only two points.

Draping a towel around his neck, Gary wheezed, "If I'd known that all it took to get you to play championship tennis was a dirty suggestion from one of your groupies, I'd have rented them by the hour weeks ago."

Drew had already gathered up his tennis bag, zipped his racket into its holder and was heading toward the stairs that led to the patio overlooking the courts. "Most of them could be rented by the hour, I'm sure."

"Don't be too hard on them. They're your fans."

"I could do with more fans who are sports writers or commentators. Among them, I don't have one. All they do is tell the world that I'm washed up. Finished. Drunk all the time."

"You *were* drunk all the time."

Drew stopped on the step above Gary and whipped around to confront him angrily. His friend's face was guileless, open and damnably honest. What he'd said was true. Drew's anger dissolved in the face of such forthright friendship. "I was, wasn't I?" he asked on an embarrassed sigh.

"But not anymore. Today you were the old Drew. Blistering serves. Damn! Every time one came near me, I saw my life flash before my eyes." Drew laughed. "Well-thought-out maneuvers, strategy to take advantage of my weak left side."

A grin split Drew's mobile mouth. "I didn't think you'd notice."

"Like hell."

They were laughing companionably as they took the last few stairs up to the patio. Drew saw at once that she was still there, a sheaf of papers strewn over the table top, a glass of mineral water at her right hand. She was scribbling furiously on a yellow legal pad. He was going to walk past her table. It was on his way to the lockers, and he would only call attention to himself if he avoided passing where she was sitting.

They were almost beside her when she glanced up at them. The glance was a reflex action, as though they had disturbed her train of thought and she was looking up involuntarily to determine the source of that interruption. But she looked directly at Drew, directly into his eyes, and the impact of her gaze made his eyes narrow on her and his ears close to Gary's chatter.

Her eyes dropped immediately back to her paper, but not before Drew had seen that they were incredibly green and surrounded by dark, bristly lashes.

That was when he made up his mind. He'd make a

wager with himself. If she were still there when he came out of the locker room, he'd speak to her. If not, well, nothing was lost. He wasn't really interested in meeting a woman, any woman. It was just that this one intrigued him. If he were honest with himself, he'd have to admit that the main reason she piqued his curiosity was because she was so *un*curious about him.

Yes, he'd leave it to chance. If she were still there when he came out of the locker room, he'd at least say hello. No harm in that.

One other thing, he reminded himself. *Don't linger in the shower.*

Arden's heart was booming like a kettledrum.

It had been a full five minutes since he'd walked within touching distance, since she'd seen his face up close and in the flesh for the first time, and still her heart hadn't quieted. She blotted her palms with the damp napkin knotted in her fists. Ice rattled in her glass when she took a sip of her lime-refreshed mineral water.

He had looked straight at her. Their eyes had met. Briefly, briefly. Yet it had been like lightning striking her to see Drew McCasslin for the first time, knowing the bond that linked them together. Total strangers to each other, yet with a common secret they would share throughout their lives.

She looked down at the court where he had just played with such brilliance. A few months before, she'd known little about tennis, especially professional tennis. Now she was almost expert in her wealth of knowledge on the subject. Certainly she had a vast amount of knowledge on the career of Drew McCasslin.

A group of four ladies came onto the court, looking ridiculous in their designer tennis clothes and extravagant gold and diamond jewelry. She smiled at them indulgently, remembering Ronald's urging that she join the tennis league at their club in Los Angeles.

"That's not me, Ron. I'm not athletic. I'm not a participator, a joiner."

"You'd rather sit in the house all day writing those little verses that you lock away and don't let anyone see. For god sakes, Arden, you don't have to play *well*. I don't care if you can play tennis or not. It's just good for my professional image, not to mention the valuable contacts you could make if you're an active member of the club. Socialize with the other doctors' wives."

He'd settled for bridge. She never was a master of the game, but she played well enough to be invited to all the tournaments sponsored by the country club, and that satisfied Ronald's demands that she mix and mingle with what he considered suitable friends for a prominent doctor's wife.

Then Joey had come along and provided her with a viable excuse for curtailing her social activities. Joey had provided her with excuses for many things. Some, she wished she could forget. Would her son, her adorable, painfully sweet, innocent son, have understood that one life-altering decision? Would he have forgiven what she couldn't forgive herself?

She'd asked his forgiveness the day the pitifully small casket was lowered into the short grave. She'd asked God's forgiveness, too, for the bitterness she felt at watching an intelligent, beautiful child waste away in a hospital bed while other robust children played and ran and got into mischief.

Shaking herself out of her emotional reverie, she took another sip of water and mentally toasted herself for playing it just right with Drew McCasslin. It was public knowledge that since he'd retreated to his carefully guarded estate on this island, he'd avoided interviews and shunned publicity of any kind.

For days, Arden had occupied herself with thinking of a way to approach him. On the long flight over from the mainland and even after her arrival on Maui, she had discarded one plan after another. The only positive thing she'd done was to acquire a room at the resort and club where he worked out every day. His privacy had been guaranteed him by the management. This was the first day since she'd been watching him that he hadn't entered the locker room from the metal door that opened directly onto the courts.

Her only option had been to play it subtly, to make herself visible and see what happened. She would pretend to ignore him. It wasn't hard to see that his more forward fans irritated him.

And today he'd noticed her. Instinctively, she knew it. She'd given an impression of casual disinterest, but she'd been aware of every move he made. He'd glanced in her direction several times, especially after executing an outstanding move. He'd never caught her eyes on him. A famous personality like Drew McCasslin wasn't used to being ignored.

In his case, such conceit was justifiable. His blond hair was too long, but it suited his dashing good looks. His trim physique didn't show the ravages of his recent bout with alcohol. The tropically tanned arms and legs, which moved with the precision and power of a well-oiled machine, were the epitome of masculine grace, and contrasting with the bronzed skin was an eye-catching dusting of tawny body hair. He was somewhat broader of chest than most tennis players, but that flaw was readily forgiven by anyone who watched the play of those muscles under his tailored white T-shirts.

It was obvious that since the tragic death of his wife, Drew McCasslin had just as soon women not notice his virile appeal. No, she had played it just right, Arden congratulated herself. Today he had looked at her. Maybe tomorrow—

"You must have a lot of friends and relatives."

Startled by the masculine voice, Arden swiveled

around; to her dismay, she found herself staring into the fly of a pair of white shorts. The sculpted bulge behind that fly could only be produced by either very brief and very tight underwear or a jock strap. Either possibility sent a hot current rushing through her body.

She dragged her eyes away from Drew McCasslin's crotch and let them scale the long torso, which was clothed in a royal-blue nylon windbreaker zipped only halfway up to reveal a coppery chest furred with golden hair. His smile was an orthodontist's dream. Straight white teeth were set in a jaw too strong to be anything but stubborn. The blue eyes were as dazzling as they were reported to be.

"I beg your pardon?" she asked in a voice she hoped didn't betray her disabling nervousness.

"You're busy writing an awful lot of something. I thought it might be postcards home. 'Wish you were here.' That sort of thing."

His voice was clear, a true baritone in pitch, unaccented, his tone strangely intimate.

She smiled, remembering her act of nonchalant indifference. "No. Not postcards. There really is no one home to miss me."

"Then no one could mind if I joined you."

"*I* could mind."

"Do you?"

Elated but not daring to show it, she paused only a heartbeat before saying, "No. I guess not."

He tossed his canvas bag beneath the chair opposite hers and sat down. Reaching across the paper-strewn table, he said, "Drew McCasslin."

She took the extended hand into her own. "Arden Gentry." She was touching him! Looking at their clasped hands, at his flesh against hers, she marveled over the wonder of this being their first physical contact when—

"Are you on vacation?" he asked politely.

She released his hand and sat back in her chair, trying to dispel a feeling of lightheadedness. "Partially. A mixture of business and pleasure."

He signaled the waiter from behind the outdoor bar. "Do you care for another?" he asked, indicating her glass.

"Pineapple juice this time," she said, smiling.

"You're a foreigner, all right. You haven't had time to grow sick of the stuff."

She wished he weren't quite so attractive when he smiled. His blatant sex appeal distracted her from the reason why she had wanted to make his acquaintance, gain his confidence, if possible, become his friend.

"The lady wants pineapple juice, and I want about four glasses of water, please," he told the waiter.

"Yessir, Mr. McCasslin. You were playing well today."

"Thank you. Hurry with the water. I'm all sweated out."

"Yessir."

"You did play well," Arden said when the waiter hurried off to get Drew's order.

He studied her face for a time before he said, "I didn't think you noticed the match at all."

"I would have to be blind and deaf not to. I don't know much about tennis, but I know you're playing better now than you were several months ago."

"Then you knew who I was?"

"Yes. I'd seen you on television once or twice." He seemed boyishly crestfallen, and Arden's smile widened. "You're a celebrity, Mr. McCasslin," she whispered reassuringly. "People all over the world know your name."

"And most of those people don't make any bones about staring at me when I'm in public." It was a gently spoken challenge.

"Like your cheerleading section down there?" She nodded toward the fenced-off area where the groupies had collected. They had since dispersed.

He groaned. "Would you believe I began working out

here because I was promised anonymity and privacy? It's also about the best court on Maui. But we didn't take into account the fact that guests of the resort have access to the courts. When word gets out that I'm practicing—" He sighed in exasperation. "Well, you see what happens."

"Most men would be flattered by such adoration."

He scoffed at that and quickly changed the subject. "What is all this, anyway?" he asked of the papers scattered across the table.

"Notes. I'm a freelance writer."

His retreat was instantaneous and physical, though he didn't move. His eyes became cold and implacable. The sensuous curve of his lips thinned into a line of aggravation. Around the frosted glass of water the waiter had just delivered, his fingers flexed in anger. "I see," he said tersely.

She lowered her eyes and picked at the paper doily under her glass of juice. "I don't think you do. I'm a writer, not a reporter. I'm not after an interview. You initiated this conversation, not I, Mr. McCasslin."

When he didn't respond, she lifted her thick, dark lashes and looked at him. He was as he had been before, smiling slightly, friendly, yet guarded, just as she was. "Call me Drew, please."

He had laid down the terms of the truce, and she accepted it. "All right, Drew. And I'm Arden."

"What kind of writer? Novelist?"

She laughed. "Not yet. Maybe someday. Right now I'm trying to peddle anything and everything until I find my niche. I'd always wanted to come to the islands but never had. I lined up several articles to write to help subsidize my trip. This way I can stay longer, see more and not have to worry about the drain on my bank account."

He liked the sound of her voice, the way her head tilted first one way then another as she talked. It made her dark hair move against her neck and bare shoulders. The wind off the ocean lifted sun-reddened strands and tossed them playfully about her face before letting them rest against skin that had been in the islands long enough to be tinted a beautiful apricot but not long enough to take on that lined, leathery look that he found repulsive. Arden Gentry had exceedingly touchable skin. And hair. And lips.

He cleared his throat. "Articles on what?"

She went on to explain that she was doing one for the travel section of the *Los Angeles Times,* another for a fashion magazine. She was also going to interview a local botanist and do an article for a gardening publication. He barely listened.

For the first time since he'd met Ellie, he was interested in a woman. It surprised him because he had never thought he'd want to be deeply involved with a woman again. Not that this would go beyond sharing a drink or casual conversation. But having met Arden, he felt that he might one day get over Ellie's death and actually seek another female companion.

He couldn't help being conscious of Arden Gentry physically. He'd have to be a blind eunuch not to be. She was a beautiful woman. And she had a serenity about her that he found appealing. He tried to concentrate on that and on her soft voice and keep his mind off other aspects of her.

From the moment he'd sat down, he'd tried not to look at her breasts and speculate whether that firm shape came from a strapless bra beneath her green cotton sundress or whether she had such a figure naturally. *What the hell. Go ahead and look.*

He voted strongly in favor of the latter theory. For with the caress of the cool wind, he could detect the merest puckering of her nipples. He felt stirrings of desire that he thought had been buried with Ellie and didn't know if he were ashamed or glad to feel them again.

He hadn't admired a woman's body since the last time he'd made love with Ellie. Gross displays of flesh did nothing to turn him on. He had the same interest in a woman's body as any man, but this . . . this was something different. It wasn't merely the flesh he found himself liking about Arden but a personality, an evident intelligence, a certain disregard for his fame.

A spark of his old mischievousness flared. It made him wonder what she'd do if he leaned toward her and said, "Arden, please don't take offense, but for the first time since my wife died, I'm not disgusted by the way my body is responding to a woman."

There had been women. Bodies. Nothing more. Procured for him by well-intentioned friends who thought that erotically talented hands and mouths would cure him of all ills. If he could remember the drunken encounters later, he'd become sick with disgust for himself.

One night in Paris, where he'd publicly disgraced himself with a humiliating defeat on the courts, he'd found his own woman. She was the most sordid of whores. She was the punishment he doled out to himself. His penance. Later, when he was sober enough, he'd wept and hoped to God he hadn't been infected with something he'd have to be terribly embarrassed about.

That had been the turning point. The last chapter in the suicidal dissipation of Drew McCasslin. No one could save him but himself.

And then, besides himself, there was Matt to consider.

"How long have you lived in the islands?"

Arden's question yanked him back into the much brighter present. "Most of my adult life. After I began winning and making money on endorsements, it seemed like the ideal place for a bachelor to live. I was living in Honolulu when I met Ellie. She—"

His words came to an abrupt halt. He looked down into his water glass, and his shoulders assumed a defensive hunch. "I know about your wife, Drew," Arden said softly. "You don't have to apologize for mentioning her."

He saw in her eyes a compassion that was unlike the morbid curiosity he was accustomed to reading in inquiring faces. That alone compelled him to continue. "Her father was a naval officer stationed at Pearl. Eleanor Elizabeth Davidson. I told her it was too much for a woman her size—she was petite—to carry the name of a first lady and a queen."

"So you dubbed her Ellie." Arden was smiling encouragingly.

He answered with a chuckle. "Yeah, much to the irritation of her parents." He took a sip of water and drew idle circles in the condensation on the side of the glass. "Anyway, after she was killed, I wanted a change of scenery, so I moved here to Maui where it's much more isolated. I wanted to protect my privacy and shelter Matt from all the curiosity seekers."

Arden's whole body went still. "Matt?"

"My son." Drew beamed.

Her throat throbbed with the thudding of her heart, but she managed to reply. "Oh, yes. I've read about him, too."

"He's terrific. Smartest, cutest kid in the world. This morning, he—" Drew bit off his sentence. "Forgive me. I get carried away when I talk about him."

"You won't bore me," she said quickly.

"Given half a chance, yes, I will. Suffice it to say that he's been the one thing in my life recently that I could take pride in. We live right on the beach. He loves it."

Arden, striving for control, stared out at the horizon. The sun was a brassy reflection on the surface of the ocean. It hurt one's eyes to look at it from this angle. The island of Molokai was a gray-blue shadow against the northwestern horizon. Palm trees swayed with rhythmic grace in the gentle wind. Frothy white waves rolled in to kiss the sandy beach before receding.

"I can see why you'd want to live here. It's lovely."

"It's been great for me. A healing place, both mentally and physically."

He wondered why he was talking so openly to this woman. But he knew why. She inspired confidence and radiated understanding. A thick, sun-bleached brow arched quizzically over one of his eyes as a thought struck him. "You said there was no one at home to miss you. You aren't married?"

"I was. I'm divorced."

"No children?"

"A son. Joey." She faced him squarely. "He died."

He muttered an expletive before he sighed and said, "I'm sorry. I know how painful inadvertent reminders can be."

"Don't be sorry. The only thing I hate is when friends *won't* talk about him, as though he didn't exist."

"I've run into that, too. People avoid speaking Ellie's name, almost as though they're afraid I'll collapse into tears and embarrass them or something."

"Yes," Arden said. "I want Joey to be remembered. He was a beautiful child. Fun. Sweet."

"What happened? Accident?"

"No. When he was four months old, he contracted meningitis. It damaged his kidneys. He was on dialysis from then on, and I thought he'd live a fairly normal life, but . . ." Her voice faded into nothingness, and they were quiet for long moments, not even aware of the peripheral noises around them—laughter from a table on the other side of the patio, the whirring of the blender the bartender was using, a gleeful shout from the tennis courts below. "He got worse. There were complications, and before a suitable organ became available for a transplant, he died."

"Your husband?" Drew asked softly.

When had he taken her hand? She didn't remember. But suddenly she became aware of his holding it, rubbing the back of her knuckles with his thumb. "We were divorced before Joey's death. He more or less left Joey in my care."

"Mr. Gentry sounds like a real sonofabitch."

Arden laughed. His name wasn't Gentry, but she couldn't agree with Drew more. "You're right; he is."

They laughed softly and privately until they became aware of it. With the awareness came a flustered embarrassment. He released her hand promptly and leaned down to pick up his gear. "I've distracted you from your work long enough. Besides, I promised to baby-sit this afternoon so my housekeeper can go shopping."

"You have a housekeeper who tends to Matt? Is she . . . good with him?" Anxiety made her voice breathless.

"I don't know what I'd do without her. We had Mrs. Laani before Matt came along. When Ellie died, she took over and moved here with me. I trust her completely."

Arden could feel the taut muscles of her body easing with relief. "It's fortunate you have someone like her."

He stood and extended his hand. "I've enjoyed it, Arden."

She shook his hand. "So have I."

He seemed reluctant to let go of her hand. When he did, his finger tips lightly dragged against her palm. He wanted to do that to her cheek, to the underside of her arm, to her shoulder. He wanted to do what her hair did, sweep the skin of her neck and chest with seductive caresses. "I hope you enjoy the rest of your trip."

Her heartbeat had accelerated; there was a tickling sensation in the back of her throat. "I'm sure I will."

"Well, good-by."

"Good-by, Drew."

He took three steps away from her before coming to a stop. He weighed his decision for a few seconds before turning back. He was going to do something he hadn't done since he'd met Ellie Davidson. He was going to ask for a date.

"Uh, listen, I was wondering if you'd be around tomorrow."

"I don't know," Arden said with cool tact. Actually, she was holding her breath, offering up a silent prayer. "Why?"

"Well, Gary and I play tomorrow morning." He shifted from one sneakered foot to the other. "And I was thinking that if you were going to be around, maybe you could watch a game or two and then we could have lunch somewhere here at the resort."

She lowered her eyes, almost closing them in jubilation.

"If you'd rather not—" he began.

"No," she said quickly, lifting her head again. "I mean, yes, that would be . . . I'd like that."

"Great!" he said, his confidence flooding back. Why the hell did it matter so much that she'd consented? He could have a woman any time he wanted one. And not for lunch. But it had been damned important for Arden to say yes. "Then I'll see you here sometime around noon?" he asked, trying to steal a glance at the legs primly crossed beneath the table. Maybe she had thick ankles.

"I'll be here."

Her ankles were gorgeous. "Bye." His lips opened wide over a devastating smile.

"Bye." She hoped her own lips weren't visibly trembling when she returned it.

His easy, athletic stride carried him quickly across the patio. She watched him go, admiring the effortless way he moved and the athletic shape of his body.

She liked him! And she was so glad she did. He was a nice man. An extraordinary man, to be sure, but a man. Not a faceless, nameless question mark in her mind any longer. A man with an identity and a personality. A man who had experienced love and pain and bore them both well.

She had won his trust, and that gave her a twinge of

guilt. Would he have invited her to lunch if she'd told him who she was? Would he have been as eager to see her again if he knew she had been the woman artificially impregnated with his semen? Would he have confided in her so openly if she had come right out and said, "I'm the surrogate mother you and Ellie hired. I bore your son."

Chapter 2

IN HER ABSENCE, THE MAID HAD CLEANED HER ROOM AND left the air conditioner going full blast. Dropping her purse and notebook on a table, Arden first adjusted the thermostat on the wall, then slid open the wide glass door that led out to her private ocean-front terrace. The room was exorbitantly expensive, but the view was well worth every penny.

She drew in a great breath, and as she expelled it, breathed a name: Drew McCasslin. Her quarry. At last she had met him, talked to him, heard him speak her son's name. Matt.

It didn't take her long to peel off the sundress and wrap herself in a terry robe. She stepped out into the embracing Hawaiian warmth and sat down in one of two chairs on the terrace. Propping her heels against the seat of the chair, she rested her chin on her knees as she stared out at the seascape.

Drew had assumed that Gentry was her married name.

23

What he didn't know was that she'd thrown off that name like an animal shedding old skin as soon as she had filed for divorce. She wanted nothing to do with Ronald Lowery, even his hateful name.

Just when she'd think the anger was finally gone, it would sneak up and grab her, as it was doing now. It was as silent and intangible as a fog, but just as blanketing, just as blinding, just as suffocating.

Would she never forget the humiliation of that night he had first broached the subject? She had been in the kitchen of their Beverly Hills home preparing dinner. It was a rare evening when Ron came home directly after office hours. But that afternoon he'd called saying that no babies were due, he'd made hospital rounds early and he'd be leaving the office in time to have dinner with her. In a marriage that had quickly proved disappointing for Arden, even having dinner together was an event. If Ron was going to try to make things better, Arden would do her part.

"What's the occasion?" she had asked when he came in carrying a bottle of vintage wine.

He kissed her peremptorily on the cheek. "A celebration of sorts," he said offhandedly. She knew from experience that he liked to keep secrets, not for the pleasure they would eventually bring someone else, but because they gave him a sense of superiority. She'd learned long ago not to press him for information. More often than not, his surprises were unpleasant.

"The pot roast will be done in a minute. Why don't you go in and see Joey? He's in the den watching 'Sesame Street.'"

"For god sakes, Arden. I just got home. The last thing I want to do is listen to Joey's chatter. Fix me a drink."

Stupidly, she had obeyed. As was her habit. "Joey's your son, Ron," she said as she handed him his Scotch and water. "He worships you, but you do so few things together."

"He can't do normal things."

She hated the way he dashed down his drink and then shoved the glass toward her with an unspoken command to refill it. "That's why it's even more important that you find—"

"Christ! I should have known that if I came home with good news, you'd have to spoil it with your bitching. I'll be in the living room. Call me when dinner's ready. *Our* dinner. I want to talk to you about something important, so feed Joey ahead of time and put him to bed."

With that, he had stalked out of the room, and Arden had taken immense pleasure in noting that his pants bagged in the seat. When she had met Ron as a medical student, he'd been proud of his athletic physique. Too many cocktail parties later, his stomach was no longer flat and trim. His buttocks were getting flatter and his hips wider. He wasn't nearly as suave and debonair as he used to be. And he knew it. All he had to fall back on now was the gynecological practice that he had sacrificed everything else for. Even her love.

She made an effort that night to be congenial and attractive when she called him into the dining room for dinner. Joey had been shuttled away after a hasty and insincere kiss from his father. The meal she'd prepared was sumptuous. In those days, she had taken pleasure in cooking.

"Well, now," she said, smiling across the table at her husband as he finished his second slice of apple pie, "are you going to tell me what we're celebrating?"

"The end to all our problems," he said expansively.

The end to all her problems would be to see Joey completely well and living the normal life of a three-year-old. But she asked politely, "What problems? The clinic's going well, isn't it?"

"Yeah, but . . ." He sighed. "Arden, you know lately I've needed to . . . relax, have some fun. All I hear day in and day out is women griping about cramps or screaming in labor."

Arden swallowed a tart rebuke. Her father hadn't felt that way about the practice he'd spent a lifetime making one of the finest in Los Angeles. He hadn't felt intolerance for his patients' pain, imagined or not, the way Ron did.

"I've been gambling a little, and well . . ." He shrugged and grinned at her with what he considered to be boyish appeal. "I'm busted. In debt up to my armpits."

It took her a moment or two to absorb what he'd just said. Then a full minute to fight down her panic. Her first thought was of Joey. His medical care was incredibly expensive. "How . . . how much in debt?"

"Enough that I might have to sell the practice or put it in hock so deep I'd never get it out no matter how many brats I deliver."

The dinner she'd just eaten almost came up. "Oh, my God. My father's practice."

"Goddammit!" Ron roared, slamming his fist down on the table so hard that china and crystal clattered. "It's not *his;* it's *mine.* Mine, do you hear me? He was a country doctor with outmoded methods until I converted that women's clinic into a modernized—"

"Factory. That's how you run it. Without compassion or feeling for the women you treat."

"I help them."

"Oh, granted, you're a fine doctor. One of the best. But you have no emotion, Ron. You don't see that woman you're treating as a person. You only care about her checkbook."

"You don't mind living here and being a member of the grandest country club—"

"*You* wanted the house and the club, not me."

"When a woman leaves my office, she feels on top of the world."

"You have a terrific bedside manner. I know that, Ron. I'm not stupid. But it's all for show. You can charm a person into thinking you care for them."

He settled back in his chair, his legs stretched out in

front of him, ankles crossed. His expression was sly. "Speaking from experience?" he drawled.

She lowered her eyes to her plate. It hadn't taken long after their marriage for her to realize that all his romancing and professions of love had been to gain himself, not a loving wife, but a well-established, well-paying practice. "Yes. I know why you married me. You wanted my father's clinic. I think you purposely badgered him until he had his stroke and died. Now you have everything you want." Her anger had been building up to this point. Now she ended on a shout. "And now you're telling me that you're about to lose it all because you've gambled it away!"

"As usual, you're jumping to conclusions and not listening to half of what I'm saying." He poured a generous glass of wine and downed it. "I've been given an opportunity to make a lot of money."

"How? Drugs?"

He glowered at her but continued. "Do you remember when I got that baby for a couple to adopt about a year ago? They wanted no hassle, no red tape, just a baby with legal documents."

"I remember," she said cautiously. What was he considering? Black-market babies? It wouldn't be beyond him. She shuddered.

"I had an appointment with friends of theirs today. A *secret* appointment. Very hush-hush. Because they're celebrities." He paused dramatically, and she knew he wanted her to beg him for their identity. Later, she would regret that she hadn't. "This couple wants a baby more than any I've seen. They've tried everything for her to get pregnant. Nothing's worked, but he's been checked out. A loaded pistol if I've ever seen one," he said lewdly. Arden listened stoically, with no change of expression. "I said I'd see what I could do about finding them a baby to adopt with no hassle. But the woman said no dice. She wants this to be her husband's baby."

"I'm not sure I follow you."

"The fruit of his loins, his seed," he intoned theatrically. "They want me to find them a suitable surrogate mother and impregnate her with his sperm. *Presto!* They have a baby."

"I've heard of surrogate mothers. How do you feel about it? Can it work? Would you do it for them?"

He laughed. "Hell, yes, I'll do it for them for the money they're talking about. One hundred thousand dollars. Fifty for the mother. Fifty for me."

Arden gasped. "One hundred . . . They must be *wealthy* celebrities."

"All they demand is a healthy baby and absolute secrecy. Secrecy, Arden. Nonreportable income. They've said they'll pay me in cash."

It was unethical, if not illegal. She couldn't imagine any woman consenting to such subterfuge. "Where will you find a woman willing to have a baby, only to give it up?"

His eyes bored into hers, and a chill slithered down her spine. For ponderous moments, they stared at each other over the corner of the table. "I don't think I'll have to look too far," he said.

Her face drained of all color. Surely he couldn't mean *her*. His own wife! "Ron," she said, hating the note of desperation and panic in her voice, "you're not suggesting that I—"

"Exactly."

She bolted out of her chair and spun away, but he was a step behind her, nearly wrenching her arm out of its socket when he spun her around to face him. His face was florid, and he showered her with spittle as he growled, "Think for once, Arden. If you do this for me, we get all the money. I . . . we don't have to divide it with anyone."

"I'll try to forget we ever had this conversation, Ron. Please let go of my arm. You're hurting me."

"You'll hurt even more if your sweet tush gets booted

out of this house you love to seclude yourself in. And what about Joey? His treatments are eating us alive. And your precious father's legacy. Are you going to let it go down the tubes because of your sterling principles?"

She yanked her arm free and would have run from him, but what he'd said made her think despite the insanity of it all. She couldn't let Ron gamble away her father's life's work. And Joey! What would they do if they couldn't afford his medical bills?

"I'm sure this . . . this couple didn't have their doctor's wife in mind when they sought you out."

"They'd never know. They don't want to know the mother and don't want her to know them. They intend to pass the kid off as their own. All they want is a healthy woman to deliver them a healthy baby. A vessel."

"Is that all I am to you, Ron? A means of bailing you out? A money-making *vessel?*"

"Take it from one who knows. You're not using that equipment for anything else. You might just as well have a baby with it."

Her whole body sagged under the weight of his insult. It was true. The infrequency of sex between them was an ongoing argument. Arden didn't have an aversion to sex. She had grown up educated to it by her father's frankness, with a respect for its sanctity, with a healthy anticipation for it. What she did have an aversion to was Ron's kind of sex. It was without foreplay, without tenderness, without love. She had submitted for years until she couldn't stand any more and had begun to make frequent excuses.

Rather than begin that stale argument, which invariably led to his near raping her, she said, "I don't want to have a baby. Another man's baby. I have Joey to consider. I'm worn out half the time when I come in from the hospital. I don't think I'm physically up to it. Certainly not psychologically."

"You're up to it if you make up your mind that you are.

And forget that crap about another man's baby. It's a biological process. Sperm and egg. Slam, bam, one baby coming up."

She turned away in revulsion. How could he be so callous about a miracle he witnessed every day? She didn't know why she was even standing there discussing this with him, except that maybe she saw it as her way out, too.

"What would we tell people? I mean, when I came home from the hospital without a baby."

"We'd tell them that the baby had been stillborn, that we were devastated and wanted no funeral service, no memorial. Nothing."

"But what about the hospital staff? There are strict rules forbidding doctors to treat family members. How do you make the switch, give my . . . the baby to a woman who wasn't pregnant and pass mine off as dead?"

"Don't worry about any of that, Arden," he said impatiently. "I'll take care of all those details. Money shuts people up. The delivery-room nurses are loyal. They'll do what I tell them to do."

Apparently, he was accustomed to such intrigue, pulling off deals. Such things were foreign to Arden, and the scope of possible repercussions made her uncomfortable.

"How do we . . . do it?"

Now that he thought she was going to comply, his excitement heightened. "First we have to make sure you're not pregnant." He smirked a nasty grin. "But then that would be almost impossible, wouldn't it? I'll show them your medical history, which is without blemish. You had no trouble with your first pregnancy. We sign a contract. I do the procedure at the office."

"What if I don't conceive?"

"You'll conceive. I'll see to it."

She shivered. "I have to think about this, Ron."

"What's to think—" he began on a shout. But when he saw her chin lift stubbornly, he softened his approach and relied on his charm. "Sure. I know. Give yourself a few days, but they want an answer by the end of the week."

She told him her answer the next morning. He was thrilled. Then she stated her conditions.

"You *what?*" he snarled.

"I said that I want half the money upon delivery, along with divorce papers, signed, sealed and delivered. There will be no intimacies between us until I deliver. As soon as I leave the hospital with my money, I never want to see you again."

"You won't leave me, baby. If anyone gets dumped around here, it will be you! You care too much about the clinic's reputation to leave me."

"I did. While father was alive, it was everything it was supposed to be. I strongly suspect that under your auspices it will gradually begin to crumble. I won't be here to see it. It's no longer something I can take pride in." She drew herself up straight. "You used me to get the clinic. Now do with it as you will. I'll have this baby because the money will allow me and Joey to be free of you. You've used me for the last time, Dr. Ronald Lowery."

He'd met all her terms. He never told her, but Arden was fairly certain that his creditors were pressuring him. A desperate man didn't have any choice but to accept conditions. When she left the hospital that day, feeling soiled and used and empty, but free, she hadn't regretted her decision. The money her nine months' job had earned her would enable her to take better care of Joey.

But now, almost two years later, she had ambivalent feelings about her decision to bear the child of a stranger. The McCasslins had had their heartfelt wish granted when she bore a baby boy. He had enriched their lives and given Drew an anchor to cling to, a reason for living when the rest of his world fell apart. Shouldn't that alone absolve Arden of any guilt she felt? Why did she continue to fault herself? In any event, it was too late now to alter history.

She hadn't moved as she reviewed the event that had finally brought her to that lovely island. Now she stood up and stretched muscles that were stiff from having been in one position so long. She spent a quiet evening in her room, writing some, mostly wondering when she would tell Drew McCasslin who she was and how she could ask him to let her see her son.

"Hi." He jogged over to the edge of the court and looked up at her where she sat at her customary table near the ledge. "You look as cool as a cucumber."

"And you look as hot as hell."

He laughed, surprised. "And that's exactly how I feel. Gary's giving me a run for my money."

"I'd say he's getting his money's worth, too." Arden had been watching the strenuous match for the last two games, and Drew was playing at what she knew must have been his full potential before grief and too much alcohol crippled his game.

He seemed pleased that she'd noticed. "Yeah, well, I've managed to get in a few good shots," he conceded humbly. "I'm working up a hearty appetite for lunch."

"Don't rush on my account. I'm enjoying the exhibition."

He bowed at the waist and trotted back onto the court, calling to an exhausted-looking Gary that rest time was over. Drew took the next game without granting a point. On Gary's serve, however, the club pro came back with a vengeance. The game went to deuce several times before Drew took two points in a row to win the match.

Ignoring the cheering girls who had again collected like bright butterflies against the fence, he comically staggered over to the wall and looked up at Arden. "Isn't the matador supposed to throw the lady the bull's ear or tail or something to dedicate the bullfight to her?"

She laughed. "I think so, yes. But please don't cut off Gary's ear."

"I don't have anything to throw you except a tennis ball. Or a sweaty towel."

"I prefer the ball."

He tossed it up to her, and she caught it deftly, bowing her head over it in regal acceptance. "Order me four glasses of water and I'll be with you in a minute."

Arden watched as he slung his bag over his shoulder and loped off in the direction of the locker room. He waved at her once before disappearing through the thick metal doors.

Had he ever thought about the woman who had borne his child, she wondered as she signaled the waiter and ordered his water and another glass of iced tea for herself. Had he ever considered how she must have felt carrying a part of him in her body? Intimacy without intimacy.

The day Ron determined she was fertile—he had taken her temperature with a specialized thermometer for several days in a row—he told her to come to his office after hours. Naked and vulnerable, she had lain on the examination table, her feet propped in stirrups while he inserted what he called a cervical cup. Then he injected the frozen seminal fluid into the receptacle. It would hold the fluid against the door of her womb until she painlessly extracted it at home. With any luck, the results would be positive.

"You're getting no more excited over this than you do over the real thing, Arden," he said, leering down at her.

"Just hurry and finish," she said wearily. His lurid jokes no longer had the power to provoke her.

"Aren't you the least bit curious? Hmm? Don't you wonder what he looks like? Who he is? I have to admit he's a handsome fellow. Are you wishing you could get a little turned on beforehand so it would seem more official?" His hand grasped her breast and squeezed painfully. "I could accommodate you. Everyone's gone home."

She slapped his hand away, and he laughed cruelly. Did he truly think that slack-lipped, insinuating smile was going to send her into the throes of passion? She looked away as a lone tear rolled down her temple. "Just finish, please."

"We do it again tomorrow," he said when she sat up.

"Tomorrow?"

"And the next day. Three days while you could be ovulating." He leaned against the table and stroked her thigh. "Then we sit back and wait and see."

She prayed that she'd conceive on that first attempt. After subjecting herself to Ron's lewdness, she didn't think she could stand to go through with it again next month. Her prayers had been answered. Within six weeks, Ron was certain that she was pregnant. He informed the couple that their surrogate mother had conceived. He told Arden they were ecstatic.

"You be damn sure to take care of yourself," he warned. "I don't want anything to mess this up now."

"Nor do I," she had said, closing the door to the bedroom in his face.

She didn't think about the life she was carrying as a baby, a personality, a human being. She thought of it only as a means to let her and Joey have a better chance at happiness, free of Ron's greed and selfishness.

During the weeks of morning sickness and on the long, exhausting days she drove Joey to and from the hospital, she tried not to resent the fetus she could never let herself love. When friends congratulated her and Ron on the pregnancy, she forced herself to smile and accept their good wishes and Ron's proprietary arm around her shoulders.

The day she first felt the infant move, she knew a moment of incredible joy. It was quickly suppressed, pushed aside, hidden in some secret corner of her mind. Only at night, alone in her room, as she spread soothing lotion on her distended abdomen did she allow herself to wonder about the child. Would it be male or female? Blue-eyed or brown? Or would it inherit her green eyes?

And that was when she'd begun to wonder about the father, about whose seed she carried. What was he like? Was he kind? Would he be a good parent? Did he love his wife? Surely he did. She loved him enough to let another woman bear his child. Had they been lying together when he collected—

"Penny for them."

"Oh!" Arden gasped, flattened her hand over her chest and whirled around to see the subject of her thoughts leaning down over her, smiling. His hand was on the top of her chair, close to her bare back.

"I'm sorry," he said, genuinely contrite. "I didn't mean to scare you."

"No, no. It's okay." She knew her cheeks were burning and that she looked as disconcerted as she felt. "I was a million miles away."

"I hope the daydream was worth the trip."

His eyes were unbelievably blue against his dark tan, and they were ringed with thick, brown lashes, gilded on the tips. His teeth flashed whitely. He smelled wonderfully of soap and an elusive and expensive cologne. Apparently, he intended to let the sun dry his hair. Damp strands lay rakishly on his forehead.

Because of what she'd been thinking, Arden didn't want to see him as a man with a face and a body. A handsome face. A sexy body. Her cheeks burned as she thought of that life-generating injection Ron had made into her body. She looked away, wetting her lips nervously. "It wasn't really a daydream," she said lightly, dismissively, she hoped. "Just musings. The surroundings are hypnotic. The lull of the surf. The sighing of the wind. You know."

He relaxed in the chair across from hers. He was wearing ivory-colored slacks and a navy polo shirt. He took a long drink from one of the glasses of ice water and said, "Sometimes I can go down to the beach in front of my house, particularly in the evenings, and sit for an hour or more without ever knowing that time has passed. It's like sleeping, except I'm not asleep."

"I think our minds have a way of shutting down when they know we need escape."

"Ah-ha, so that's what you were doing. Trying to escape me."

Arden laughed, thinking that no woman in her right mind would want to escape a man who looked like him when he smiled. "No. Not before you buy my lunch, anyway," she teased.

"That sounds like Matt. He demands a treat before he grants a hug and a kiss." When he saw her startled expression, he cursed under his breath. "Arden, ah . . . hell. Arden, I didn't mean that the way it sounded. There are no strings attached to this lunch. I mean . . ."

"I know what you meant," she said, smiling again. "And I didn't take offense. Truly."

He partially lowered one eyelid as he assessed her mouth, making no secret of the fact that it appealed to him. "It bears thinking about, though, doesn't it? Kissing, that is."

"I don't know," she said gruffly.

She had debated all morning over what to wear. Now she wished she hadn't been quite so adventurous. For months after Joey's death, she had wallowed in misery, letting herself become slovenly. Before she embarked on this mission, she had exercised diligently, begun eating right, worked on her nails, her complexion, had her hair cut and bought a new wardrobe of coordinates that stretched her limited budget. She was amazed at the results. Had Ron repressed her that much? She looked better than she ever had. That day was no exception.

The black, elasticized, strapless tube top clung provocatively to her breasts, detailing every nuance of their shape. The trim white skirt was fashionably cut and buttoned down the left side from waist to hem. She'd left the buttons undone halfway up her thigh. Her legs looked tanned and silky against the white cloth. Her sandals were flat-heeled black patent leather and had thongs that wrapped around her ankles. Her only jewelry was a white bangle bracelet and large white hoops in her ears.

Standing in front of the mirror in her room, she had thought she looked smart. Smart and chic. Why was she now feeling she had dressed seductively?

Because Drew's eyes, taking a long, appraising tour with evident appreciation for everything he saw, made her feel seductive. She knew he could detect the hardening of her nipples. She'd never thought of herself as a sensual person, but now, with those azure eyes lazily tracking her, every sensory receptor in her body seemed to be going wild.

"Maybe we should start with lunch and go on from there," he said when his eyes eventually returned to hers.

"All right."

Chapter 3

HE ESCORTED HER TO ONE OF THE RESTAURANTS IN THE resort. With a deference reserved for VIPs, the maître d' seated them at an ocean-view table. Though the luncheon diners were dressed in casual clothes for the most part, there was an underlying elegance to the room with its mint-green and peach décor, black lacquered chairs and vases of fresh flowers scattered throughout.

"Cocktails, sir?" the waiter asked.

"Arden?"

"A virgin Mary, please."

"Perrier and lime," Drew said to the waiter, who backed away with a silent nod.

Drew reached for a bread stick, snapped it in two and handed her one half. "Did you order that on my account?" he asked in clipped tones.

"What?" She bristled at his curtness. "The drink?"

"The drink that isn't really a 'drink.' If you want something else, order it." He had the appearance of a tightly wound coil about to spring. "I promise not to grab it from you and guzzle it down. I'm past the sweating and shaking stage." As though to prove that, he was taking inordinate care in buttering his half of the bread stick.

Arden set her bread stick on the plate and folded her clenched hands in her lap. "I'll order what I please, Mr. McCasslin." Her frigid declaration brought his head up. "If anyone knows your name, he knows you had a drinking problem. But please don't talk to me like I'm some missionary who has appointed herself to rescue you from demon rum. If I didn't think you were past your sweating and shaking stage, I wouldn't be here with you in the first place."

"I've made you mad."

"Yes, you have. And I'll thank you never to do my thinking for me again."

The waiter brought their drinks and placed menus in front of them. Arden stared levelly at Drew across the table. She was nettled and was making no secret of it.

"I'm sorry," he said when the waiter withdrew. "I'm sensitive to criticism, even though lately I've deserved every word of it. I've become the classic paranoid, looking for slights when none are there."

She was studying the pattern of the silver and cursing herself for being so prickly. Did she want to win his friendship or scare him off? When she lifted her green eyes, they had softened considerably. "I'm sorry, too. For years I let my husband do my thinking and speaking for me. It's a dangerous rut for a woman, or anyone, to get into. I think we touched sore spots at the same time." Diplomatically, she smiled and lifted her glass. "Besides, I *like* tomato juice."

Laughing, he raised his own glass and clinked it against hers. "To the loveliest lady on the island. From now on, I'll take everything you say or do at face value."

She wished he had composed another toast, one that had less to do with honesty, but she smiled back at him.

"What do you like to eat?" He opened the embossed menu.

"Name it."

"Liver."

She burst out with a spontaneous laugh. "That's the one thing I *won't* eat in any form or fashion."

His grin was wide and white and wonderful. "Good. I can't stand the stuff, either. I think this friendship was predestined."

As Arden scanned the menu, she couldn't help thinking that Matt would probably grow up hating liver, too.

She ordered a shrimp salad that was served in a fresh pineapple boat garnished with avocado and orchids. It was almost too pretty to eat. Drew had a small filet and garden salad. During lunch, they got acquainted. When asked, Arden told him that her parents were dead, that her mother had died while Arden was studying creative writing at UCLA and that her doctor father had died of a stroke a few years after that. She went into no details, especially on her father's gynecological practice.

Drew had grown up in Oregon, where his mother still lived. His father had died some years before. Drew had begun playing tennis in junior high school.

"That was before very many public schools had tennis teams. When the coach saw that I had a knack for the game, he asked me to be on the new team he was setting up. I really preferred baseball, but he kept pressuring me, so I gave in. I soon became obsessed with getting better. By the time I got to high school, I was winning local tournaments."

"But you went on to college."

"Yes, much to the consternation of my manager, Ham Davis, who took me on in my sophomore year. Exams were always getting in the way of practice and play, but I knew my body wouldn't let me play tennis, at least not competitively, the rest of my life, so I thought I'd better prepare for the day when I couldn't."

"You caught up, though, didn't you? Once you started playing the circuits, you were an instant winner." She plopped the last chunk of papaya in her mouth. They had ordered fresh fruit compotes for dessert and were finishing them and sipping coffee.

"I had some good years." He shrugged modestly. "I had the advantage of a few years maturity, too, and didn't stay out all night and carouse like some players do the first time they tour." He took a sip of coffee. "The system is unbalanced. When you first start out, it's expensive as hell. Transportation, lodging, food. Then, when you make it, when you're winning prize money and getting endorsement contracts, everything's paid for."

He shook his head, laughing. "I risked losing some valuable contracts when even the best of tennis shoes couldn't keep me from stumbling onto the court after a drinking binge."

"You'll get them back."

His head came up to search her eyes. "That's what Ham says. Do you really think so?"

Was her opinion so important to him, or did he need any form of encouragement? "Yes. Once they see you play the way you've been playing, once you've won a tournament or two, you'll be back on top."

"There are younger guys every day to take my place."

"Can't hold a candle," she said with a dismissive wave of her hand.

He smiled crookedly. "I wish I had your confidence in me."

"Uh, Mr. McCasslin, excuse us, but . . ."

A dark scowl wrinkled Drew's thick blond brows as he turned in his chair to see the couple standing timorously behind him. They wore matching Hawaiian shirts in a gaudy floral print and labeled themselves tourists in myriad, unmistakable ways. "Yes?" At best, Drew's greeting was chilly.

"We . . . uh . . ." The lady hesitated. "We were wondering if you'd give us your autograph for our son. We're from Albuquerque, and he's just now getting into tennis, and he thinks you're wonderful."

"He has a poster of you in his room," the man said. "He—"

"I don't have anything to write on," Drew said, and rudely turned his back on them.

"I do," Arden chimed in, noticing the embarrassed, discomfited expressions on their sunburned faces. She reached into her bag and took out the tennis ball Drew had tossed her from the court. "Why don't you sign this for them, Drew?" she suggested softly, extending the ball to him.

At first, his eyes were hooded and rebellious, and she thought he might very well tell her to mind her own damn business. But when he saw the gentle chastisement in her eyes, he smiled and reached for the ball. Taking the pen the woman had found in her purse, he scrawled his signature on the fuzzy surface of the tennis ball.

"Thank you so much, Mr. McCasslin. I can't tell you what this souvenir will mean to our son. He—"

"Come on, Lois, and let the man enjoy his lunch. We hated to bother you, Mr. McCasslin, but we just wanted to tell you we can't wait to see you play again. Good luck."

Drew stood and shook hands with the man and kissed the lady's hand, an action that almost caused her to faint, if her fluttering eyelashes were any indication. "Good luck to your son, too. Have a nice vacation."

They ambled away, studying their precious souvenir and murmuring how nice he'd been and that all those reporters who said he was nasty and belligerent were wrong.

Drew looked over at Arden, and she prepared herself for a blistering put-down. Instead, his voice was husky when he asked, "Are you finished?" When she nodded, he put his hand under her elbow and helped her from her chair. They left the restaurant and didn't speak until they were wending their way through the landscaped pathways that connected the various buildings of the resort.

"Thank you," he said simply.

She stopped on the path and looked up at him. "For what?"

"For subtly warning me that I was behaving like a bastard."

She found his eyes too compelling to look into, so she studied the third button on his shirt, but was instantly distracted by the wedge of chest hair above it. "I shouldn't have interfered."

"I'm damn glad you did. You see that's another thing I'm overly sensitive about. For months after Ellie died, I was hounded by reporters for a 'comment' every time I stuck my nose out the door. Soon I became furious whenever someone even recognized me in public."

"I can imagine that having such a high public profile can be trying." What did that hair feel like to touch? It was a gorgeous golden color against his tanned skin.

"Under the best of circumstances it's trying. Under the worst, it's hell. When I was at my lowest, I had crowds jeering at me from the spectator stands, throwing things at me because I was playing so badly. Irrationally, I blamed them. My fans were deserting me because I drank, and I drank because my fans were deserting me. It was a vicious cycle. I'm still wary when people approach me, thinking they may very well have an insult to throw in my face."

"What I just witnessed was nothing short of unabashed hero worship." Forcing her eyes away from his chest and her mind from the erotic thoughts it incurred, she looked up at him. "You've still got thousands of fans just waiting for you to get back on the circuit."

He stared down into her sincere face for a long while and almost got lost in the swirling green depths of her eyes. She smelled of flowers. She looked both cool and assured, yet warm and giving. He raised his hand, intending to touch the sable hair that blew gently against her cheek, but changed his mind and dropped it back to his side. At last, he said, "Meeting you is one of the nicest things that's happened to me in a long time, Arden."

"I'm glad," she said, meaning it.

"I'll walk you to your room."

They went through the lobby of the main building. At the elevator, he said, "Wait here for me. I'll be right back."

Before she could wonder what he was doing, he had dashed off. She punched the up button but had to let two empty elevators go before he came running back carrying something wrapped in white paper. "Sorry," he said breathlessly. "Which floor?"

They took the elevator up, and Arden's female curiosity over his package was killing her. His eyes were dancing. If this was to be a surprise, she wasn't going to spoil it for him.

At her door, she stuck out her hand. "Thank you for a lovely lunch."

He didn't take her hand. He unwrapped the paper and shook out a plumeria and orchid lei. Dropping the wrapping negligently on the hallway floor, he held the lei over her head.

"You've probably been presented with dozens of these since you've been here, but I wanted to give you one."

The heady fragrance of the flowers and his nearness made oxygen scarce. Her senses reeled. Emotion congested her throat, but she managed to strangle out, "No. I've never had one. Thank you. The flowers are beautiful."

"You enhance the flowers."

He slipped the ring of perfect blossoms over her head and settled it gently on her bare shoulders. The fragile petals were dewy and cool against her skin. He didn't withdraw his hands but laid them lightly on her shoulders. Confusion and conflicting emotions swamped her, and she bowed her head.

The man and everything about him overwhelmed her, filled her head, her heart. He subjected her body to a lethargy that was foreign but so delicious. She longed to succumb to it and sag against his hardness. The flowers lying on her breast trembled with her erratic heartbeat. Tentatively, she touched them with palsied fingers.

In her peripheral vision, she saw his fingers reaching toward hers, and then they brushed, touched, entwined. His were dark with springy golden hairs on the knuckles. They were warm, sure, strong. She raised her head and looked at him with eyes as dew sparkled as the flowers.

"*Aloha,*" he whispered. He leaned down and kissed her first on one cheek, then the other. He rested his lips against the corner of hers. There, with his beard-roughened cheek lightly touching her, he sighed her name. "Arden."

His thumbs traveled over her collarbone, while his breath fanned her temple and teased her ear. "Now that lunch has been dispensed with . . ."

Oh, no! she groaned silently as her heart sank. *Here comes the sleazy proposition.*

He pulled back and released her shoulders. "How about dinner?"

Even as she dressed for the evening, she knew she should have begged off when Drew asked her for the date. It would have been logical for her to have said, "I'm sorry, and it sounds wonderful, but I should stay here tonight and work on an article."

Instead, she had heard herself say, "I'd love to, Drew." He had smiled and turned toward the elevator. She had entered her room in a cloud of romantic feeling. It hadn't taken long, however, for her to remember why she had contrived to meet Drew.

For a few minutes, while his hands had been touching her and his breath stirring her hair, she had forgotten her son. She had been thinking of Drew not as her son's father but solely as a man, a man she realized she was dangerously attracted to.

After her dismal marriage and hideous sex life with Ron, she had thought she'd never be interested in having a relationship with a man again. It came as a shock to her how much she was anticipating another few hours in Drew's company. And for all the wrong reasons.

It would have served her purpose better had Drew not been so sexually appealing . . . and widowed . . . and lonely himself. Wouldn't it have made her task less complicated to find her child's parents both alive and well, the father a jolly sort? Short, soft, round and balding? At the outset, the looks and personalities of the couple hadn't been a factor. She'd been interested only in locating the child she'd given birth to but had never seen. It hadn't been easy.

It was like opening a wound every time she remembered the gray, rainy day she had buried Joey. Never in her life, not even after the deaths of her father and mother, had she felt so alone. After obtaining her divorce, she had devoted herself to taking care of Joey. For the last few months of his life, he had been hospitalized. She watched him deteriorate with each day and struggled against praying for the death of another child so Joey might have the needed kidney. God couldn't be expected to grant such a prayer, so she never actually verbalized it.

When at last the time came, he had died as sweetly as he had lived, asking her please not to cry, saying that he would save her a bed next to his in heaven. For hours after he'd breathed his last, she held his thin hand in hers and stared into his peaceful face, memorizing it.

Ron had put on a performance of abject grief at the funeral service for those few of his friends who had attended. Arden was sickened by his hypocrisy. Valiantly, Joey had hid his disappointment each time Ron failed to come to the hospital to see him, as promised.

After the funeral, Ron cornered her. "Do you still have any of that money you screwed me out of?"

"That's none of your business. I earned that money."

"Goddam you, I need it."

She couldn't help noticing that the ravages of dissipation were becoming more and more pronounced. He wore desperation like a banner. It generated not the least amount of compassion in her.

"That's your problem."

"For god sakes, Arden. Help me. Just this once and I promise—"

She had slammed the limousine door in his face and demanded that the driver leave immediately. Even at his son's funeral, Ron's thoughts were only for himself.

For the next several months, she was so immersed in grief that she didn't know one day from the next. She lived in a vacuum of despair. Only on paper could she communicate her feelings, reconcile herself to them. An essay she wrote on losing a child was sold to a ladies' magazine, and it won public acclaim. She was asked to write others but had no ambition to do so. She felt that she was only filling time until her own death, for she had nothing else to live for.

Except that other child.

It came to her quietly one day. She *did* have a reason for living. Somewhere in the world, she had another child. It was at that point she made up her mind to find it. Never was it her intention to disrupt the child's life. She wouldn't be that cruel to parents who had gone to such great lengths to get that child. She only wanted to see it. To know its name, its sex. She had asked Ron to give her anesthesia just before the moment of delivery so she'd never remember the birth itself or inadvertently learn anything about the child she had borne for someone else.

"What do you mean there are no records?" she had demanded in frustration on her first attempt to gain information.

The administrator's face remained unperturbed. "I mean, Mrs. Lowery, that your records seem to have been misplaced and I've yet to locate them. In a hospital this size, these things happen."

"Especially when an influential doctor asks you or pays you to 'misplace' a file. And my name is Ms. Gentry!"

It was the same story everywhere. Birth records both at city hall and at the hospital had mysteriously disappeared. But to Arden it was no mystery at all who was responsible for such a puzzling loss of efficiency.

She didn't know the attorney who had drawn up the official papers. But he had to have been hired by Ron and therefore wouldn't tell her a thing if she found him. Ron, guessing correctly that after Joey's death she'd feel compelled to locate her second child, had gone before her, putting everyone involved on guard against feeding her one scrap of information.

The obstetric nurse who had helped her through her labor was her last resort. She found the nurse working in a charity clinic that specialized in abortions.

Arden could detect her fear immediately when the nurse spotted her as she left the clinic one afternoon. "Do you remember me?" Arden began without preface.

The nurse's furtive eyes darted around the parking lot as though looking for some means of escape. "Yes," she whispered fearfully.

"You know what happened to my baby," Arden guessed, intuitively knowing the statement to be a fact.

"No!" Earnest as the answer was, Arden knew she was lying.

"Miss Hancock," she pleaded, "please tell me anything you know. A name. Please. That's all I ask. Just a name."

"I can't," the woman cried, and covered her face with her hands. "I can't. He . . . he watches me, told me that if I ever said anything to you, he'd tell them about me."

"Who watches you? My ex-husband?" The woman jerked her head up and down in confirmation. "What is he using to blackmail you? Don't be afraid of him. I can help you. We can turn him over to the police—"

"No! My God, no. You don't . . ." She choked back racking sobs. "You don't understand. I was on . . . I had a little trouble with Percodan. He found out about it. He had me fired from the hospital but got me a job here. And . . ." Her narrow shoulders shook. "And he said if I ever told you anything, he'd turn me over to the police."

"But if you're clean now. If you . . ." Arden's voice trailed off when she read the guilty admission in the woman's shattered face.

"Not just me. My old man would die without . . . his medicine. I have to get it for him."

It was useless to pursue that channel. Arden sank back into a black pit of self-pity and despair. One day bled into another with no real differences between them. That was why she was sitting on her living room sofa staring vacantly into the television screen one Saturday afternoon. How long she'd been there, she didn't know. What she was watching she couldn't have said.

But suddenly something caught her attention. A face. A familiar face the camera loomed toward. And just as closely, Arden's brain focused on it. Shaking off the leaden depression, she turned up the volume on the set. The program was a sports show. The day's featured event was a tennis tournament. Atlanta? Somewhere. Men's singles match.

She knew that face! Handsome. Blond. Broad white grin. Where? When? The hospital? Yes, yes! The day she left with nothing but a purse with fifty thousand dollars cash in it. There had been a commotion on the outside steps. Reporters with microphones and cameras. Television crews crawling over the marble steps for better vantage points.

They were all there to see the beautiful couple leaving the hospital with their new baby. The tall blond man with the dazzling smile had a protective arm around his petite, equally blonde wife, who was holding a squirming bundle of flannel. Arden remembered the joy they radiated and had known a stab of envy at the loving way the man smiled down at the woman and child. Tears had blurred her eyes as she shoved her way through the crowd toward the taxi that had been called for her. She had refused Ron's offer to take her home.

She hadn't thought of that scene until then. And *this* was the man. She listened to what the commentator was saying as the man's body arched into his serve.

"Drew McCasslin seems to be making a heroic effort here today after his crushing defeat in Memphis last week. We've seen a steady decline in his performance over the past several months."

"Much of that has to do with the personal tragedy he suffered this year," another off-camera voice said charitably.

"No doubt."

Drew McCasslin lost the point, and Arden read on his lips a vile expletive that should never have been televised. Apparently, the director thought so, too. He picked up another camera angle that showed McCasslin at the base line, concentrating on the ball he was bouncing methodically. The serve was brilliantly executed, but the line referee called it out.

McCasslin axed his aluminum racket against the court and lunged toward the referee's high chair shouting vicious curses and insults. The television network judiciously went into a commercial break. After the virtues of an American-made car had been touted, they rejoined the match.

Arden hung onto every word as the commentators smugly excused McCasslin's behavior as a result of his grief over losing his wife in a grisly automobile accident in Honolulu where the couple lived with their infant son. McCasslin played, surly and belligerent, and lost the match.

Arden went to bed that night thinking about the professional tennis player and wondering why she was so intrigued by him, having only seen him once. It came to her in the middle of the night that she *had* seen him more than once. She sat bolt upright in bed, her heart racing, her mind spinning out of control. She couldn't grasp the thoughts before they eluded her.

Slinging off the covers, she paced the room, pounding her temples with agitated fists. "Think, Arden," she commanded herself. "Think." For some reason, it was terribly important that she remember.

With agonizing slowness, the pieces fell into place. She'd been in pain. Lights, moving lights. That was it! She was being rolled down a hospital corridor on a gurney, and lights flashed by overhead. She'd been on her way to the delivery room. It was almost over. All she had to do was deliver the baby and she'd be free of Ron forever.

She'd seen the couple out of the corner of her eye as she was pushed past a shadowed hallway. The light had caught on their two blond heads. She'd turned her head slightly. Neither of them noticed her. They were smiling, clinging to each other happily, whispering excitedly and secretively. What was wrong with that picture? Something, but what? *What?*

"Remember, Arden," she whispered as she slumped down on the side of the bed and clasped her head with both hands. "They were happy just like any other couple having a baby. They—"

Everything stopped at once. Her breathing. Her heartbeat. Her whirling thoughts. Then they started up again, sluggishly, gaining momentum as the dot of light at the end of a dark tunnel grew larger until the conclusion blasted into her mind. *The woman hadn't been pregnant!*

She hadn't been in labor. She'd been standing out in the hall talking in excited whispers with her husband. They had had about them an air of secrecy, like children plotting a marvelous prank.

The McCasslins were wealthy. They were recognized

world-wide. He was handsome, as Ron had said the father of her baby was. They had left the hospital with a newborn child the same day Arden had left.

She had had their baby.

Arden wrapped her arms around herself and rolled back and forth on the bed in solitary celebration. She knew she was right. She had to be. All the pieces fit.

She sobered considerably as she remembered the other fact she'd learned that day. Mrs. McCasslin was dead. Arden's son—the sports announcers had said Drew McCasslin had an infant son—was being reared without the loving care of a mother and by a father who wasn't mentally or physically stable.

Drew McCasslin became Arden's obsession. For months, she read everything she could about him past and present, spending hours in the public library poring over microfilms of sports pages that featured stories about his heyday. Daily, she read of his decline.

Then, one day, she read that he had gone into semiretirement. His manager was quoted as having said, "Drew knows his game has slipped. He's going to concentrate on restoring it and spending time with his son at their new home on Maui."

That was when Arden had begun planning to go to Hawaii to somehow meet Drew McCasslin.

"And now that you've met him, what are you going to do about him?" she asked her mirror image.

She hadn't counted on being susceptible to his charm and good looks. "Remember why you're here, Arden. Stay objective," she told her reflection.

But it mocked her from the mirror. She didn't look like a woman striving for objectivity. The strapless jade silk dress did nothing to disguise her figure. The fuchsia belt encircled a trim waist and drew attention to the round curves above and below it. The cream-colored blazer she wore over the sheath only made more suggestive the expanse of bare shoulders it covered. She was wearing the lei instead of jewelry, The flowers almost matched the color of her belt. She had pulled her hair back into a neat chignon, but its severity was compromised by wavy tendrils that had escaped to lie on her neck and to form a soft brush of bangs over her forehead.

The woman who looked back at her with smoky green eyes looked like a prime candidate for a tempestuous love affair.

"My God," she whispered as she pressed cold, trembling fingers to her forehead. "I've got to stop thinking of him this way. It'll ruin everything. And I've got to stop him from thinking of me as a . . . a . . . woman."

He would need discouraging. She knew that with every feminine instinct she possessed.

He had loved his wife. Probably still did. But everything about him spoke of intense virility. He wasn't the kind of man who could live without a complementing feminine presence for long.

The electricity between them—and she could no longer convince herself that it wasn't there—threatened her plan. That plan had been to meet him and win his confidence as a friend. When she had proved she didn't mean to threaten his relationship with his son, she would tell him who she was and make her request. "I would be forever grateful if you'd let me see my son now and then."

Hold that thought, she told herself when she heard his knock on her door. *Objectivity,* she reminded herself, and resolved to put away any other thoughts about Drew McCasslin.

It was impossible, however, to keep that promise to herself when he looked so handsome in tailored navy slacks, a beige sport coat that was almost the same color as his collar-length hair and a baby-blue shirt that matched his eyes.

Those eyes were doing their fair share of looking. They went all the way from the top of her head to the heels of her lizard sandals and back up again. They stopped short of her face and paused in the vicinity of the lei. Arden got the distinct impression they weren't looking at the blossoms but at the shape of her breasts beneath them.

"You do a lot for those flowers," he said in a gravelly voice that confirmed what she had suspected.

"Thank you."

"You're welcome." Only then did he lift his eyes to hers and smile. "Ready?"

Chapter 4

THEY HAD DINNER DATES EACH NIGHT AFTER THAT FOR THE next three. Arden knew she was making the difficult impossible but couldn't bring herself to refuse his invitations. She and Drew were growing closer, true, but in the wrong way. There was no room in her scheme for romance. So, on the fourth night, she begged off, using the lame excuse of working on her article about the chances of tropical plant survival in less tropical climes, an article she'd already mailed.

Instead of directing her thoughts away from Drew, she spent that evening wondering where and with whom he was having dinner. Was he home with Matt? With a friend? With another woman? She doubted it was the last. When they were together, she held his undivided attention.

"Am I moving too fast, monopolizing your vacation time, horning in on someone else's territory?" he had asked when she declined his dinner invitation. The ques-

tion was spoken lightly, almost jokingly, but she knew by
the frown wrinkling his eyebrows that he was serious.

"No, Drew, it's nothing like that. I told you the day I
met you, there is no one I'm accountable to. It's just that I
think we might need a night away from each other. I don't
want to monopolize your time, either. And I really do
have work to do." Skeptically, grudgingly, he had accepted her refusal.

She was terrified of what was happening to her each
time they were together. She was flirting with disaster and
knew it well, but the hours she wasn't with him had
become colorless and monotonous. He had never kissed
her except for that one time when he gave her the lei.
Beyond common courtesies, he never touched her. Yet he
made her feel giddy and young and beautiful. All those
emotions were symptoms of falling in love. And that
simply couldn't be. She had come to Maui to see her son.
That was her main goal, and Drew McCasslin was only the
means to that end.

Still . . .

The morning after their evening apart, she meandered
in the direction of the tennis courts, swearing to herself
that she wasn't going there to see him. He might not even
be playing.

He was guzzling Gatorade when he spotted her. He
tossed the bottle to Gary and trotted over to her.

"Hi. I was going to call you later. Dinner tonight?
Please."

"Yes."

His rapid-fire invitation and her spontaneous acceptance
surprised and delighted them both. They laughed together
softly, shyly, all the while drinking in the sight of each
other.

"I'll pick you up at seven-thirty."

"Fine."

"Are you going to watch me play?"

"For a while; then I must go back to my room to work."

"And I promised Matt I'd play with him on the beach."

Whenever he mentioned the boy's name, her heart lurched with eagerness. "I'm not keeping you away from him too much, am I?"

"I don't leave in the evenings until he's bedded down for the night. He doesn't miss me. He makes sure I'm the second one in the house awake every morning."

She laughed. "Joey used to do that, too. He'd come into my bedroom and peel open my eyelids, asking if I was awake."

"I thought only Matt knew that trick!" They laughed together again; then he said, "I'm losing momentum. I need to get back, but I'll see you tonight."

"Play well."

"I'm trying."

"You *are*."

He winked at her before rejoining the patient Gary, who hadn't wasted his time, but had been flirting with their covey of spectators. Arden wondered if she looked like just another groupie to anyone observing her and Drew. The thought made her uneasy. *Was* she just another groupie?

She wasn't quite ready when Drew knocked on her door. Despite her subconscious thoughts about him all afternoon, she had become inspired and had worked fast and furiously on one of her articles. She'd barely allowed time for a bath and shampoo before he arrived.

She was still zipping the back of her dress as she raced for the door. "I'm sorry," she said breathlessly as she pulled it open. He was leaning indolently against the jamb as though she hadn't kept him waiting a full minute already.

He took in her flushed cheeks, stockinged feet and general appearance of disarray and smiled. "It was worth the wait."

"Come in. I'll be ready as soon as I get on my shoes and

jewelry. Did you make reservations? I hope we don't
lose—"

"Arden," he said, closing the door behind him and
catching her by both shoulders. "It's okay. We've got
plenty of time."

She took a deep breath. "Right. I'll slow down."

"Good." He laughed and released her. He took a
cursory look around the room, finally focusing his gaze on
her as she stepped into high-heeled sandals. Flattening one
hand against the wall to brace herself, she lifted one
slender foot to adjust the strap. Her movement was
graceful, innately feminine and unconsciously provocative.

He took in the smooth length of her silk-encased legs.
The muscles of her calves were clearly, but softly, defined
as she stood on the balls of her feet. They would fit in the
palm of his hand perfectly, he thought.

Catching a glimpse of the weblike lace that bordered the
hem of her slip, he smiled at the sheer womanliness of it.
And as she leaned down, he couldn't help noticing the
precious weight of her breasts filling and pulling taut
the bodice of her dress. The deep V neckline revealed the
shadowy velvet cleft between her breasts. Mentally, he
placed his lips there and pressed them against the fullness
on each side of it. Immediately aroused, he ordered his
unwilling eyes to safer ground.

Her hair always seemed soft and touchable even when it
was pulled back. That night she'd worn it loose, and his
fingers tingled with the desire to caress the dark strands, to
test their silkiness and then to see if her complexion was as
soft as it looked. All over.

"There," she said, pushing herself away from the wall
and going to the long, low bureau opposite the king-sized
bed.

Drew hadn't allowed himself to think about the bed, to
think about the alluring body he was examining so closely
lying naked on that bed.

"Jewelry." She was rummaging through a satin travel jewelry carrier.

Her sleeveless dress was of some clingy, soft aqua material that conformed to nicely rounded but not overdeveloped hips. Anything she wore looked terrific no matter how dressy or casual. He thought she could be wearing jeans and a sweatshirt and give them as much class as a *haute couture* ensemble. She'd also look great in nothing at all.

Damn! He was thinking about what he'd promised himself he wasn't going to think about.

Her fingers worked deftly to clip gold earrings onto lobes he now fantasized about touching with his tongue. His heart began to hammer when her breasts lifted and swelled above her dress as she raised her arms to clasp a slender gold chain around her neck.

"Here. Let me," he said unsteadily. He moved up behind her. For a moment, before his fingers took the ends of the chain from hers, they stared at each other in the mirror. Her arms were still raised, her breasts still high and voluptuous, the tender undersides of her arms displayed, making her pose both wanton and vulnerable.

She lowered her arms slowly as he took the chain from her hands and ducked his head to work the intricate clasp. When it was fastened, she hurried to move away.

"Wait." His hands gently held her. "Your zipper's stuck."

"Oh." She barely had enough air to utter the word. In her effort to make the sound, it came out as a soft exclamation.

With tantalizing slowness, he eased the zipper down. Air cooled the flushed skin of her back. Motionless, not daring to draw a breath and break the sensuous spell, she stood, letting him draw the tab of the zipper all the way to her waist. His eyes, matching the leisureliness of his hand, charted its descent. The bare expanse of smooth skin let him know that there was no bra between her and the bodice of the dress.

Again, his eyes met hers in the mirror. They were dark and smoldering, like the purest of blue flame. And in her own eyes was the glassy sheen of desire.

His tense body radiated silent sexual messages. She knew that if she moved back but a fraction of an inch and let her hips brush the front of his trousers, she'd feel him hard and primed with passion. She doubted they would go to dinner. It was her decision.

But going to bed with Drew was out of the question. Bringing sexual involvement into this already untenable situation would be lunacy. And in some secret corner of her mind, she feared she might be disappointed. Or worse, he might be. Ron's scathing criticism of her sexual prowess haunted her.

It would be best to keep things on an even footing. Friendly. Wasn't it possible for a male and female to be nothing more than platonic friends? Wasn't that what she'd originally wanted from Drew McCasslin?

Wisely, judiciously, with cowardice, she lowered her head and shook it slightly. He got the message and pulled the zipper up. "A loose thread got caught. All done."

"Thank you," she said, stepping away.

She wasn't going to get off that easily.

"Arden?"

She picked up her purse before turning to face him. "Yes?"

"It's been a long time since I've been around feminine clutter, watched a woman I care for dress. I didn't realize until now how much I've missed living with a woman."

She looked away, out the wide windows where palm trees were blackly etched silhouettes against an indigo sky. "Living alone has disadvantages for a woman, too."

He took a step closer. "Like what?" It was a low, urgent whisper.

This had to stop. And it was up to her to see that it did.

She raised her eyes to his, forced them to twinkle mischievously and determinedly grinned a gamine smile. "Like not having someone around to unstick a zipper."

His disappointment in her answer showed in the slight relaxing of his shoulders, but he smiled a gracious surrender, alleviating the crackling tension in the room. "See? What would all you liberated women do without us?"

That cheerful, bantering mood stayed with them as he drove his Seville along Maui's narrow highways. The Kaanapali Beach area was one of the few developed regions on the island. It was studded with elegant hotels, restaurants and clubs.

Drew brought his car to a stop under the porte-cochere of the Hyatt.

"Ever been in here?" he asked as he joined her on the curb after a valet had assisted her out of the car.

"No, but I wanted to see it before I went home."

"Prepare yourself. It's like no other hotel in the world."

That was readily apparent. Most other hotel lobbies had ceilings. This one did not. The ceiling of the lobby, which was many stories high, was a starry sky. The lobby was landscaped to represent a rain forest, profuse with tropical trees and blooming plants. When it did rain, the effect was true to life. The areas that were covered were elegantly decorated with huge Chinese vases that dwarfed even Drew. Priceless rugs and oriental antiques gave the hotel a palatial aspect without detracting from the casual, homey atmosphere.

They crossed the immense lobby, Drew giving her far too little time to gaze into the elaborate shops and galleries before whisking her down a curved staircase into the Swan Court.

"I feel like a country bumpkin in the city for the first time. Is my mouth hanging open?"

"I like bumpkins," he said, and squeezed her waist. "And your mouth, like the rest of you tonight, looks delectable."

She was glad the maître d' chose that moment to escort them to a candlelit table beside the pond, where swans glided across the surface with the haughty disdain of royalty. As were most of the restaurants on the island, this one was open-air. It looked out on a small lake complete with waterfall and lava rocks.

The patrons were dressed in evening clothes, and Arden was glad she'd selected her dressiest dress to wear. Drew seemed to guess her thoughts. "Don't be too impressed," he whispered from behind his menu. "In the mornings, this room is swarming with people in swim suits and thongs at the breakfast buffet."

She let the ambience of the room soak into her and was only vaguely aware of Drew signaling the waiter.

"Would you like wine with dinner, Arden?"

She met his challenging stare levelly. "Yes, thank you."

He ordered an expensive bottle of white wine. She refused to show her surprise. In all the times they'd been together, he'd never drunk anything alcoholic.

"I drink an occasional glass of wine at dinner," he said.

"I didn't ask."

"No, but you were probably wondering if I can handle it."

"I asked you once before not to do my thinking for me. You're a big boy. You know if you can 'handle' it or not."

"You're not afraid that I'll go on a binge and become drunk and disorderly?" He was teasing.

She tossed down her own gauntlet. Leaning toward him, she whispered. "Maybe I'd like you to become a little disorderly." Moths had an instinct for flying directly into flames.

Drew's eyes narrowed seductively. "It wouldn't take even a sip of wine to make me completely unruly."

She backed off before her wings could be singed. "But I trust you not to."

He allowed her retreat. The tone of his voice told her he was willing to change the subject. "You have every reason to be concerned. I've been drunk and disorderly more this last year than I've been sober. I don't think I'll ever live it down." He clenched his teeth as strongly as he clenched the fist that lightly thumped the table top. "God, I'd give anything to undo some of the things I did."

Arden was well acquainted with the frustration and self-loathing he was feeling. Decisions were made; decisions were regretted. Most were irrevocable. "We all make mistakes, Drew, and later wish we could redo it all. We can't. We have to live with our decisions." Her voice became painfully introspective when she added, "Sometimes for life."

He chuckled softly. "That sounds so defeatist, hopeless. Don't you think we're given second chances to make things right again?"

"Yes. Thank God, yes. I think we *make* our second chances. We either try to turn our mistakes around or learn to live with them."

"That's the loser's way. To give in."

"Yes. And you're a winner."

"I couldn't live with the garbage I'd made of my life. I had to do something about it."

"So did I," she muttered to herself.

"Pardon?"

Should she tell him now? Now? He'd brought up the subject of personal failures and attempts to rectify them. He was doing that in his own life. Surely he'd understand her own desire to correct her mistakes. Wouldn't he? What if he didn't? What if he stormed out and left her alone and she never saw him again? She would never see Matt, either. No. Better to wait until after she'd at least seen her son once. Then she'd tell Drew she was Matt's mother. Then, not now.

She sat up straighter and flashed him a brilliant smile. "Why are we having this gloomy conversation? Here comes the wine. Let's not dwell on past mistakes tonight."

Their veal was scrumptious, as were all the dishes that

went with it. They had only the one bottle of wine, and half of it was left when they finally brought the two-hour dinner to an end. Full and satisfied, yet feeling as light as a feather, Arden seemed to float up the staircase. She wasn't drunk on wine but on the romantic atmosphere and the magnetism of the man beside her.

At the lobby cocktail bar, a pianist was playing love ballads on a white baby grand. An ocean breeze swept through the lobby, stirring the leaves of the trees and carrying with it the perfume of pikaki and plumeria.

They paused beneath a softly glowing lamp. "Enjoy the dinner?" he asked, taking both her hands in his and swinging them back and forth.

"Um-huh." She was looking at his hair and wondering what it would feel like to run her hands through it, to twist it around her fingers when passion rendered her mindless. She contemplated his mouth. The most erotic scene she'd ever seen in a motion picture was a camera-close view of a man's mouth on a woman's breast. She remembered vividly the tender flicking of his tongue as it circled a dusky areola, the flexing of his cheeks as he gently sucked the nipple, the moist caress of his lips on the soft flesh. That was what looking at Drew's mouth brought to mind, and her whole body flushed hotly with the fantasy.

Ron had never taken time for such foreplay, had never asked what she'd like. She probably wouldn't have liked it with Ron. She thought she'd like it very much with Drew.

"What?"

"What?"

"Did you say something?" Drew asked. His eyes were scanning the features of her face, lingering on one a long while before moving to another.

"No," she whispered. "I didn't say anything."

"Oh. I thought you said something." He was studying her mouth now, and if she had blushed at her own fantasy, she would have disintegrated with embarrassment had she known where *his* fantasy placed *her* mouth. To safeguard his sanity, he pulled a curtain over the erotically detailed mental picture. "What would you like to do?"

"Do? I don't know. What do you want to do?"

Oh, God, don't ask! "Go dancing?"

"That sounds fun," she said, coughing lightly and making an unnecessary straightening gesture down the front of her dress. Activity. That was what they needed. When they stood still, they became absorbed in each other to the exclusion of everything else.

"There's a club downstairs. I've never been there, but we can give it a try."

"Fine."

He led her down yet another staircase, this one brass banistered and reminiscent of the turn of the century. Pushing open the tufted leather door, they were greeted by a smiling hostess, a blast of disco music, a rumble of conversation and laughter and a cloud of tobacco smoke.

Drew looked down at her in silent query. She looked up with the same question in her eyes. Simultaneously, they turned on their heels and went back up the stairs. They were laughing by the time they reached the lobby.

"We must be getting old," Drew said. "The music of that single piano sounds better to me."

"To me, too."

"And I don't want to shout to be heard." He leaned down and placed his lips on her ear to whisper, "I may say something I wouldn't want anyone else to hear." When he pulled back, the burning glow in his eyes reinforced the intimacy of his words. A shiver of excitement feathered up Arden's spine. "Would you like something to drink?"

She shook her head. "Why don't you show me the pool?"

Clasping her hand and linking their fingers, he led her out onto the terraced rock pathways that wound through a veritable Garden of Eden. The paths were lit by widely spaced torches. Their flames flickered drastically in the wind. The swimming pools were an architectural masterpiece built on several levels around a lava-rock grotto.

Arden responded appreciatively to everything he pointed out, but she didn't really care what he said or what she saw. It was marvelous to hear his voice near her ear, to catch the fragrance of his warm breath, to feel the protective strength of his hard body as he directed her footsteps with subtle movements. Her pulse seemed to beat with the pagan rhythm of the surf as it pounded the shore only yards away.

Lovers lurked in the shadows, embracing, whispering. It was tacitly understood that privacy was the goal of anyone walking through the garden at that time of night. And when Drew stopped and pulled her behind a sheltering rock draped with a clinging vine, she made no protest.

"May I have this dance?" he asked with mock formality.

She laughed, trying to keep a straight face as she answered, "Yes, you may." She walked into his arms, and for the first time since they met, she knew the thrill of holding him, of being held.

He held her in the traditional waltz position, his arm around her waist and their joined palms at shoulder level. Her hand rested on his other shoulder. They couldn't move much without sacrificing this precious, private space, and both knew the invitation to dance had been issued only to provide them with an excuse to hold each other. So they swayed to the rhythm of the mood music wafting from the piano in the lobby bar.

Minutes ticked by, and one song drifted into another, and still they clung together, their eyes never wavering from each other's face. Their bodies, looking deceptively serene, were raging on the inside, clamoring for closer contact, yearning and straining until finally her breasts brushed against his chest.

He uttered a small groan and closed his eyes in exquisite pleasure. When they opened again, hers had been shuttered by the most fragile, lavishly fringed eyelids he'd ever seen. He wanted to kiss them. Instead, he brought his hand up from her waist and increased the pressure on her back until first the delicate crests, then the full mounds of her breasts were flattened against his chest.

Her eyes opened slumberously, and she moved her hand from his shoulder to the back of his neck. Her fingers threaded through the adorably shaggy blond hair that lay on his collar. Never taking his eyes from hers, he brought the hand he held to his mouth and brushed the knuckles with his lips. Back and forth, he caressed that dainty ridge, leaving it moist with the vapor of his breath.

Gradually, he lifted her arm and placed it over his shoulder and behind his neck. Then his hand glided down the underside of her arm, down her ribs and around to her back. He drew her close.

"You know how hard it's been for me to keep my hands off you, don't you?"

"Yes," she said throatily, responsively arching her body to meet his.

"I've wanted so badly to hold you, Arden."

"And I've wanted so badly to be held."

"All you had to do was ask," he whispered before he buried his face in her hair, nuzzling her with his nose and chin and mouth. "You smell so good, feel wonderful. Your complexion is beautiful. Honest to God, I've imagined every inch of it. I've wanted to see you, touch you, taste you."

A tremulous sigh shook her whole body as she nestled her face in the curve of his throat. Her hands tightened around his neck, and she took a step closer. His rasping groan of ecstasy was emitted through tightly clamped jaws. One of his hands stole down her back, paused briefly at her waist, then lowered to conform to the curve of her buttocks. Without separating himself from her, he managed to alternate their feet until one of his legs rested between hers, one of hers between his.

He was hard. And warm. So warm Arden felt his heat searing through their clothes, burning into her body and melting it against his. Holding her still with one hand on her hip, he rubbed himself against her. Her sharp, startled cry was muffled against his shirt front.

"I'm sorry, Arden. I don't mean to be crude, but God, it feels so good."

"Drew—"

"Do you want me to stop?"

"Drew." She threw her head back to look boldly into his face. "No." She shuddered. "No." Then, a bit hysterically, a bit deliriously, and quite desperately, she begged, "Kiss me."

His mouth came down on hers with the same kind of desperation she had voiced. It was a violent kiss, an explosive release of pent-up longing and withheld emotion. His lips ground into hers almost brutally, but she welcomed the rough caress, for she'd never felt more alive. She was a butterfly bursting free of a dreary chrysalis, a prisoner of despair and dark unhappiness seeing the light of life for the first time.

He lifted his head and looked down at her with shining blue eyes. His breath was ragged, labored. It matched hers. She could feel his rigid virility against that part of her that seemed to be throbbing with joy.

By an act of will, he controlled his raging impulses and let his hand come up to cradle her jaw with heartfelt tenderness. He ran the pad of his thumb along her bruised lower lip and frowned his regret. She smiled her forgiveness.

When next his lips met hers, it was with the merest touch. He skimmed over them with soft, moist lips whose comforting caresses became a gently building torment.

"Drew." His name was a plea from the bottom of her soul.

"I was rough. I didn't mean to be."

"I know."

"You make me wild with need of you."

"Take what you want."

A moan of animal pleasure rumbled in his chest as his mouth descended once again. His tongue was a sweet aggressor. It traced her bottom lip, bathing it with the nectar of his own mouth. She picked it up with her own tongue and murmured her approval. He placed his mouth against hers and opened his lips slowly. She did the same. For long moments, they waited there, savoring their expectation, their accelerated pulses, their aroused sexes.

Then his tongue pressed home, embedding itself snugly in her mouth. He withdrew, pressed again. Again and again, until Arden thought for certain she would die. She could feel her body flowering open, preparing for love. Her nipples grew hard and sensitive against the cool, sensuous cloth of her dress.

His kiss became playful. His tongue darted around her mouth. He teased, explored, stroked, probed, at varying tempos and angles and with such skill that she clung to him weakly and called his name softly when she had to tear her mouth free to breathe.

The heels of his hands inched up her ribs to find the sides of her breasts. With soft pressure, he squeezed them together. They nearly overflowed the V of her neckline, and he whispered accolades to them. He pressed hot kisses into the fragrant flesh. His tongue delved into the deep cleavage in a caress so evocative that Arden's body was washed with a delightful sense of shame.

She had needed this all her adult life. She had needed a man to show her what it was to be adored, loved for what she was, admired for her femininity. Not until she met Drew had she thought of herself as an attractive woman. From the beginning, his every look, every gesture, had told her he thought she was extremely sexy and desirable. He'd been honest and forthright about it from the beginning.

But she hadn't been.

What she was feeling now was pure and honest, but would he believe that later? When he learned she was Matt's mother, she would have so many things to answer for. Did she want to add luring him sexually to that list? The thought sickened her. She had to reverse this headlong plunge into sexual involvement immediately or forever be the object of his scorn.

"Drew," she murmured against his lips, which had returned to hers.

"Hmm?" He was lost in his caress.

"Drew," she repeated more stridently, and placed her hands against his shoulders. "Don't—" His hand was sliding beneath the strap of her dress, easing it down. She panicked. If she didn't stop this now, she wouldn't be able to. Her only recourse was to make him angry. He was beyond reasoning with.

"Stop it!" She slapped his hand away and yanked herself free of his embrace.

His face registered total bewilderment. He blinked his eyes rapidly until he could focus on her clearly. She watched as his initial befuddlement changed to irritation. "All right," he said tightly, "you don't have to treat me like a disobedient child. I had every right to think you were enjoying my kisses."

She avoided looking at him. "Kisses, yes, but I'm not one of the groupies you—"

"Is that all you think this is?" He raked a hand through his hair and worked with frustrated, ineffectual fingers at his necktie. "Is it?" he demanded.

Angering him had been her intent, but she hadn't counted on contending with such a volatile temper. She stammered to explain. "I . . . I—"

"Well, okay, then, but what sets you apart from the others? Huh? You've been more than available, and there were no strings attached. What else was I supposed to think? Or are you different because you never intended to go 'all the way'? No sex, just spiritual support for my much-publicized lost soul." He was furious. "Was that it? Was I a charitable case you took on?"

Arden was finding it difficult to keep a leash on her own temper. "As I pointed out to you the first day, you approached me, not the other way around. As for taking you on as a 'case,' I don't care if you go straight to hell or drink yourself to death or stumble and fall on every tennis court in the world. I frankly doubt if you're worth saving."

He ignored her, cocking his head to one side as if seeing her in a new light. "Maybe you're not so different, after all. Groupies want to sleep with a celebrity to elevate their own egos. Was sleeping with me going to shore up your shattered confidence after a failed marriage?" He thrust his face to within an inch of hers. "What's the matter? Chicken out?"

Fury bathed her world red. "You conceited ass. I'm not some frustrated divorcée. I was all too glad to get rid of the man I had. And I'll think long and hard before wanting another one. And if my confidence *were* shattered, which it's not, it would take a lot more than sleeping with a washed-up tennis bum to restore it. You can keep what's in your pants, Mr. McCasslin. I've lived without it for thirty-one years. I think I can go at least another thirty-one."

She whirled away from him and stumbled down the darkened path. He caught up with her and growled, "You're going the wrong way."

She tried to wrench her arm free, but he wouldn't let her. She wasn't going to engage in an undignified tug of war, so she let herself be escorted through the lobby. They waited in hostile silence for his car to be brought around. Not one word was said on the drive back to the resort where she was staying.

"I can find my way, thank you," she said as she pushed open the door the instant he braked the car to a stop. Not looking back, she rushed to the elevator and to her room. He didn't follow her.

Only when her anger had been spent in a fit of door
slamming, drawer rattling and cursing did she realize what
she'd done.

Matt!

She had ruined all chances of meeting him now. Tears
rolled down her cheeks in torrents, and she pledged to
herself repeatedly that it wasn't for losing Drew but only
for losing her son again.

Her eyes were puffy and burning when she tried to pry
them open the next morning. She rolled over and bur-
rowed her face in the pillow. When the second loud knock
sounded on her door, she groaned. "Go away, maid."

A third knock, more imperious, shook the whole room.
Arden cursed the maid's ambition. She saw that her only
option was to go to the door and tell the maid to come
back later.

She rolled out of bed, groping for the walls, since her
eyes seemed to have been glued shut with tears. They
came open wide when she peered through the peephole
and saw Drew standing on the other side of the door. She
watched as he knocked again. This time, he said, "Arden,
open this door."

"Not on your life."

"So you *are* awake."

She appreciated his cheerful tone of voice as much as
she would appreciate a splinter under her thumbnail. "I
don't want to see you, Drew."

"Well, I want to see you. To apologize. Now open the
door or everyone on this floor is going to hear an apology
that will wake them up faster than a good strong cup of
coffee."

She gnawed at her bottom lip while she weighed her
options. She wasn't up to seeing him. The night before, he
had been insulting, and she wasn't ready to forgive him.
And even if she were, she knew she looked like the devil.
Her eyes were probably red and swollen and her hair

tangled. When she met him face to face again, she wanted to be at her haughtiest best.

On the other hand, she'd deliberately made him angry. No man, no matter how easygoing normally, could be expected to be in the best of humor after being sexually thwarted. She had spent half the night tearfully berating herself for letting her relationship with Drew jeopardize her chances of seeing Matt. Swallowing her pride was a small price to pay for that, wasn't it?

She flipped open the dead-bolt lock and opened the door a crack. "I'm not dressed."

"You're dressed," he said, taking in the collar and sleeves of her blue and white striped oxford cloth nightshirt.

"If you insist on seeing me, I'll meet you in the lobby. Give me—"

"Haven't got the time." His grin was both devilish and winning. "Come on, Arden. Let me in."

Reluctantly, she opened the door and preceded him into the room. The door was closed softly behind him. He took in her dishabille in one lazy glance. Her bare feet and legs made her feel nervous and uncomfortable. The nightshirt wasn't revealing, but she suddenly wished the hem fell below the middle of her thighs. Self-consciously, she crossed her arms over her chest and tried to look bored.

"You're right. I'm a conceited ass." He brushed past her and went to the window, opening the drapes without her permission and flooding the room with a blinding sunlight that made her squint.

"I was acting like a horny teenager, grappling and groping in the dark. Hell"—he sighed, rubbing the back of his neck—"no wonder you thought I saw you as no more than a groupie. That's how I was treating you. And when you said no, I don't know why I said the things I did. I didn't mean them. They weren't accurate, and I knew it." He glanced over his shoulder to see that her militant stance hadn't relaxed one iota.

"The only excuse I can offer," he went on, "is that soon after Ellie died, I was surrounded by women who thought they could cure me of my grief. I got the impression they saw themselves as some kind of sexual social workers out to save me from my self-destruction. And to them I'd be no more than a notch in the bedpost."

Arden lowered her arms and relaxed her posture. She'd had that same kind of response from men after her divorce. Friends of Ron's, divorced themselves, began calling, offering her their "help." "No, thank you," she had said until they finally gave up.

"Anyway," Drew was saying, "that's why I had to see you first thing this morning. The minute I pulled away from here last night, I knew I'd acted like a jerk. You should have kicked me in the groin or something."

"I thought about it."

He laughed. "Well, it might not have changed my mind immediately, but you would have gotten my attention."

She laughed, too.

"Now that we're friends again," he said hurriedly, clapping his hands together, "why don't you go over to Oahu with me for a few days."

"What—"

"Just a minute," he said, holding up both hands to ward off her objections. "There are still no strings attached. I'll only be there a few days. I've got a suite of rooms reserved. Maybe you'll get an idea for an article." It was a weak argument, but he was in a rush to convince her.

"But I can't just move out of here. I—"

"I'm not suggesting you do. Pack only what you'll need. We'll tell the manager that you'll be gone for a few days but want to keep the room."

He stepped closer and clasped her hands. "I like the way you look in that nightshirt," he said in a sexy drawl, "with your hair all mussed up and your cheeks blushing pink. You have the sweetest mouth I've ever tasted. And I really can't believe I was stupid enough to let a good thing like last night end so badly."

"You're a bully, did you know that? You have your nerve coming in here this morning after the things you said to me last night, telling me how good I look when I know I must look like hell." Her outburst made him smile, and that fueled her anger. "Do you always get your way?"

"I'm a competitor, Arden, and I like to win." The fierceness in his eyes told her she was his next goal. While she was held dumb struck by his handsome appeal and the earnestness of his expression, he urged softly, "Come to Honolulu with me. We'll get to know each other better."

She wanted nothing more but knew she was only letting herself in for more trouble. Taking a deep breath, she shook her head. "Drew, I don't think—"

"Please. Besides, it'll give you a chance to know Matt."

Chapter 5

SECONDS TICKED BY WHILE SHE STARED AT HIM SPEECHLESS-ly. The arsenal of arguments she had been stockpiling in her mind tumbled. Finally, she stammered, "M . . . Matt's going?"

"Yeah, he's the main reason we're going. It's time for a checkup at the pediatrician. He needs a booster shot. And Mrs. Laani was complaining the other day that he's growing so fast he doesn't have any clothes. She's planning an extensive shopping trip."

Arden's mind was thrown into chaos. It was going to happen! She was going to see her son, spend time, *days*, with him. For months, she had waited for this moment, dreamed about it, imagined how she'd feel. But the panic that seized her now was unpredicted. That was all she felt—cold, blind panic. Now that what she'd prayed for was here, she was terrified of it.

She began trying to talk her way out of it. "This is a family trip, and I wouldn't want to interfere. He . . . Matt might not like me. Mrs., uh, Laani, is it? She might resent your bringing a . . . me along."

"It *is* a family trip, but I happen to be the head of the family. Mrs. Laani lectures me on just about everything, including the deficiency of a nice—and I stress nice—lady in my life. She's eager to meet you. And Matt's only twenty months old. He loves anyone who feeds him." His hands cupped her head. "Please come, Arden. If I didn't think it was a good idea, I wouldn't have asked." His voice deepened perceptibly. "I don't want to be away from you even for a few days."

Oh, God, why wasn't she jumping up and down with glee? Why was she hesitating? Did she feel guilty? Was that the emotion that had a stranglehold on her heart and wouldn't let go to make room for others? Drew was gazing down at her with naked longing. He was looking at her as a woman he was growing romantically attached to, not as the surrogate mother he and his beloved wife had hired. How long could she go on tricking him?

"Drew, I'm not sure going with you is a good idea."

"Are you still angry about last night?"

"No, but—"

"I don't blame you for being mad. I said terrible, insulting things." His thumb stroked her cheekbone. "I was wrong, but everything you said was true. I behaved like an ass. I am conceited. I am accustomed to getting my way and am likely to throw temper tantrums if I don't. I am a washed-up tennis bum."

"No! That's not true. I said that to deliberately hurt. No other reason."

He sighed. "Whether it's true or not remains to be seen. What I am is a man who finds himself attracted to a woman when he never thought he'd feel that way again. I'm scared as hell of you, Arden, and of what I'm feeling. Don't make it so damn hard on me. I'm trying to adjust to being a human being again, to act like one and not like a wounded animal. Sometimes I have lapses. Last night was one of those times."

"I'm not playing coy, Drew."

"I know that."

"I wasn't last night, either."

He kissed her gently. "I know that, too."

"There's a reason why I shouldn't go."

"You've given me no reason. I don't think there is one. Not a valid one, anyway. Come with us. The plane leaves in an hour."

"What?" she gasped, shoving him aside and checking the digital clock on the bedside table. "An hour! Oh, Drew . . . I can't . . . Why didn't you say . . . I'll never get ready—" She stopped abruptly when she realized she'd just consented.

He laughed at her startled expression, and dropping down on the bed, picked up the telephone. "You'd better hurry. I'll call down for coffee."

By the time she stepped out of the shower, he was tapping on the bathroom door. "Room service." She eased the door open a crack and took a cup of coffee from him. "Thirty minutes," he said. "Want me to toss a few things in a suitcase for you?"

The thought of his handling her intimate garments set off a chain reaction that ended in a flush of warmth between her thighs. "No. I'll be out in a jiffy."

She sipped the coffee and tried to keep her hands from shaking while she applied her makeup. She told herself her jittery nerves were the result of a short, virtually sleepless night. But not a little of her tenseness had to do with standing naked only a few feet and one door away from Drew. And most of it had to do with the fact that in less than an hour she'd meet the son she'd carried for nine months but had never seen.

Drew was dressed in a pair of casual khaki slacks and a loosely woven white cotton sweater with wide sleeves that he'd pushed up to his elbows. Arden had taken a pair of raw silk slacks and a matching top with dolman sleeves into the bathroom with her. She wound her hair into a loose French braid down the back of her head and tucked the ends under at the nape. Not great, but the best she could do in a hurry.

When she came out of the steamy bathroom, she looked nervously toward Drew, who was slouched in a chair near the glass terrace door perusing the morning newspaper. He tipped down a corner of the paper to look at her and whistled long and low. "How'd you do that so fast? Take casual clothes, shorts, swim suit, something to wear to dinner, but nothing fancy."

She began folding things into a shoulder bag, her mind clicking off the accessories that went with each outfit. She became all thumbs and butterfingers when she began packing her underwear in the bag. Though he still held the paper up in front of him, Drew's eyes weren't on the print. Arden could feel him watching her every move as she packed lacy panties and flimsy brassieres. When she shot him an accusing glare, he flashed her a broad, guileless grin.

"All set," she said as she zipped the bag, in which she'd managed to cram not only clothes but also makeup, jewelry caches and shoes.

"Amazing," he said, standing up and glancing at his wafer-thin watch. "And just on time. We're meeting Mrs. Laani and Matt at the airport. Mo, who takes care of the grounds of the house, is going to drive them. We'll take the resort's limo, if that's okay. I hated to leave my car at the airport for that long."

"That's fine." She set a natural straw hat with a wide, floppy brim over her head and slid on large square sunglasses. "Remember, I'm accustomed to traveling on a shoestring budget."

"You certainly don't look like it," he said as he carried

her bag down the hall toward the elevator. He took in every fashionable detail as they waited for the elevator. "I approve," he said softly.

"Thank you," she whispered back.

Once inside the cubicle, he said, "I forgot something."

"You left something in the room?"

"No. I forgot this." He bent his knees to put his height on a level with hers, tilted his head under the brim of her hat and slanted his mouth over hers.

His lips moved but little, but she felt their sweet pressure all along her body. His tongue barely breached her lips to touch the tip of hers, but he could have been teasing her finger tips, her nipples, secret places deep inside her, for she felt the titillating caress in all those places.

When he pulled back, she was exceedingly warm and tingling. "You fogged up my sunglasses," she said in a husky voice.

"Sorry?"

She shook her head. He was well into a second kiss when the elevator door whooshed open. Flustered, Arden said, "I've got to make arrangements about my room."

"I'll save us a place in the limo."

She waded through the crowd at the concierge's desk. Naturally, it was jammed that time of day, with guests either checking out or checking in or making reservations for various excursions via land, sea or air to other parts of the island. She cast several anxious glances over her shoulder toward the front doors before it was finally her turn.

Hastily, she explained that she wanted to pay for the days she had occupied her room but wanted to keep it until she returned in three days. After repeating her request several times, she finally made herself understood over the hubbub. The harried clerk found her registration card, ran her credit card through his machine, smiled at her toothily, wished her a good trip and expressed his gratitude for her business. She felt uneasily that she'd been dismissed, but before she could get the clerk's attention again, Drew was calling to her.

"Arden, the limo's waiting."

"I'm coming," she called back, and made her way through the crowd until he clasped her hand and pulled her toward the door.

"No problems?"

"No."

"Good. We're barely going to make it."

Once they were seated in the limo and speeding toward the airport, she realized that in just a few minutes she would see her son. Her heart was pounding in her chest, and her breathing was shallow.

"You're not scared of flying, are you?" Drew asked, mistaking the source of her obvious nervousness.

"No. I don't mind flying, although I prefer the larger jets."

"I like the smaller airplanes because I can see more. Besides, this airport, such as it is, is only five minutes from home. And it's a good commuter airline. I know just about everyone on staff by now."

Kaanapali Airport, as Drew had said, wasn't much compared to major city airports. The building was about the size of a self-service gas station. But it was a beehive of activity. As each plane landed and disgorged its nine passengers, another would be taking off.

The resort's van pulled up with a jarring halt. Drew hauled her bag onto his shoulder, stepped out ahead of her and offered her a hand to help her down.

"They should be somewhere . . . Ah, there they are." His chin lifted, indicating that Arden should look behind her. She drew in a great amount of air, squeezed her eyes shut momentarily and turned around. She had to lock her trembling knees to keep them from buckling under her. Drew hadn't noticed. He was walking away from her toward a grove of trees. "Matt," he shouted.

Arden saw him, and her heart turned over.

He was wearing a white shirt and a pair of bright-red shorts with a bib and shoulder straps that crisscrossed over his back. White knee socks encased stocky calves. He had on white high-topped shoes. The pumping chubby legs came to a weaving halt when Matt heard his father's voice, and he turned around, squealed and came racing back in the opposite direction toward Drew. A woman in a white uniform, who was as wide as she was tall, came huffing along behind him on amazingly small feet for someone her size.

Arden had eyes only for the blond boy who almost toppled over in his excitement before he barreled into his father's legs and was swooped over the tall man's head.

"Hey, you little dynamo, slow down or you're going to skin your knees again," Drew said, shaking the boy, whose peals of laughter filled the morning air.

"Up, up," he shouted.

"Later," Drew said, swinging him down to hold him in the crook of his arm. "I want you to meet a lady. Arden," he said, turning to the pale, transfixed woman beside him, "this is Matt."

Her eyes were rapacious, trying to devour as much of him as she could. She searched for something familiar but found little. His coloring was his father's: blond hair, blue eyes. There was a squareness to his chin that reminded her a little of her father.

She saw none of herself, but she could not have been more certain that this was her son. She knew by the way her breasts expanded, as though filling with the milk that had never been allowed to come. She knew by the contracting of her womb as she remembered each time she felt the movement of a fist or a foot or laughed at a case of prenatal hiccups that echoed through her own body. She knew because of her yearning to touch him, to clutch his sweet, young, healthy body to her.

"Hi, Matt," she rasped out.

The child stared back at her with candid curiosity. "Say *aloha*, Matt," his father directed him, nudging his stomach.

"O-ha," he mumbled before turning in Drew's arms and shyly burying his face against his father's neck.

Drew closed his arms tight around his son and rubbed his back. He looked at Arden over Matt's blond curls. "We're still working on etiquette," he said, smiling apologetically.

"Mr. McCasslin, I thought I'd let him run off some energy before the airplane ride," the nurse panted as she came up to them.

"Good idea. Mrs. Laani, I want you to meet Ms. Gentry. She's our guest for the next several days."

"*Aloha*, Mrs. Laani," Arden said, dragging her eyes away from the soft skin on her son's nape. She used to tickle Joey there with her mouth. "Getting sugar," she called it.

The middle-aged Polynesian woman was eying her with open curiosity. She seemed to like what she saw, for her round, unlined face split into a broad grin.

"*Aloha*, Ms. Gentry. I'm glad you're coming with us. Sometimes two men are too much for me to handle."

"Fine," Drew said. "Your job is to handle Matt. Let Arden handle me."

Arden blushed beneath her hat, but Mrs. Laani laughed gustily. Arden liked her instantly. Despite her size, she was neat to a fault, her uniform crisply starched. Her hair was cut short and permanently curled to form a dark, silver-threaded wreath around her head.

One of the employees of the commuter airline stepped out onto the porch. "Mr. McCasslin, we're ready for your party to board now."

"Did you get all the luggage on board?" Drew asked the attendant, who checked them off the passenger list.

"Yes, sir, we sure did."

"Add this," he said, handing the man Arden's bag.

"I don't mind carrying it on board," she offered.

"No, ma'am," the attendant said. "The seats are too small. All luggage has to go in the back."

A man in shirt-sleeves, whom Arden determined was their pilot, slapped Drew on the back. "When are you going to treat me to another match? I finally recovered from the last one." As they chatted, they made their way onto the tarmac to the waiting plane. Drew was still carrying Matt on his shoulders. Arden had yet to take her eyes off him. She was grateful that the confusion of boarding the airplane provided her with an opportunity to stare at him without anyone noticing.

Mrs. Laani's bulk could barely squeeze through the narrow door of the aircraft. She sank into one of the seats in the back so she wouldn't have to wedge herself through the aisle.

"Care to ride in the copilot's chair this morning?" the pilot asked Drew.

He grinned boyishly. "You know that's my favorite seat." He turned to Arden. "Do you mind sitting beside Matt?"

She shook her head, not trusting herself to speak. She took the window seat so Matt wouldn't feel so confined. Drew buckled him into the seat beside hers and just behind his. "There we go, hot shot. You can be the navigator, okay?"

Matt smiled, revealing eight pearly teeth. His excitement wavered when the pilot started the noisy engines. His back went ramrod straight, his eyes widened, and his lower lip began to tremble. Arden placed her hand on his knee, and when he looked up at her fearfully, she smiled. Drew turned around, winked at the boy and reached back to pat him on the head.

Matt sat still and stiff until the plane gained altitude and he was convinced he was in no immediate danger. Only one stranger had boarded the plane with them, and he had fallen to sleep immediately. As had Mrs. Laani. Matt grew

restless and strained against his seatbelt. After first checking with Drew and the pilot, Arden released it.

"Just don't let him crawl around too much," Drew told
her. "If he gets too rambunctious, pass him up here."

"No. He'll be fine." Drew went back to his conversation
with the pilot, and she devoted her attention to Matt, as
she had longed to do. In typical little-boy fashion, he
couldn't sit still. He twisted and turned in his seat, tried to
stand up, wobbled unsteadily and sat back down. He
investigated everything.

Arden watched each movement, adored it and savored
it for the time when she'd have to leave him again. She
hadn't made plans beyond this point, beyond getting to see
her son. But she knew she couldn't uproot him from the
life he had. She couldn't do that to his father, and she
knew it wouldn't be best for Matt, either. For right now,
she only wanted to love Matt, silently and secretly, but
love him as only a mother could.

When she patted her lap, he paused for only a moment
before climbing up into it. He studied her closely and
reached out and poked the lens of her glasses with a damp
fist.

"Thanks," she joked as she took the glasses off to clean
the smudged lens. "Between you and your dad, I'm having
a hard time seeing out of these."

He grinned and pointed toward the back of Drew's
head. "Dad."

"Yes," she exclaimed, laughing. She touched his cheek
and marveled at how soft it was. His hair, too, curled
softly around her fingers. It was only several shades away
from platinum, and as he grew older, it would darken to
the wheat color of Drew's. Lovingly, she ran her hands
over his dimpled arms and let him wrap tight, damp fists
around her fingers. Quoting a nonsense rhyme, she made a
game of squeezing his knees until he giggled. "A good
child, a good child / As I suppose you be, / Will neither
laugh nor cry / At the tickling of your knee."

When he didn't resist, she pulled him into her arms and
held him close. She hugged him as tight as he'd allow. He
smelled of baby soap and clean clothes and sunshine. Mrs.
Laani took good care of him. He was spotless; his fingernails were well trimmed. Arden loved the sturdiness of his
body. Joey had been so pitifully frail. When she left Matt,
she'd leave knowing that he was healthy and normal.

And like any normal, healthy little boy, he rebelled
against so much affection. He squirmed away from her,
taking her hat off in the process. Playfully, she placed the
hat on his head, and it all but swallowed him. They played
peekaboo from under the floppy brim for a while. Inspired, she put the glasses on his nose. He had to hold his
head still to keep them from slipping off, and she could see
his eyes rolling back and forth behind the lenses to watch
her as she took a compact from her purse. When she held
the mirror up to him, he crowed with glee.

"Dad, dad," he called, getting to his feet in Arden's lap
and hitting Drew on the head. The hat and glasses were
knocked askew, but Matt didn't notice.

Drew turned around and burst out laughing at the
comical sight. "You look worse than E.T. in the wedding
dress," he hooted. Matt bobbed up and down until he
became a little too wild and had to be calmed down. When
he eventually tired of the hat and glasses, Arden placed
them in his chair and took him back on her lap.

The droning motors of the plane and her gentle maternal stroking of his hair lulled him, and soon his head was
resting heavily on her breasts. She couldn't believe that
she'd been blessed with this moment. It was more than she
had allowed herself to hope for. He liked her, trusted her
instinctively, enough to fall asleep against her.

She could feel the rapid beating of his heart against hers
and thought of the irrevocable and eternal bond that
bound them. There was none other like it in the universe,
that between mother and child. Her body had nourished

him, breathed for him, sheltered him. Emotion such as she'd never known welled up inside her.

Drew glanced at them and did a double take when he saw the rapt attention Arden was giving his son. She was absorbed in the small hand she held in hers, massaging the tiny knuckles. As though she sensed him watching her, she raised her head, and he was further startled to see tears pooling in her eyes. She smiled at him tremulously, then once again lowered her eyes to the boy sleeping on her bosom.

The pilot landed the plane expertly and taxied toward the terminal. As soon as he cut the engines, he excused himself and hurried to the back of the aircraft to assist Mrs. Laani out. The other passenger left as soon as he located his briefcase.

Drew eased himself down on the edge of the seat next to Arden's. He studied her for a moment with probing blue eyes before he spoke. "I see you two have taken to each other."

"I hope so. He's dear, Drew. So dear. A wonderful little boy."

"I think so."

Lightly, she ruffled the blond curls. "Was he a good baby?"

"Ellie and I didn't have anything to compare him to, but we thought so. He was hard to come by. We wouldn't have cared if he'd squalled all the time."

Her next question would be like stepping off a high diving board into a vat of fire. The quantity of adrenaline that pumped through her veins was the same as if she were. "Ellie had a difficult time having him?"

There followed a significant pause. She continued to stare down at the sleeping child, noting each eyelash that rested on his flushed cheeks.

"Not exactly," Drew said slowly. "She had a hard time conceiving him."

"Oh." It relieved her conscience somewhat to know that Drew had chosen to lie, also. How far could she fish before he became suspicious? "Does he look like his mother?"

"Ellie was blonde," he answered noncommittally. "I think he takes more after me, though."

Arden looked up at him then and smiled, though there were still tears in her eyes. "As a proud father, you're biased."

"I'm sure that has a lot to do with it," he answered with a hint of self-mockery. "I can't really tell how much he looks like his . . . mother."

Arden looked away again, quickly, before he could see her wounded expression. But he saw the tear that rolled down her cheek. Raising her head with a gentle fist under her chin, he lifted away the tear with his finger tip.

"Because of the son you lost?" The question was asked with such tenderness and compassion that a new, unnamed emotion blossomed in her chest. She was stunned by it. Stunned and frightened.

Now, now, she said to herself. He had presented her with the perfect opportunity to tell him that she had just now *found* her son, that she had borne this boy whose life Drew treasured. But the words wouldn't come. He might yank her son away and never let her see him again. He might think that she'd been using him all this time to get to her son.

Wasn't that what she had done?

No, no! She cared as much for the father now as she did for her child. She couldn't hurt Drew, not when he had just gotten his life back in order and regained his self-confidence. No. She couldn't tell him yet. Later. When the time was right, she'd know it.

"Yes," she said. "Because of the son I lost."

Drew nodded in understanding. Matt's breath whistled through his cherubic mouth. He had left a trickle of saliva on Arden's top.

"He's getting your blouse wet," Drew whispered in the

still silence. He couldn't have honestly said which he found the most captivating, his son's sweet mouth or the sweet place it rested against. Her breast was plumped out from the weight of Matt's head and looked maternal and comforting, and he longed to touch it, to stroke its full softness.

"I don't mind." And she didn't. She didn't care if the child irreparably stained every garment she owned as long as she could continue to hold him.

Entranced, she watched as Drew's index finger reached toward his son's cheek. He brushed it lovingly, then moved toward the open baby lips and picked up the beads of moisture that lingered there. Fascinated both by what she was seeing and the love that was bubbling inside her, she watched the finger trail slowly from the child's mouth to the wet spot on her breast. He touched it, but had she not been watching, she might not have known it, so light was that touch. Then, moving with excruciating slowness, he turned his hand and cradled his son's head, placing the back of his hand against Arden's breast.

A shudder of emotion rippled through her, and a soft half sob escaped her trembling lips. Her eyes were made blind by collecting tears. Drew's head snapped up, and his blue eyes pierced into her wide green ones.

"Arden, don't cry anymore." Without moving anything but his head, he joined their mouths together. This kiss wasn't restrained like the one in the elevator earlier that morning. This one was rife with emotions, any one of which would have been sufficient to tear down all their defenses.

His tongue delved deeply and was received into the snug warmth of her mouth. Without thinking about it, her hand came up and pressed Matt's head to her breast, trapping Drew's hand between them. Now she was holding them both. The son. The father. So long dreamed about, speculated on. Ever elusive. Now her flesh could feel them both; her senses could luxuriate in the sounds, smells and sights of them. Their bodies were the most beautiful in the world to her. With one, she had created the other.

Drew groaned softly, and his lips twisted over hers. With his fingers, he caressed his son's head. It wasn't accidental that his fingers were also moving against Arden's nipple with the same pressure his tongue applied inside her mouth. His passion coursed through her, down her throat and straight into her body until it touched her femininity and bathed it with liquid heat. And she knew then what it would have been like had they made Matt in the conventional way, and she felt cheated, bereft at not having had the full knowledge of that miracle.

"God," Drew moaned as he pulled away at last, lifting the still-sleeping Matt into his arms. "If you go on kissing me like that, I'll start crying myself. And for an entirely different reason."

He helped her out of the airplane into the balmy sunlight. The sleeping Matt was draped over his shoulder. With his free hand, Drew clasped hers, and they made their way to the terminal.

Their suite of rooms at the Sheraton was spacious and faced the ocean with an unrestricted view of Diamond Head. There was a sitting room that separated the room Mrs. Laani and Matt would share from Drew's bedroom. Arden had the room across the hall from his.

"Here's a key to the suite if you should need one," he said on their way up in the elevator. "Make yourself at home anytime." He pressed the key into her palm, making his meaning implicitly clear. When Arden had the nerve to glance at Mrs. Laani, she saw that the woman was beaming a smile. Arden knew they'd both be disappointed if they expected her to use the key.

They got the worst over first. As soon as they had eaten lunch and Matt had taken a short nap, Drew and Mrs. Laani left with him for his appointment with the pediatrician.

Under the hotel's wide breezeway, as they were getting into the car Drew had leased at the airport, he clasped Arden's hand. "We'll be back in about an hour. You're sure you'll be all right?"

"Yes, but I wouldn't mind going along." In fact, she wanted desperately to go with them but knew it would seem unnatural to press the issue.

"That's generous of you, but I wouldn't force this on anyone." Drew laughed. "Matt's not the most cooperative of patients. Shop, sightsee and we'll meet you back in the suite by five o'clock."

"Okay," she said resignedly. He kissed her quickly on the cheek, and they sped away.

Matt was obviously miffed at both Mrs. Laani and his father when they brought him back to the hotel. He treated them as enemies who had put him through a terrible ordeal. He would have nothing to do with either of them during the early dinner they ate at one of the coffee shops in the hotel complex. Only Arden was allowed to cater to him.

"You're only making it worse," Drew said as she fed ice cream to Matt after his dinner. "He'll think you're his fairy godmother or something."

Arden almost dropped the spoon but managed to recover. She looked pleadingly at Mrs. Laani and Drew. "Let me spoil him. He's had a hard day."

The child was querulous with everyone by the time dinner was over, and Drew firmly suggested they make it an early night.

"As soon as Matt's in bed," Mrs. Laani said, "I'd like to go out for a while. My sister wanted me to come see her and meet my niece's fiancé."

"That's fine with me," Drew said.

"Why don't you go on now," Arden rushed to say. "I don't mind putting Matt to bed. In fact, I'd love to. There's no sense in your postponing your visit."

"Are you sure you know what you're letting yourself in

for?" Drew asked her, his brows creasing over skeptical eyes.

"Yes." Arden turned to Mrs. Laani. "Go on. Matt and I will get along fine."

It was settled, and Mrs. Laani left a few minutes later. Between the two of them, Drew and Arden managed to get the cross little boy bathed and snapped into pajamas. Arden almost regretted that he was so fractious and sleepy. She would have loved to have played with him longer.

It was she who laid him in the portable crib the hotel had provided and patted his back until he fell asleep. Drew had already withdrawn into the other room. She stayed by the crib until Drew called to her.

When she joined him in the sitting room, he was leaning back in the sofa with his feet stretched out in front of him. He had changed into a pair of shorts and a T-shirt. He was barefoot. Arden admired the bunched muscles in his arms and legs, the rippling ridges of muscle on his chest. She loved, too, the way his body hair shone golden against his bronzed skin in the soft lamplight.

"Come here and crash," he said, extending his hand. "I'd get up and come get you, but I'm pooped."

She laughed and sank down beside him on the sofa. "A big strapping boy like you being worn out by one twenty-month-old!" she teased.

He grunted. "He can wear me out faster than a tennis match. Incidentally, I've got to practice while I'm here. Want to watch me tomorrow morning?"

"Of course."

"We'll make good our escape before Matt realizes we're gone. Mrs. Laani can take him to the park or something. Right now I'm feeling very jealous of my son for absorbing so much of your attention." He turned to face her, letting his eyes take in her pleasantly rumpled appearance. As he had been sure she would, she made even domesticity look elegant.

"You shouldn't," she said, wishing she had the courage to brush the wayward strands of hair from his forehead. "The reason I like him so much is because he's related to you."

His eyes gleamed with pleasure. "Is that right?"

"That's right." It was true. She loved Matt not only because he was her son but also because he was Drew's. It only stood to reason that she loved Drew as well. But what kind of love? Was it merely because he was Matt's father? No. She was in love with this man, and it had nothing to do with Matt.

He was looking at her in the same intense way she was surveying him. "This is twice today my son has gotten you wet." His finger traced the damp patterns that Matt's body, wet from his bath, had left on the casual blouse that had replaced her traveling clothes.

His hand paused at the top curve of her breast, and his eyes met hers. "From the very beginning, you were no casual pickup, no quick lay. Tell me you know that."

Shaking her head and closing her eyes briefly, she said, "Yes, I know that." She dared to meet his gaze again, knowing as she did that she was making an error in judgment. Her conscience screamed at her, but she ignored it because she wanted him so badly. "Last night, I was afraid."

"Of me?"

"Of . . . this."

"And now?"

She shook her head, and his face tightened with emotion. His hand moved down, over the swelling mound of her breast. He looked at what he touched in a way that endeared him to her. She got as much pleasure from watching the delight in his eyes as she did from the stirring way his hand caressed her. When he raised his head, his eyes were smoldering with desire, and he held her captive in that swirling inferno. He was looking directly into her eyes when his finger tip grazed the tip of her breast. It ripened beneath his touch. They cried each other's names simultaneously.

His mouth came down hard on hers as his arms enfolded her. She locked her hands behind his neck and opened her lips to his tongue. It mated with hers, rubbing and pressing and thrusting, intimating the most primitive of lovemaking.

"God, but you're sweet," he whispered against her throat. He nuzzled her neck, left tiny love bites on the fragile skin, tasted her with the tip of his tongue.

He palmed the generous fullness of her breast, kneaded it tenderly, then sought the nipple with his thumb. He worried it to tight perfection before ducking his head and taking it between his lips. Even through her clothes, the moist fury of his mouth surrounded her, drove her mad with its sensuous tugging cadence.

She lay back against the cushions, urged down by his reclining weight. His desire strained against the cloth of his shorts. She felt it against her thigh and thrilled to it. Her hands slipped under his T-shirt and began working it up even as he began to unbutton her blouse. His mouth returned to hers for quick sipping kisses. "I want to love you. Now, Ellie, now."

Arden froze.

Drew jerked upright when he heard the words leave his mouth. *What had he said?* It took only one look at Arden's chalky face to know.

He vaulted off the couch to his feet. The heels of his hands dug viciously into his eye sockets as his face contorted into a feral scowl of rage and agony.

When he could no longer contain it, a vile expletive erupted from his mouth.

Chapter 6

THEY WERE PETRIFIED BY SHOCK. DREW'S BLASTING CURSE had left a vacuum of silence behind it, like the absence of oxygen immediately following an explosion, like the sulfurous charge in the air after lightning has struck. They were held paralyzed in that deadly quiet void.

When at last he spoke, his voice carried a great weariness with it. "I'm sorry, Arden." He raised his arms in helpless appeal. "Dammit, what else can I say but that I'm sorry?"

Arden stood like a somnambulist, swayed slightly, but at last was able to propel herself toward the door, rearranging her clothes as she went.

"Arden." He said her name softly, apologetically, but when she didn't turn around, he repeated it with more force. When she didn't stop then, he lunged after her. "Arden," he said, grabbing her arm and turning her around. "Listen—"

"Let me go, Drew." She kept her head averted, her voice iron hard and cold.

"Not until you've listened to an explanation."

She laughed without humor. It was a hollow, lifeless sound. "I think this poignant scene is self-explanatory." She struggled against his tenacious hold. Had she not been so civilized, she would have clawed, kicked. She was frantic to get away. "Let me go," she shouted. "I don't belong here. I don't know why I'm here. It's wrong. Let me go." She was bordering on hysteria but couldn't contain it and fought the manacle of his hand around her upper arm.

"You *do* belong here because I invited you. I want you here with me and Matt."

"You want Ellie here!" she screamed up at him.

His face, which had been working with anger at himself and frustration over her misunderstanding, went completely blank. Her cruel words erased all expression. The steely fingers around her arm relaxed, and his arm fell to his side. "Ellie *is* here," he whispered. "That's the problem."

He returned to the sofa with trudging footsteps. Slumping down onto it, he laid his head against the back cushions and closed his eyes.

The moment Arden flung her hateful accusation in his face, she would have given heaven and earth to recall it. As he turned away from her, she reached out a comforting hand, but pulled it back. The last thing he would want now was her pity. But she couldn't leave without saying something.

"What I said was unforgivable, Drew."

He scoffed with the same bitterness she had shown only moments before. "What *I* said was unforgivable. I know you feel insulted. Don't. You should feel flattered." He opened his eyes and looked at her. "I'd like to explain."

"You don't have to."

"I want to." His tone was determined. She nodded.

He stood up and walked to the wide glass door. Sliding it open, he let the scent and sound of the Pacific Ocean fill the suddenly stifling room. "Honolulu is where Ellie and I met, where we lived when we were married. I can't come back here without having a million places and things remind me of her or something she said or something we did."

"I know what that's like. After Joey died, sometimes the memories were so strong, I would think I'd hear his voice."

He shook his head in aggravation. "She's been on my mind since we arrived. We used to take Matt to the pediatrician together, you see. Tomorrow I'm taking him to visit her parents." Arden didn't want to acknowledge the stab of envy that pierced through her. "And all day, I've felt like . . . like I was being unfaithful to Ellie."

"Because of me?"

"Yes."

Sorry as she was about what she'd said to him, she felt he'd slapped her in the face again. "Is that supposed to make me feel better?" she asked scathingly. He pivoted around, and she saw again that flicker of impatience in his eyes. Actually, she preferred it to the haunted vacancy that had been there moments before.

"It might if you wouldn't fly off the handle, if you'd let me tell you a few things before you jump to conclusions."

"You make me sound like an unscrupulous home wrecker."

"Dammit, will you *listen?*" He muttered a curse and shoved strands of hair off his forehead. "There have been other women, Arden. Since Ellie and before you."

"I'm feeling better all the time."

He frowned at her sarcasm before going on. "Too many women. One-night stands. Faceless, nameless women that I was later glad I couldn't remember." He closed the distance between them and peered closely into her eyes to emphasize his next point. "They meant nothing. Nothing," he said, slicing the air with his hands. "My desire for them was a biological function, nothing more. What I did with those women could be described in the coarsest of terms because that's all it was. I didn't feel I had betrayed Ellie, at least not our love, because there was no emotional involvement for me."

He took a breath that expanded his chest almost enough to touch her. His voice lowered in pitch and volume. "You're the first woman I've felt guilty about."

Her outrage receding, she wet her lips nervously. "Why?"

"Because with you there *is* an emotional involvement. With you it wouldn't be just . . ." He searched for a less abrasive word, shrugged and said bluntly, "Screwing." He placed his hands on her shoulders and drew her closer. "It would be loving. I'm falling in love with you, Arden. I'm surprised by it. Actually dismayed. And I don't quite know how to handle it."

She swallowed the knot in her throat. "You still love Ellie." There was no inquiry in her voice; it was a simple statement of fact.

"I'll always love her. She was a part of my life. But I swear to God I'm not trying to replace her with you. The two of you are too totally different. Nothing alike. So please don't think that because I spoke her name while I was loving you, I superimposed her image over your body. I wasn't thinking of her. I was immersed in you, only you."

He brought his hands up to her face and alternately stroked her cheekbones with his thumbs. "It's just that this is the first time since her death that my heart has been an integral part of having sex. Speaking her name was a conditioned reflex, because I haven't felt that emotional and spiritual rush since I last held Ellie. Not until you. Don't assign any Freudian implications to it, please."

"I reacted out of conditioned reflex, too. My pride was stung," she cried. "Any woman's would have been."

"Or any man's. I'm not diminishing my error. Believe me, I know it was ghastly. I just want you to know where it was coming from. Tell me you understand."

When he was close like this, she couldn't think, so she stepped away from him and stared out the glass door herself. She wondered if he would be telling her all this if he knew who she was. If she identified herself as the surrogate mother he and Ellie had hired, would he still want to make love to her? How could she ever hurt him and risk losing him by telling him the truth?

"I do understand, Drew. You and Ellie had a rare and special marriage." She could have added, "She loved you enough to let another woman have your child."

"Yes, we did. I was faithful to our vows." He laughed softly. "On tour, that's not always easy. There are opportunities every day. Whatever you want, it's available."

He came to stand beside her, propping himself in the door frame by leaning into it with his shoulder. "Ellie traveled with me when she could, but not all the time. Sometimes I wanted sex. Badly. And there were plenty of women who would have obliged. But I knew how rotten I'd feel afterward. And it would be more than just feeling guilty for being unfaithful. After having experienced sex as a part of love, I really didn't want it any other way. I didn't want it reduced to a merely physical exercise."

He glanced at her quickly. "I'm not a saint. There were times when I was strongly tempted. Particularly if I'd played well, won a match and wanted to celebrate. The adrenaline would be pumping, and I'd want . . . want to make love."

She looked away, out over the ceaseless surf. Quietly, she said, "I can see how one would go with the other. How physical stamina would give you more energy . . . make you . . ."

His laughter this time was genuine, and he cupped her chin with his hand and turned her face back to his. "I know what you're thinking, Ms. Gentry."

"I'm not thinking—"

"You're thinking that since I was playing well that first day we met and since you were sitting there on that patio all cool and serene and appealing as hell, I automatically wanted to hop in the sack with you and work off some excess energy."

She blushed and hated herself for being so transparent. Drew smiled wider, knowing he'd been right on target. "Well, I'll admit I was aroused from that first day. I've given making love to you a lot of thought since we met, particularly after our first lunch date. You looked so untouchably sophisticated, yet you nearly drove me to distraction in that little black top that fit like a second skin over your breasts."

She gasped softly in surprise, but he continued. "Arden, here," he touched the fly of his shorts, "I've been ready to make love since I first saw you. Here," he touched his temple, "I know it's time I loved again. It's here," he said, indicating his heart, "that I'm in conflict."

"You don't hold a monopoly on that," she said, brushing past him and going back into the room. "Hasn't it occurred to you that this might be different for me, too?" She whirled on him. "I'm not accustomed to accompanying men on three-day vacations." Her eyes darted past him as she said in a quieter tone, "The only man I've slept with was my husband. Before or after we were married. It was a lousy marriage. In every way." She hazarded a look toward him. He was listening closely, his eyes trained on her.

"He and I didn't love each other the way you and Ellie were lucky enough to. And when the marriage was over, I gave all the love I had to give to Joey. When I lost him, too, I felt empty, depleted of emotion, a shell with no soul inside. Until . . ." She raked her bottom lip with her teeth and cautioned herself not to reveal too much.

"Anyway, I'm not ready to gamble with my heart, either. I've lost my parents, my husband, such as he was, and my son. I don't know that I'm ready to risk loving anyone else."

"The odds don't look particularly promising when

you're risking it on a has-been tennis bum and his orphaned son."

"Don't say that about yourself," she said fiercely. "You're *not* a has-been and certainly not a bum. And Matt is—"

She broke off when she saw the grin tilting up one side of Drew's lips. "You've just put your foot in it, Arden. You care more than you want to admit."

She lowered her eyes in chagrin. When she raised her eyes again, he could see that they were brimming with tears. "I'm afraid, Drew."

He went to her and wrapped his arms around her. His large, strong hand cradled her head and pressed it into his shoulder. "What are you afraid of?"

Afraid that if you find out who I am you won't believe how much I've come to love you. I wanted my son, but now I think I want you more, and that's wrong of me. Isn't it? I don't know. I don't know.

"I'm afraid to let myself love again."

He pulled away only far enough to look down into her face. He squeezed his hand between their bodies and placed it over her heart. "You have so much love to give. I can feel it, beating here, trying to get out. Don't be afraid to let it go." He lowered his head, and his lips made a pass across her brow as his hand cupped her breast and made a caressing circular motion. "God, Arden, but it would be easy and right for us to love each other."

Yes, it would be so easy. Her body gravitated toward his as naturally as the river flowed toward the falls. And just as perilously, she wanted to hurl herself over the cliff of conscience and principle.

But would it be *right?* Would he feel it was right if he knew that their meeting hadn't been dictated by fate but had been contrived by her for the purpose of finding her son? She tamped out the fires of desire that were already rekindling.

His lips hovered above hers, but she placed her fingers

over them. "Don't, Drew. Not now. If we ever make love, I want everything to be perfect. It wasn't that way for me with my husband." Before she could say more, his mouth stopped her. It was a kiss that promised loving him would be beyond her previous experience and her wildest imagination.

Shakily, she went on when he lifted his lips from hers. "Until such a time, we have our private wars to wage. I don't want you to blame me for any guilt feelings you might have over Ellie."

"You're not to blame," he whispered into her hair. "I blame only myself."

She maneuvered her mouth away from the seductive persuasion of his. "Let's continue being just close friends for the present. Please?"

He sighed his disappointment, but she knew he was going to agree. His smile was wry. "You're making it hard on me." His nose nuzzled her ear. "In case you didn't catch it, there's a pun in there."

"I caught it," she said dryly, pushing him away. "It was in exceedingly bad taste."

"I told you I wasn't a saint."

"Then I'd better clear out while my virtue is still intact. What time do you practice in the morning?" They arranged to meet and have a quick cup of coffee before driving to the courts.

At the door, he caught her waist with both hands. They were indomitably possessive as they squeezed lightly. His eyes swept her breasts and lingered. She focused on the hollow of his throat.

"Arden, do you honestly believe we're going to remain just good friends?"

Her eyes took in the sensuous shape of his mouth. "No."

His voice was slurred with longing when he replied, "Neither do I."

*   *   *

They were friendly the next morning when they met, the tension of the evening before having been dispelled. Drew kissed her briefly on the mouth as he cheerfully greeted her. When they arrived at the courts at the appointed time, he introduced her to his opponent. Bart Samson was a retired professional, Drew's senior by fifteen years, but he could still play a mean game of tennis.

They played on municipal courts, which surprised Arden, but she didn't remark on it. She sat on the splintery bleachers and watched the match. She had brought along a tablet and pen, should she want to work on an article, but took very few notes. Drew's superb game held her attention.

"Thanks for the workout, Bart," Drew said to the man as they strolled toward the parking lot when they were through.

The older man ran a towel over his face and around the back of his neck. "Thank *you*. You whipped me, but it was great tennis." He looked at Arden before he said, "Why don't you meet me at Waialee tomorrow? This"—he indicated the less than perfect courts—"isn't where some-one of your caliber should be playing. Everyone at the country club would love to see you again, Drew."

"Thanks, Bart, but no. Not yet." He took Arden's hand. "If you'd rather not play here with me, I'll under-stand," he said frostily.

"I don't deserve that," Bart replied quietly and without rancor. "Here tomorrow morning at eight." He nodded to Arden before sliding into his Mercedes and starting the motor.

They were almost back at the hotel before Arden said, "You and Ellie were members of Waialee Country Club, weren't you?"

"Yes, why?" he asked, momentarily taking his eyes off the rush-hour traffic.

"Nothing. I just wondered."

At the next stop light, he leaned toward her. "My not

wanting to play there has nothing to do with Ellie or you or
our old friends seeing you and me together. They'd all be
delighted with you, I'm sure. The reason I don't want to
play there is because I made a spectacle of myself the last
time. I'm not ready to face the club set yet. Okay?"

"Not okay. You should go back and play there with your
head held high. Talk to old friends. You've got absolutely
nothing to be ashamed of, Drew."

He studied her for a time, grudgingly admiring the
wisdom of what she said and appreciating her vote of
confidence in him. "Give me a kiss."

"No."

"Because I'm sweaty and stinky?"

"No. Because the light turned green about thirty seconds ago and all the cars behind us are honking."

He cursed softly as he released the brake and continued
the drive back to the hotel, scowling at Arden's soft
chuckles. The moment they opened the door of the suite,
they knew something was wrong. Matt, tears streaming
down his face, came running to his father, arms out-
stretched.

Drew scooped him up. "What the hell . . . ?"

"Mrs. Laani!" Arden cried, crossing the room swiftly
when she saw the woman lying on her back on the sofa,
one forearm across her eyes, the other across her stomach.
She was moaning pitiably. "Mrs. Laani," Arden repeated,
going down on her knees beside the sofa and touching the
woman's arm, "are you ill?"

"I'm so sick," she groaned. "The baby, he's hungry and
wet . . . but, I'm sorry, Mr. McCasslin," she said when
Drew walked into her range of vision. "I couldn't get up.
My stomach." She closed her eyes again in misery.

Matt had stopped crying and was hiccupping against
Drew's shoulder. "Do you need to go to the doctor? Could
it be appendicitis?"

"No. I had my appendix out years ago. It's . . . at my

sister's house. They all had this virus. I guess I caught it. I don't want Matt to get sick."

Arden was touched over Mrs. Laani's concern for the child. "Don't worry about him. He'll be fine. We need to get you feeling better. Can I get you something?"

"You're a nice *wahine,*" she said, squeezing Arden's hand. "Thank you, but I don't want anything except to get out of here and keep all of you from catching this. Mr. McCasslin, I called my sister and asked if I could stay with her until I'm well. My brother-in-law is coming to pick me up. I hate to desert you, but—"

"That's all right," Arden said, intervening again. "I can take care of Matt. When is your brother-in-law coming to get you?"

"He should be downstairs now."

"Drew, give Matt to me and I'll get him some breakfast. You help Mrs. Laani down to the lobby. Is that her bag? Here, carry it for her."

"Yes, ma'am," he said as he followed her instructions. Despite his worry over his able housekeeper, whom he'd never seen in less than perfect health, his eyes were twinkling with amusement at the way Arden was taking charge.

They were still sparkling when he returned after escorting Mrs. Laani down to meet her brother-in-law. Arden was helping Matt eat his cereal. There was a small refrigerator in the suite, and Mrs. Laani had stocked it with juice, milk, fruit, cheese and snacks so Matt wouldn't have to be taken to a restaurant for every meal. The hotel management had provided them with a small assortment of dishes and silverware.

"How is she?" Arden asked.

"Miserable, but relieved that she's separating herself from Matt. He was her main worry. She expects that if she lives for the next twenty-four hours, she'll survive."

"I think so, too. It's probably just a bug."

"And in the meantime—"

"I'll take care of Matt."

"I can't let you do that."

"Why not? Don't you trust me with him?"

He placed his hands on his hips in exasperation. "Yes, I trust you with him, but I didn't bring you along to take over as nursemaid."

Feeling glowingly content, with her child on her lap and his father looking ruggedly handsome in his sweat-damp tennis clothes, she cocked her head to one side and asked impishly, "Why *did* you bring me along?"

"To woo you into bed with me."

She laughed. "Well, before you proceed, would you please go take a shower?"

He looked down at himself, grinned abashedly and said, "Oh, yeah. That might be a good idea."

By the time Drew had showered, she had Matt bathed and dressed. "If you'll give me just a few minutes, I'll be ready, too." She'd told him she needed some things for Matt, and they'd decided to make a short shopping expedition. "Let me pop into my room and I'll be right back."

"I was meaning to talk to you about that."

"About what?" she paused to ask as she was sailing out the door.

"About your room. Wouldn't it be more convenient if you moved in here?"

She fixed him with a doubtful stare. "Convenient for whom?"

His smile fell on her like warm sunshine. "For you. And Matt, of course."

"Oh, of course."

"Think about it," he said, shrugging with feigned nonchalance.

"I already have. The answer is no."

She met them in the designated place in the lobby ten minutes later, looking amazingly well put together after having dressed so quickly. "I like those stretchy little tops you wear," Drew said in her ear as he draped an arm around her shoulders. Matt was walking with independent importance a few steps ahead of them.

"This is a sundress," she said, smiling her pleasure.

"Yeah, but it's made like that top you had on that day at lunch. I loved it because—"

"I know. You've already told me."

"Because it—"

"It's high fashion."

"Because it shows your nipples when they contract. Like now."

"Stop it." She tried to sound indignant and failed.

"It makes me wonder what color they are and how they'll feel against my tongue."

She made a whimpering sound. "Please, Drew, stop talking that way."

"Okay. I will. But only because those two sailors are ogling you in a way that makes me want to knock their heads together. The last thing they need to see is that limpid look in your eyes. It's the biggest come-on I've ever seen, and a man would have to be dead not to notice it." He all but snarled at the two hapless sailors as they walked past them. Then he hissed in her ear. "You've got great legs, too." She laughed.

He was highly irritated that one of the items on the shopping list was disposable diapers. "Matt's supply is running low," Arden explained.

"I want to get him out of diapers, but Mrs. Laani says he's not ready to potty train yet."

"And she's right. It can be traumatic if you try to train a child too early."

"I know," he grumbled, shoving his hands into the pockets of his navy blue shorts. The lean muscles of his thighs looked sculpted. "It's just that he'll seem officially a son when we can go into the men's room together."

She rolled her eyes heavenward. "The male ego. I can't

believe it. I've changed him numerous times and seen him in the bathtub twice. He's officially your *son*."

Drew's eyebrows arched wickedly. "You think he inherited something from me?"

Her cheeks flamed scarlet. She spoke over his hearty laughter. "He might train more quickly if you'd take him into the bathroom with you now and again. Maybe he'd begin to get the idea."

"You're changing the subject."

"You're right."

He kissed her soundly but quickly. "I'll take your suggestion to heart—it sounds like a good idea that I should have thought of myself."

When they returned to the hotel, Arden carrying their parcels and Drew carrying Matt, it was time to clean him up for lunch with Ellie's parents. Arden was dismayed to find that most of her belongings had been moved into the bedroom formerly occupied by Mrs. Laani.

"Remind me to compliment the manager of the hotel on his staff's efficiency."

"Drew," she said, rounding on him, "I won't stay here with you tonight."

"Not with *me*. With Matt. He's in a strange place. He'll feel better with someone in the room with him."

"Then you sleep with him."

He placed an index finger over her lips. "You're too smart for your own good." His eyes followed his finger as it moved over her lips. "Please. Nothing will happen that you don't want to happen. I promise."

In the end, she relented. Actually, being able to spend the night in the same room with her son was like being given a gift.

"You can go with us," Drew repeated for the third time when he and Matt were ready to leave for lunch.

She shook her head as she ran a fine brush through Matt's curls. "No, Drew. I couldn't."

"It wouldn't matter to me. I'd like for them to meet you."

She could tell by his inflection that it was important she believe him. "Thank you for that. But I wouldn't want to spring up from nowhere and probably spoil the visit for them. I know they're looking forward to it."

"They are. Matt's their one and only grandchild."

Then they don't really have one, do they? she thought to herself. "Was Ellie an only child?"

"Yes. She moved to the mainland to wait for . . . until Matt was born. They wanted her to . . . uh . . . to have him here, but she wanted to have him in Los Angeles. Anyway, when we brought him home, they were ecstatic. He'll be a demon tonight. They spoil him rotten."

So, even Ellie's parents didn't know that her pregnancy had been a hoax. Did anyone know besides Drew and herself? And Ron, of course.

"What will you do while we're gone?" he asked her.

"Work on an article. I checked with the hotel, and they have a spare typewriter they'll let me use." Drew had discouraged her from carting her portable along. "Or I may go to the pool and work on my tan."

"Wear something modest. I don't want a stray man with dishonorable intentions to get the idea you're available and take it upon himself to make your acquaintance."

She propped her fists on her hips. "That's how I met you."

"That's what scares me."

The sun was hot, baking into her body. It felt marvelous. The breeze off the ocean was cooling, so only her skin, lightly glossed with tanning lotion, was warm from the afternoon sun. She had tuned out the sounds of laughing tourists, playful children, boisterous teenagers, and listened only to the pounding surf. Its rhythm was so hypnotic that she could almost feel her body undulating to the beat.

Was it the surf that caused that restlessness in the lower part of her body? Or was it the thought of Drew's kisses, his caressing hands, his tongue in her mouth and licking her skin? He had introduced her to a world of sensuality she'd never known before. Until she met him, she had thought that sphere existed only in the imaginations of poets and dreamers, romantics who wished life could be better than it was. But this world of sight and sound and smell and taste and breathless excitement did exist. If one were fortunate enough to find the right partner to share it. It wasn't a world that could be experienced alone.

For much of her life, she'd been alone. Now her life was so full it frightened her. She was with her living son. *Her son.* And she loved him as passionately as she had loved Joey. She took advantage of every excuse to touch him, to snuggle him to her, to breathe in his delicious smell, to marvel over his powers of reasoning and his physical dexterity.

And she was coming to love, even more passionately, the man who had fathered him.

She was both joyful and sad. Joyful over having found them and loved them. Sad because she knew she couldn't have them. Everyone she had ever loved, she had lost. They would be lost to her, too. The day would come when she'd have to give them up. But until that day, she'd bask in their presence.

"Oh!" she exclaimed, coming bolt upright on her beach towel and knocking Matt down into the sand on his bottom.

"Code," he shrieked, giggling and shaking another ice cube onto her bare stomach.

She gasped again, sucking in her stomach and reaching for his cup of ice at the same time. "Yes, it's 'code,' and as smart as you are, I don't think you could have thought up this prank."

She turned around to see Drew squatting on his heels behind her, grinning like a Cheshire cat. The sight of him in light blue swimming trunks took her breath away as effectively as the ice cubes on her burning skin. The breeze tossed his blond hair, making him look wild and reckless and consummately male.

"Guilty as charged," he said, smiling broadly.

"I thought as much."

"But Matt was all for the idea."

"Like father, like son."

He walked around her to sit on the end of her beach towel. Matt had tottered toward the water and was taking tentative steps into the surf. "I thought I told you to wear something modest. If that's your idea of modest, you need a new dictionary."

Out of contrariness, she had put on the most provocative of her swim suits. It was of black crocheted cotton yarn lined with flesh-colored material. The top was two triangles held together with braided strings. The bottom was brief and narrowed on the sides of her hips to a single strand of braid.

"I'm not going to let you bully me. Besides, no one has bothered me. Until now," she said pointedly.

"Do I bother you?" The seductive pitch of his voice and the way his eyes took in every erogenous part of her body sent her senses into pandemonium.

Before she could voice a suitable comeback, Drew was hailed from the low brick wall that separated the hotel's pool area from the beach.

"Drew! Drew, is that you?"

Drew's eyes searched the crowd to see who had called to him, and Arden saw a mixture of vexation and caution when he identified the man. Unenthusiastically, he raised his hand and waved. "I'll be right back. Do you mind watching Matt?"

"Not at all," she said, more concerned about the grim shadow on Drew's face than the active little boy.

Drew cursed mentally as he weaved his way through the sunbathers on the beach to the steps leading up to the patio surrounding the pool. Of all the people to spot him. The last person he wanted to see. Jerry Arnold, manager of the tennis program at Waialee Country Club.

"Hello, Jerry," he said, extending his hand.

"Drew—God, man, it's good to see you." The man pumped his hand. "You're looking great since I last saw you."

Drew smiled grimly. "Well, that's not saying a helluva lot, is it? The last time you saw me, you had me by the shirt collar and you were dragging me out of the locker room, asking me not to come back. I wasn't so drunk that I don't remember."

Jerry Arnold was a head shorter than Drew and much stouter. At one time, he'd played on the pro tour, but he knew before coaches or anyone else kindly told him that he didn't have what it took to play competitive tennis. He'd surrendered his dreams graciously and done the next best thing. He worked with those who did. "I'm sorry, Drew. You gave me no choice."

"I don't blame you, Jerry. You should have revoked my membership and whipped my ass."

"I couldn't," the man said, smiling. He rubbed his jaw in remembrance. "You've got a mean right hook."

Drew chuckled softly. "I was violent and abusive. I'm sorry."

"So was I. I hate to see talent like yours going to waste." His eyes probed Drew's. "I'm hearing terrific things."

"Oh?"

"You're on the way back."

"Yes, I am."

"Prove it."

Drew had been watching Arden and Matt wrestling in the sand. She had beautifully slender thighs and a nicely rounded tush. It took a bold challenge like Jerry's to snap his eyes and his attention away from that. "What did you say?"

"I said prove that you're on the way back up."

"How? By coming back to the club? Bart Samson already asked me this morning. I told him no."

"By coming back to the club . . . and playing an exhibition match. Tomorrow."

Drew's mouth went dry, and his hands involuntarily knotted into fists that matched the knots forming in his stomach. "I can't," he whispered, terrified.

"You can. I need you to. McEnroe was supposed to be here to play in a match for charity. Muscular dystrophy. Fifty dollars a pop for tickets. He sprained his thumb in—"

"I read about it."

"So his coach says no playing. Not even exhibition. I need you, buddy. And you need this match."

"Like hell I do."

"Like hell you don't. You've got to start sometime, Drew. Prove to all those who didn't have faith in you that you can climb right back into that number-one seed."

"Not this year. Next, maybe." He hated the way his insides were churning, the way his hands had become slippery with sweat, the acrid taste of fear in his mouth.

"As I said, you've got to start sometime. I talked to Bart. He told me you were here. He said you ran his tail into the ground this morning, said he couldn't return but half your serves."

"What are you, a cheerleader? Are you asking me to play in this match because you need a warm body on the court to save your face, or do you really care about my floundering career and yet-to-be-seen comeback?"

"Both." The man stared up into Drew's taut face, conceding nothing. He was being brutally honest. At least Drew could appreciate that.

Drew was the first to look away. "I don't know, Jerry."

"Look, if I thought you'd get out there and make a fool of yourself, I wouldn't ask. For both our sakes. You've got your head on straight again. I see you've got a new chick. So—"

"She's not a *chick*," Drew said between his teeth.

Jerry's eyebrows expressed his surprise at Drew's rabid defense. He cast a look at the woman on the beach. She was playing with McCasslin's boy. Jerry returned his gaze to Drew, whose anger was still simmering behind glacial eyes. "I'm sorry. I didn't mean to give offense." His face took on an earnestness that couldn't have been faked. "Drew, I don't care if it's a *guy* you're seeing. I'm glad of whoever or whatever is going to bring you back to where you should be. On top."

Drew let the muscles of his body relax. He was surprised at his possessive, protective attitude toward Arden; it had momentarily overruled his better judgment. He'd been almost ready to kill Jerry for slighting her. In that moment, he realized the extent of his feelings for her. It thrilled him. It also imbued him with confidence.

"Who's playing?"

"Teddy Gonzales."

Drew's curse was terse and explicit. "Thanks, Jerry." He sighed heavily, his flicker of optimism extinguishing.

"Yeah, I know, he's your arch rival."

"And eleven years younger. With eleven years more stamina."

"And you've got eleven years more experience. He's a hothead, Drew, an egomaniac. Play with strategy; work on his emotions." Jerry eyed him shrewdly. "Scared?"

Drew stated crudely just how scared he was, and Jerry laughed out loud. "Good. That'll make you play better. Say I can count on you, Drew. You need this match more than I do. If I didn't think so, I wouldn't have asked. I swear to God I wouldn't have."

"Thanks, Jerry." For a brief moment, they looked at each other in honesty and friendship. Drew sought out Arden's graceful form. Just then, she turned toward him and smiled. Matt stumbled in the sand. Her arms were there to help him up. "Can I tell you tonight, Jerry?"

"Sure. I'll call around eight." He clamped his hand on Drew's shoulder and squeezed it tightly. "I hope you'll say yes. Oh, and Drew," he paused to add after he'd taken several steps, "your lady is very pretty."

Drew made his way back to the beach towel and dropped down on it. He tousled Matt's hair and hugged him tightly before the boy toddled off toward the water. Only then did Drew look at Arden. God, she was beautiful. Just looking at her filled him with an assurance that replaced the fear. If he sat and stared at her long enough, would all of it disappear?

"A friend?" she asked softly.

"I wonder." She didn't pry, but he could see the question in her green eyes. "He wants me to play an exhibition match at Waialee for muscular dystrophy. Tomorrow. Against Teddy Gonzales."

"Are you going to play it?"

"Do you think I should?"

"Absolutely."

Chapter 7

HE WANTED TO BE TALKED INTO IT. ARDEN KNEW THAT. HE was nervous and keyed up as they left the beach and returned to the suite. He couldn't stand still. While she bathed sand off Matt, Drew paced the bathroom.

"I don't know if I'm ready."

"Maybe you're not." She would play devil's advocate. If she tried to encourage him, he'd only dig in stubbornly and keep refuting every positive thing she said. Then should he be defeated, he'd have her to blame for talking him into playing.

"On the other hand," he contradicted himself, "I'll never know, will I, until I start playing competitively again."

"That's right."

"But *God!* Tomorrow. Why couldn't it be next week?"

"Too bad it's not. Then you'd have all week to stew over it."

He wasn't really listening or he would have caught her

caustic tone. Pacing, he was tapping his thumbnail against his front teeth. His brows were creased. "But if I had a week to think about it, I'd probably talk myself out of it."

"Probably," she said, hiding a smile.

"Maybe it's best that I have to make a hasty decision."

"Yes, maybe."

He stalked her as she carried Matt into the bedroom to dress him. "I'll have to call Ham. He's been after me for months to start playing, even in penny-ante tournaments. But he might not think this exhibition match is a good idea."

"No, he might not."

"But I should mention it to him, anyway," Drew said, heading for the phone. "I'll call him right now."

His manager was thrilled and said he'd try to get a plane out of Los Angeles so he'd be there in time for the match the next day.

"It *would* be Gonzales." Drew had ordered a succulent cut of prime rib but had eaten virtually none of it. Arden had ordered for Matt and herself when it became apparent that Drew was too preoccupied to do so. "The last time I played him, he laughed at me. The bastard turned toward the crowd in the bleachers, spread his arms wide in a gesture of dismay and *laughed.*"

If Drew was looking for pity, he'd have to look elsewhere. Coddling was the last thing he needed. "It's unfortunate it couldn't have been someone less intimidating than Gonzales. Then people, sports writers and such, could say you were playing it smart and safe, that you weren't biting off more than you could chew."

"They'd say I was a coward," he said, viciously stabbing a piece of meat with his fork and then wagging it in her face as he made his next point. "No, maybe it's a good thing it's Gonzales. At least they can't say I'm afraid to play."

A vengeful light glowed in his eyes, but when he saw

Arden's knowing smile, his face softened, and he lowered the threatening fork to his plate. "What time is your friend calling for your answer?" she asked softly.

"Eight o'clock."

"Then we'd better get back to the suite." She wiped Matt's mouth free of mashed potatoes.

They had eaten early in deference to Matt's bedtime. As soon as they returned to their rooms, his busy day caught up with him, and he was more than ready for bed. Drew's mind was still on his dilemma even as he helped Arden get Matt settled for the night. The telephone was ringing when they walked back into the sitting room after switching off Matt's bedroom light.

Drew froze, staring at the phone for several seconds before purposefully striding across the room and lifting it to his ear. "Hello," he barked. "Oh, hello, Mrs. Laani."

Arden saw his shoulders sag with relief even as she felt her own relax. "That's good to hear. We've missed you, but Arden has a knack for controlling Matt." He glanced over his shoulder and winked at her. "Well, if you're sure you feel well enough. Don't rush back on our account . . . No, that will be fine. As a matter of fact, I might be playing a match tomorrow, so it would be convenient if Matt were taken care of . . . Okay . . . Rest tonight and we'll see you then."

He hung up. "She says she can come back tomorrow. She'll be here in the morning to take Matt shopping. Her sister will drive them."

Arden knew a pang of disappointment. She would have loved to be included on the shopping trip. Selecting clothes for her son, as she'd never been able to do before, would have been a joy. But she saw no way she could arrange to go. Besides, if Drew played the match, which she felt sure he would, she wanted to be there.

"I'm going to say good night, Drew."

He stopped his pacing and looked at her blankly. "Now? It's not even—"

"I know, but you need time alone. To think."

He crossed the room and put his arms around her waist. "I've been acting crazy since I talked to Jerry today. I'm sorry. I haven't meant to ignore you. You're not angry, are you?"

"Of course not! Give me a little credit, Drew. You're trying to make a monumental decision. Your distraction is understandable."

"But I don't want to be distracted from you," he whispered, nuzzling her neck. "I can use your advice and support. Stay with me."

"No. No one can help you make this decision." How well she knew about making pivotal decisions. The night she'd paced her room from dusk until dawn trying to decide whether to go along with Ron's scheme or not had been the loneliest and most frightening night of her life. Responsibility for the decision had rested solely on her shoulders. No one could make Drew's mind up for him. And she wouldn't be his crutch. This time he had to stand alone, or he might never stand again.

"What should I do, Arden?" he asked, pressing his face into her hair.

She pushed him away. "Do you want to play tennis professionally again?"

"Yes, until I can retire on top and not because I can't hack it anymore. Life spans on the professional circuit are short. There is always going to be someone younger and better. I'm resigned to that. But I wanted to finish in a top seed, not in the shadow of ridicule."

"Then I think you know what you should do."

"I should play." A grin broke across his mouth. "I'll play."

The telephone rang again, and this time there was little doubt who was calling. "Good night," Arden said, slipping into the bedroom and closing the door behind her.

She couldn't hear Drew's conversation, but she could detect the assertiveness in his voice. She was smiling as she picked up her tablet and pen and began making notes on the article she was going to do for the food section of the *Los Angeles Times* about simple Polynesian recipes.

When she awoke, Matt's crib was empty. She sat up and blinked rapidly, trying to orient herself in the strange room. Flinging off the covers, she went to the window and peeped through the crack in the draperies. It was before sunrise. The calm ocean was a pink and violet reflection of the sky.

The bedroom door was open. She tiptoed through the sitting room to the other side where another bedroom door stood ajar. The room she peered into was rose tinted with the encroaching dawn. Unlike the bedroom she had shared with Matt, this one didn't have two double beds but a king-size one. Matt had curled up beside his father. Both were sleeping soundly.

Compelled by something stronger than common sense or prudence, Arden crept farther into the room toward the bed. Matt was on the far side of it. His rump, looking plump and out of proportion because of the overnight diaper under his pajama bottoms, was nestled against his father's chest. He was snoring softly through slightly parted lips.

Drew's arm was draped over his son's body. The hand that dangled in front of Matt's chest was lean and slender, with long tapering fingers. The faint morning light picked up the fine golden body hair dusting his arm. Even in repose, that arm looked sinewy and capable of tremendous power.

Arden's eyes misted over with high emotion as they traveled up the length of that arm to a set of wide shoulders. He was facing away from her, but she feasted on the beauty of his back. It was a smooth expanse of tanned skin and contoured muscles that she longed to touch with her finger tips . . . her lips?

His spine curved downward, and she followed its course

to the shallow dip of his waist. She could see only a suggestion of his buttocks above the covering sheet. Below his waist, his tan was only a slight shade lighter than over the rest of his body. A ribbon of sensation spiraled up through her center at the thought of the nude sunbathing he must have done to acquire that tan.

His hair was a tumbled mass of blond strands on the butter-colored pillowcase. Moving around the bed to view his face, she admired the well-fashioned length of his nose, the mouth that declared his sensuous nature and the chin that proclaimed masculine authority. His lashes were spiky and thick, lighter on the ends than at the base, where they were almost black. It was a face that made women sit up and take notice whether they knew him by reputation or not.

Each time they went out, Arden could feel the envious stares of other women. Covetous eyes would take in the man, the woman close by his side and the child between them. Arden knew that most guessed they were a family. Biologically, yes, they were a family. But in truth . . .

Reminded once again that she was an interloper, she turned away silently. She took two steps before she was pulled up short by a swift tug on her floor-length nightgown. Twisting around in alarm, she saw that Drew was awake. He had rolled away from Matt and was facing the edge of the bed, the hem of her nightgown wrapped in his fist.

His eyes were slumberous, lazy, as were his movements as he slowly wound the fabric around and around his fist, reeling her in, shortening the distance between them until her knees bumped into the mattress. His hold on her nightgown was unbreakable. But not nearly as unbreakable as the hold his eyes had on hers. It rendered her motionless while his free hand slowly peeled back the sheet.

Her breath started coming in shallow pants. The sound of her heartbeat, loud and irregular, thundered against her eardrums. A lassitude as heavy and binding as chains claimed her limbs, yet she felt infused with energy.

In one lithe motion, Drew rolled to a sitting position on the edge of the bed, careless of his nakedness. His eyes were still fixed on Arden's, and neither seemed capable of turning away.

He positioned her between his spread knees. His thighs, hard and warm, pressed against the outside of hers. Giving in to an impulse she'd had since she first met him, she raised one hand and let her fingers sift through his sleep-tousled hair. He indulged her for a few moments before catching her hand and bringing it to his mouth.

His kiss was tentative at first, a mere brushing of his lips against the cushion of her palm. Then his tongue tickled the sensitized skin, and she broke out in goose flesh. Soon his mouth was searing her palm and setting off a chain reaction of startling sensations. Like heat-seeking devices, sensual impulses found the hidden target of her sex, and it exploded under the onslaught.

He nipped and kissed each finger tip, her wrists, sending a wave of heat up her arms and into her breasts. They ached with sexual excitement. They filled and overflowed the ecru lace cups of her nightgown.

After appreciating them with his eyes, Drew let his hands drift across her breasts. His flesh touched hers through the dainty lace, and a wildfire of longing swept Arden's body. His fingers caressed her lightly until her nipples flushed and pouted. Leaning forward, he grazed her breasts with his lips, then rested his head against the lush curves, nuzzling her, breathing in her sleepy, warm scent. His head dropped lower, burrowing into her svelte stomach.

One of his hands went to her back and gathered up a fistful of cloth. He added to it until her nightgown was a tight, revealing nylon sheath that encased her body and made her feel more exposed than nakedness could have made her feel. His eyes flickered over her like tongues of flame. He spotted the indentation of her navel and kissed it, outlining the small crater with an impetuous tongue. She watched the damp spot on her gown grow as he kissed her there again and again. Her knees trembled. Her hands had long since found their way to his shoulders. Now they tangled in his hair as his head moved lower along her sleek feminine form.

She held her breath against a whimper of passion when his index finger traced the diagonal groove above her thigh. Her head fell back, and she instinctively arched into him when he treated the other side of the triangle to the same torturous caress. Then he kissed the spot where they met, and the foundations of her world crumbled and fell away and left her suspended without a foothold. Clutching his hair, she sobbed his name.

The hand at her back released the material of her gown and tunneled through her hair as he stood up. His mouth fell on hers, hot and hungry. But with surprising temperance, his tongue made exquisite love to her mouth.

In one sweeping motion, she was being carried in his arms, through the sitting room toward the other bedroom. She felt his desire against her hips. She had seen it, rooted in a nest of dark gold. Like the rest of him, his sex was splendid.

And she knew the act would be. And just as surely, she knew she couldn't afford it.

She wanted him. Every cell in her body was crying out for surcease from this fever that afflicted her. She ached for him to fill that void that yawned wider each time they touched. Her breasts yearned for the sweet suckling of his lips and the indulgence of his tongue. But this wasn't the time. If they made love now, it could spell disaster for them both.

Unaware of her hesitation, Drew stood her next to the bed and began to caress her anew. His hands closed over her buttocks and urged her forward. Her instinct was to grind herself against him, but she resisted.

There were so many reasons why this couldn't happen now. Would their lovemaking affect the way he played his all-important match that afternoon? What if the act reminded him of Ellie? If making love with her wasn't as good as making love with his wife had been, would he feel only disgust afterward? Or if it were better, would he feel guilty? Either way, he'd be thinking about that and not his game.

Afterward, when she told him who she was, he'd never believe that she hadn't merely bartered her body for the sake of being with her son. No, she couldn't make love to him until he knew everything about her.

Once she had made love to Drew, what then? Supposing he won that afternoon after having had sex with her? He might thank her for helping him get back on his feet and bid her a cheerful farewell. Or if he lost, he might blame her for distracting him. In either case, she'd lose him. She'd lose Matt.

No. No. No. She couldn't gamble everything away, even though she wanted him desperately.

"Beautiful," he was murmuring against her throat as he slid the straps of her nightgown down. "I was dreaming of you, woke up wanting you. Then to see you bending over me, watching while I slept. Oh, God, Arden . . ."

"Drew . . . no . . . ah . . ." His lips had found her breasts, and his tongue was sponging them. "No, please." Her hands went to his shoulders and pushed. He didn't budge.

"So pretty," he whispered, folding his hand around a breast and lifting it to his mouth. His lips moved back and forth across the nipple. "I knew you'd be beautiful. Let me see all of you," he rasped, trying to peel the nightgown the rest of the way down.

"No," she grated, and pushed herself away from him.

Grappling with the slippery nylon, she tried to replace the straps of her nightgown on her shoulders. "No," she said more softly, eying him warily. She could tell by his swaying stance and glassy eyes that her negative message hadn't quite registered yet.

"No? What do you mean 'no'?"

She wet her lips and twisted her hands together in front of her. She'd thwarted him once, and the repercussions hadn't been pleasant. "I don't think we . . . you should . . . before a match. I've heard it's bad for athletes to . . . uh, you know . . . before . . ."

He laughed and took a step toward her. His finger charted the curve of her cheek. "If that were the case, there would be a helluva lot fewer athletes. Arden—"

"No, Drew, please don't," she said, moving away from the caressing hand he'd placed on her hip.

"What's the matter with you?" For the first time, she noted a touch of asperity in his voice. It sounded tight with rising impatience. "Don't tell me you're not in the mood. I know better." He glanced down at her nipples, and she felt her blush start there and stain the rest of her chest and neck like spilling ink. "Why did you come creeping into my bedroom if you didn't want to make love to me?"

She found the arrogant tilt of his chin and the lordly tone of his voice infuriating. "I was checking on Matt. I was worried when I woke up and he wasn't in his crib."

"You know he can climb out of his crib. Besides, one quick look would have let you know he was in bed with me. You didn't have to stand there at my bedside breathing heavy for five full minutes to confirm that Matt was with me."

"Breathing . . . You . . . I . . ." she sputtered.

"That's right. Admit it. Believe me, if I'd found you naked in bed, I'd have been breathing heavy, too. I don't think we've made any secret of the fact that we find each other sexually attractive. So what's the problem?"

"I've already told you. I don't think it's a good idea when you have that match to play today."

"Why? Are you afraid to commit yourself before you know if you're sleeping with a winner or a loser?"

Rage swept over her in a fiery tide that made the hair on the back of her neck stand on end. She caught him on the cheek with her palm in a cracking slap. The resultant silence reverberated in the room until she regained control of herself enough to say, "That was unfair to me, Drew. Cruel, selfish and unfair."

"Well, you don't exactly play fair, either, Ms. Gentry," he hissed. "Coming on like a nymphomaniac one minute and freezing up like an offended vestal virgin the next—twice, I might add—is not my idea of fair play."

She shook with fury. "Well, then, obviously you're not enjoying this game, and neither am I."

"I'm beginning to think that's all this is to you. A game. What's behind this charade you've been putting on?"

He was so close to the truth that she was seized by panic. She stared at him, genuinely frightened that he might somehow, freakishly, stumble onto the truth. It took her a moment to realize that the knocking that echoed through the suite wasn't her heart but someone at the door.

Drew turned away from her, tearing a towel from the rack in the bathroom and wrapping it around his waist before he went to answer the door. It was Mrs. Laani. Arden rushed into the bathroom and locked herself in before the housekeeper could see her.

In five minutes, she had gathered up those of her belongings that were in Matt's room. Mrs. Laani was alone in the sitting room, watching television until Matt woke up. Arden could hear the shower running in Drew's bathroom.

"I'm glad you're feeling better," Arden said, a plastic smile on her face as she edged toward the door. Mrs. Laani could be gregarious and was usually endearing, but

Arden didn't think she could stand the chatter that morning. "Tell Drew I said good luck on his match."

"But Ms. Gentry, he—"

"I'll see you later."

She ducked into the relative safety of her room, showered and dressed quickly in a sundress, took up her straw hat and sunglasses and was on her way in less than fifteen minutes. All morning she poured her energy into the article she was writing, interviewing chefs in several noted restaurants. And all the while she was checking her wrist watch.

Drew had been right. She hadn't played fair that morning. She shouldn't have upset him before his match. What he didn't know was that she hadn't played fair all along. After their first meeting, she should have confided in him, told him who she was. Instead, she had insinuated herself into his life, his personal *and* professional life. She belonged in neither.

But she had fallen so deeply in love with him. That was the factor she hadn't counted on.

Oh, God, what am I going to do about it? she asked herself.

She took a noon break, stopping at a coffee shop and ordering an egg salad sandwich, which she didn't touch, and a glass of iced tea that was becoming watery with melted ice cubes.

There was no solution but to leave. Leave Drew. Leave her son. What good was she doing them? Drew wanted her in his bed but still loved his wife. Arden couldn't settle for that. She'd lived for years with a man who didn't love her. If she ever lived with another, it wouldn't be a one-sided affair. Never that again.

Matt was a happy, well-adjusted, healthy boy who had a mother figure in Mrs. Laani. Drew was dragging himself out of his self-imposed exile and back into the world of championship tennis. He was a good father to her son. She could only cause strife in their lives.

She had what she'd originally set out for. She knew who her son was. Maybe she could call Drew periodically, as a friend, and check up on Matt. He might even come to see her on the mainland and bring Matt with him.

Drew would think she had left over their "lovers" quarrel. So much the better. If he pursued it, that could be her explanation. Things hadn't worked out. *I'm sorry, Drew, but these things happen all the time. You understand. But I'd still like to be your friend, keep track of you and Matt.* Yes, better to leave now before he learned the truth.

She left the coffee shop with her mind made up. She'd go back to Maui. With only one more article to write, she could return to California within a week. She glanced at her wrist watch, and acting on impulse, hailed a cab. There was one more thing she had to do.

"Waialee Country Club," she said briskly as she slid into the taxi.

The crowd was silent. Collectively they held their breath. The pent-up tension and anxiety were almost palpable. The sun was hot, but no one seemed to notice. Everyone's attention was focused on the tennis court.

The two players were as oblivious to the heat and their soggy clothes as they were to the crowd. They, too, were intent only on the match. It was the third and final set, each having taken one. It was five games to four, and Gonzales was in the lead. It was his serve. If he won the game, he'd take the match.

He had sauntered onto the court to a cheering crowd. His dark Latin good looks contrasted with the whiteness of a broad, flashy smile. He was a champion and comported himself as one. His attitude toward his opponent as they shook hands at the net was one of cocky self-assurance. He'd swiftly changed his attitude when he'd barely won the first set six to four and then lost the second seven to five.

He was no longer concentrating so much on pleasing the crowd and posing for the sports photographers. He was trying to win the match, and it was requiring all he had to give.

He went up on his toes and fired a stinging serve into the box. The ball came whizzing back. A heated volley ensued. He slammed the ball into the far corner of his opponent's court and took the point.

"Fifteen love," the umpire intoned.

Arden swallowed hard and dried her hands on the already limp skirt of her sundress. It was full and loose, and she was grateful that she hadn't worn anything more confining. Perspiration rolled in rivulets down her stomach and thighs, and only a portion of it could be attributed to the heat. It was literally a nervous sweat.

Jerry Arnold had hailed her the moment she stepped out of the cab. He had been sent by Drew to take her to the seat reserved for her. "His manager's with him," Jerry informed her excitedly, though she hadn't inquired. "It's like old times. He's calm but angry, you know? That's good. Anyway, he wanted to make sure you were here. If you need anything, ask one of the staff to fetch me."

"Thank you," Arden had said, a trifle confused. Had Drew expected her even after their argument that morning? And who was he angry with? Her?

He had walked onto the court looking breathtakingly handsome in his tennis whites with that familiar logo on the breast pocket and shorts. His trade-mark bandanna was rolled and tied around his forehead. Blond hair fell over it.

The tennis enthusiasts weren't impressed. He had received desultory applause. The spectators were carefully reserving judgment. They had paid their fifty dollars to see McEnroe and were disappointed. Would this be just another blood bath for Drew McCasslin?

Drew hadn't seemed affected by the lack of enthusiasm.

His eyes had scanned the crowd until he spotted Arden. He had nodded coolly. He hadn't looked at her since.

Drew took the next point, and Arden closed her eyes. *Just two more, Drew, and you've held him. Just two more.* Gonzales aced him on the next serve. "Thirty fifteen."

Gonzales got overconfident. He didn't expect the next return to come from Drew's lethal backhand. He lunged one way, the ball went the other.

"Thirty all."

The crowd shifted nervously and began to applaud. Arden heard supportive shouts directed to Drew, and her heart swelled with pride. He had been spectacular throughout the match. Even if he lost, he'd played excellent tennis.

Gonzales won the next point. "Forty thirty. Match point."

An exhausting volley won Drew another point. Gonzales cursed viciously in Spanish. "Deuce."

Arden's knuckles were white, her bottom lip chapped from raking it with her teeth. Gonzales's serve was but a blur. Arden thanked God when Drew found it with the sweet spot of his racket. But he overshot his mark. The ball hit past the base line.

"Advantage Gonzales. Match point."

Leaning over, Drew braced his hands on his knees. His dripping hair fell over his forehead as he hung his head and breathed deeply. Then he positioned himself for his opponent's next serve. Gonzales put all he had into it. Drew returned it with miraculous precision. They whacked the ball back and forth until the spectators were dizzy with watching. Neither made a mistake. Each outguessed the other, dodging to the far side of the court, then racing to the other. Then a ball caught Gonzales in the corner of the court. His perfect forehand landed on the ball squarely and sent it jetting to the opposite corner.

Drew reacted immediately. With the speed of a cheetah,

he propelled himself toward the ball. When he saw he couldn't beat it, he took one final lunge. His body was like a neat arrow slicing horizontally through the air, his racket extended as far as he could reach. That photograph would later win one sports photographer a journalistic prize.

Drew's racket touched the ball, without the necessary momentum. It had enough impetus to reach the net, but touched it and fell back into Drew's court. Landing, he skidded across the court leaving a trail of blood on his elbow and forearm.

No one moved. No one made a sound. With memorable courage, Drew picked himself up and heaved a deep breath. Then, slowly, with dignity, he walked toward the net, his right hand extended for a congratulatory handshake.

Bedlam broke out. Cheers went up, a roar of approval. Not for the victor but for the vanquished. Photographers and tennis enthusiasts of all ages poured onto the court . . . and they were all headed for Drew!

Arden's eyes filled with tears as she watched while hundreds of people surged around him in celebration. He was back. He was on top again. That last desperate effort proved that he was willing to give whatever it took to be a champion again.

She could leave him now. He'd be all right.

She pushed her way through the crowd, got a cab and had it wait for her at the hotel long enough for her to retrieve her bag before going on to the airport. She caught the same commuter airline that the McCasslin party had flown over on. Tears bathed her cheeks when she remembered the heavy pressure of Matt's head on her breasts and Drew's drugging kiss after they'd landed. She'd always remember that moment when she'd had father and son together.

The concierge's desk at the resort was peculiarly quiet. Then she remembered it was the dinner hour. A young woman greeted her warmly. "Good evening. May I help you?"

"I'm Ms. Gentry. I have a room, though I've been on Oahu for the last couple of days. I'd like my key now. Room 317."

The girl tapped something into a computer terminal. "Room 317?" she asked.

"Yes," Arden responded, feeling all the emotional turmoil of the day like a bag of bricks on her back.

"Just a moment, please."

There was a whispered conference between the girl and the desk manager. They kept glancing over their shoulders at Arden, who was becoming more and more vexed with each passing minute.

"Ms. Arden?" The man with whom the desk clerk had conferred came up to her.

They were extremely sorry, but there had been some kind of miscommunication. They were under the impression that she had hastily checked out of the resort. She'd paid with her credit card. The things she'd left in the room had been stored at her request in the resort's offices.

"But I didn't check out!" she argued. "I told the man I was coming back. I only paid for my room so you wouldn't think I'd skipped out."

This mistake was entirely their own. They had given that room to another guest who was planning on a two-week stay.

"I liked that room, but if you've already given it to someone else, there's not much I can do about it. I'll take another. I'm very tired—"

There was another unfortunate problem. The resort was full.

"Are you telling me that you don't have one single room to give me after booting me out of the other one?"

They regretted that that seemed to be the case. What they would be happy to do was to call the other hotels and resorts to see if they could find lodging for Ms. Gentry. They would be happy to drive her there in their van.

"Thanks," she said tersely. "I'll wait over there," she said, pointing to a group of chairs that was so visible from the desk that they couldn't pretend to forget her.

A half hour went by, and the reports were becoming repetitive and discouraging. "Every place we've called is full. But we're still trying."

She was resting her head on the back cushion of one of the chairs, going over her options, when her head snapped up. Drew was stalking through the door of the resort with grim determination thinning his mouth. He was dressed in shorts as usual and a windbreaker, unzipped halfway down as usual. His hair had been shampooed since the grueling match, but it had been mussed by the wind. There was a nasty-looking fresh scab on his arm and elbow. He did a double take when he saw Arden sitting in the lobby chair.

He stopped in front of her, put his hands on his hips and glared down at her. "I've been looking all over two islands for you. Where the hell did you go after the match?"

"The answer's obvious, isn't it?"

"Don't play cute with me. Why did you run out?"

"Why? Because we had a fight this morning." She came to her feet and put as much strength behind her glare as he had in his. "I want out from under your bullying ways and bad temper."

His mouth crooked into a smile. "You ought to get mad more often. It does great things for your eyes."

She was ready with another angry outburst but was interrupted. "Ms. Gentry!" The desk manager came trotting up to her waving a piece of paper. "We found you a room—"

"Keep it," Drew snapped, swiveling around to face the luckless man and virtually nailing him to the floor with a blue stare.

The hotel man looked up at Drew cautiously, then

glanced inquiringly toward Arden. "But Ms. Gentry said she needed a room and—"

"I said to keep it." Drew turned to face her again. "She's coming home with me." His eyes softened as they looked into hers. Then he added quietly, "Please."

Chapter 8

HE TOOK HER STUNNED SILENCE AS CONSENT. BEFORE SHE knew what was happening, Drew was issuing orders that all her belongings be taken out of storage and put in the trunk of his Seville, which was parked outside. He picked up the shoulder bag she'd taken with her to Oahu, and curving his hand around her arm, escorted her out the door. The staff couldn't have been more accommodating, fetching and carrying for him, repeatedly apologizing for having inconvenienced his friend.

She let herself be settled into the front seat of his car but sat with stiff dignity until they had driven away from the resort's entrance gates and onto the dark highway.

"Drew, I won't argue about this. I'm not going home with you. Please drive me to another hotel. I'll find a room."

"I won't argue about it, either. It's crazy for you to go chasing through the night trying to find a place to sleep when I've got three or four empty bedrooms. Besides, I'll let you have one free."

"Free?" she asked archly, leaving no doubt of her meaning.

He brought the Seville onto the narrow shoulder of the highway with a shower of gravel and a screech of tires. He braked jarringly. The momentum pitched her forward. On her way back, she was caught up against him.

"No. Not free. It's gonna cost you." His hand trapped her jaw, holding her head still. For ponderous moments, his lips hovered over hers. She expected a punishing, brutal kiss. Instead, it was excruciatingly tender. His tongue applied delicate pressure to her lips until they parted. He practiced that evocative thrusting rhythm that splintered her with shards of desire. She felt her body melting along the strength of his, her resolve to leave him dissolving just as surely.

When he lifted his head, he lovingly brushed back silky strands of dark hair from her cheek. "Consider your rent paid for as long as you want to stay."

"No other compensation will be required?"

His eyes coasted over her face, down her throat, back to her mouth. "Not unless you want to give me a gift, a gift you know I want but which I'd never take from you or bargain with you for."

She touched his hair, ran her finger along the brushy bar of his brows. "You played . . ." Emotion choked back her words as she remembered his brilliant last effort to save the match. "You played stupendously. I was so very proud. I ached with pride."

"Then why did you run away from me, Arden? Didn't you know I'd want to see you more than any person in the world when that match was over?"

"No, I didn't know that. You were so angry after . . ." She lowered her eyes. It was a gesture that was unconsciously seductive and made his senses reel. "After what happened this morning," she mumbled, "I thought whatever friendship was developing between us was over. I couldn't bear not being at the match, but I didn't think you'd want to see me anymore."

He lifted her hand to his mouth, and pressing it to his lips, spoke against her fingers. "I was mad as hell. But you must concede that when a man is as . . . uh . . . ready to make love as I was and then it's called off, he can't be expected to be in the best of moods." He delighted in the shy smile that curved her mouth upward. "And I wasn't in the best frame of mind to begin with. Hell, why mince words? I was scared, scared to death, to face Gonzales in that match."

"By the end of it, Gonzales was afraid of you."

His grin was spontaneous and wide. "Thanks, but that's not the point right now. The point is, I'm sorry for flying off the handle this morning. You certainly had every right to say no."

"I shouldn't have let things go so far before I did."

His eyelids drooped alluringly. "Think about that next time. I can't say what would have happened if Mrs. Laani hadn't knocked on the door." His lips took hers once again. This time, there wasn't even a heartbeat of hesitation in her response. Her mouth moved against his in generous reciprocation.

"What will she think about having a house guest? And I'm only staying tonight. Tomorrow, I'll have to look for another room."

"I've got twelve or fourteen hours to convince you otherwise," he said breezily as he slid back under the steering wheel and turned on the ignition. "As for Mrs. Laani, she's been throwing daggers at me all day with those beady eyes of hers, grunting instead of speaking and in every way possible showing her displeasure with me for making you run away."

"Did she and Matt have a successful day of shopping?"

"By the number of boxes we brought home, I'd say so," he said, laughing. "Which brings up another point. This afternoon, Matt went to the door of the room you'd occupied and began pounding on it shouting, 'Ah-den. Ah-den.' That's when Mrs. Laani started sniffing with indignation every time she looked in my direction."

If there had been any remaining doubts in Arden's mind, they vanished when she heard that her son missed her. How could she turn down this opportunity to live with him for even a brief span of time?

Could she be blamed later? She hadn't manipulated Drew into the invitation; only a martyr would say no to it. Hadn't she earned the privilege of having her son for a little while? Didn't all those months of mental anguish, of wondering who he was and where he was, of having no image of him, entitle her to *something?*

And Drew. She loved him in a way she'd never imagined loving a man, intellectually, spiritually and physically. Her love encompassed all that Arden Gentry was. It was a love without hope for a future, but that made it no less genuine, no less fierce. The next few days—she didn't really think she'd leave in the morning—would have to last her a lifetime. She'd not refuse them. She deserved a little selfishness.

They entered his estate from the back, since the front of it faced the Pacific Ocean on the western shore of Maui. They drove through iron gates that swung open when he pushed a transmitter and automatically closed and locked behind them.

The sweeping lawn gently sloped downhill several hundred feet toward the beach. It was well past twilight, but Arden could see vast shadows of the banyan trees that mushroomed over the yard like giant umbrellas, their ropelike roots draping from stout limbs. Plumeria trees, with their yellow, pink or white blossoms, perfumed the evening air. Ti plants, wood rose cloaked with yellow blooms, orchid trees and other flowering shrubs banked lush beds of flowers. Giant oleanders provided hedges and lent the estate total privacy.

The house itself—what could be seen of it behind its veil of blooming vines—appeared to be alternating walls of sand-colored brick and glass. Wide verandas led into rooms left open to the evening air and cooled by the ocean breeze.

"It's gorgeous," Arden said, stepping out of the car without waiting for Drew to come around and open her door. The wind flirted with her hair and filled her nostrils with the scent of flowers and sea.

"I bought it on sight. Come on in. I'll send Mo after your bags."

He led her around to the ocean side where they entered the living room through an opening in the glass wall. Tall stained wood shutters, which had been pulled open and stacked together, could be used to close off the glass to provide privacy or protection from the weather. Quarry tile floors were polished to mirror perfection and dotted with oriental rugs.

The furniture emphasized comfort, not formality. The upholstered pieces were done in a nubby, oatmeal-colored fabric. Brightly colored pillows in varied prints and stripes provided splashes of color. Fresh flowers filled vases and bowls strategically placed around the room. An ebony grand piano stood in stately dignity in one corner; a stone fireplace filled another. Tables were of glass or wood and trimmed in brass. It was one of the most gorgeous rooms Arden had ever seen, and it set the tone for the entire house.

"Formal dining room, breakfast room and kitchen through there," Drew said, pointing. "My office is on the other side. Powder room behind the stairs."

The open staircase had solid oak steps and a banister inlaid with strips of brass. Drew led her up to the second floor.

"I'm going to put myself back in favor with my housekeeper and my son by bringing you home to them."

They went down a wide second-story hallway, and Drew pushed open a door. Mrs. Laani had somehow wriggled her bulk into a rocking chair and was singing softly to a sleepy Matt.

He sat up instantly when they entered the room. The moment he saw his father and Arden, he flung himself out of Mrs. Laani's arms and hurled himself across the room. He all but tackled Arden, wrapping his chubby arms around her calves. Drew, smiling, lent her support as she knelt down to embrace the boy.

"Hello, Matt," she said, combing her fingers through his halo of blond curls. "Have you been a good boy today? Hmm?" Earlier today she'd planned to leave him. Now she had been granted a few more precious hours. She gathered him to her and hugged him hard. Her eyes grew cloudy with tears when she felt his arms going around her neck and returning her hug.

Pushing her away, his stubby finger found a button on his pajamas, and he declared proudly, "But-n."

"Oh, how clever you are," Arden cried, hugging him again. She searched her own bodice, then realized that her sundress didn't have any buttons. "Well, sometimes I have buttons, too," she said, laughing.

"He's been a terror, so don't you dare compliment him," Mrs. Laani said. "Trying clothes on him is like trying to dress an octopus." She was attempting to maintain a demeanor of solid authority, but she was beaming at Drew and Arden. "You two must be hungry. Mr. McCasslin wouldn't stop to eat before he had us pack up everything and hustled us out to the airport to catch the last flight for the evening. I swear I never saw him in such a hurry." Drew glared at her and cleared his throat threateningly, but she only smiled back, her round dark eyes flashing merrily.

"Don't you have something you could be doing?" he growled.

"As I was about to suggest," she said huffily as she

squeezed herself out of the chair, "if the two of you will bed down Matt—and you're welcome to him—I'll fix you a light supper." She folded her arms over her massive bosom and eyed Drew. "I take it you offered the young lady dinner."

He caught her less-than-subtle rebuke. "Arden will be our house guest for . . . as long as I can talk her into staying. Will you please ask Mo to get her bags out of the car?"

Mrs. Laani waddled to the door of the nursery. "And which room shall I tell him to put them in?" Her indifference was far too overdone to be authentic.

"In the guest room you think most appropriate," Drew said.

Arden hid her confusion and flaming cheeks by carrying Matt to the rocking chair and continuing where Mrs. Laani had left off. When the housekeeper had left the room, Drew squatted down in front of the chair and rested his hands on Arden's knees. Their eyes met, and an electrical spark arced between them.

"I think Mrs. Laani knows I have the hots for you."

"Drew!" Arden exclaimed.

"And I think she knows you have the hots for me."

"Hot," Matt said, wrinkling up his brows and blowing on his hands. The two adults laughed.

"I'm glad he can't interpret that in the context you said it," Arden said chastisingly.

"But you do, don't you?"

"Do what?" She pretended interest in the design on Matt's pajamas.

"Never mind," Drew said in a voice rife with promise. "We'll continue this discussion later." He slapped Matt lightly on the thigh. "Well, son, are you glad to have your favorite girl back?"

Unaware that he was answering his father's question, Matt laid his head against Arden's chest and yawned broadly.

"He's had quite a day," Arden said, feathering his cheek with the back of her finger.

"Don't spend all your sympathy on him. Save some for me. I've had a helluva day, too."

She looked at him and smiled gently, a madonna's smile. "You certainly have. This is the first of many tremendous days for you, Drew. I'm sure of it. What happened after the match?"

"I was a captive of the press for about an hour. Everyone wanted to know the gory details of my life this past year—why I became a recluse. They wanted to know if I was on the wagon."

"And what did you tell them?"

"Yes. I told them that the drinking had been the result of my wife's death. That I had come to my senses about six months ago and since then had been working like hell until I felt ready for a day like today."

"You were more than ready. When will you play again?"

He outlined the schedule of tournaments Ham was lining up. "I'm still going to take it slow for a while. I can't catch up this year, but next year I think I can make an impressive showing."

"How many years did you win the Grand Slam?" The research she'd done before coming to Hawaii had taught her that the Grand Slam referred to winning the Australian Open, the U.S. Open, Wimbledon and the Paris Open.

"Twice. With two years in between. I'll never do that again, but it won't matter, Arden. As long as I know I'm playing the best that I can, the winning's not so important anymore. I've won the really important battle."

She reached out to touch his hard, sun-tanned cheek. She could almost feel the new strength and confidence he'd found within himself. Just as her fingers brushed the line of his jaw, she jumped in surprise and uttered a sharp cry.

Matt had curiously slipped his hand into the wrapped bodice of her sundress to investigate something he'd never seen before. He had found her breast and its coral nipple an intriguing formation. He was lightly pinching it between his fingers.

"But-n, but-n," he said in proud discovery.

"Matthew!" Arden gasped, taking his hand away from her and refolding her dress.

Drew fell backward on the floor laughing. "He hasn't been around very many women."

"He's been around Mrs. Laani," Arden said, not daring to meet Drew's dancing eyes.

"Come, now, Arden. You and Mrs. Laani are hardly built alike. Matt saw something new and wonderful and had to check it out."

"Well, perhaps before he does too many things like that, you ought to have a man-to-man talk with him."

Drew rolled to his feet and scooped the boy into his arms, carrying him toward the crib. "Yes. I believe I should." He placed his mouth directly over Matt's ear and said loud enough for Arden to hear, "Son, you've got excellent taste in women."

Mrs. Laani had set a table in the "casual" dining room. Drew looked at his housekeeper from under reproving brows when he noted the candlelit table. She bustled around busily, ignoring his glower.

"I thought this would be cozy and restful after such a long, tedious day. I hope you like salmon, Ms. Gentry."

"Yes. That sounds wonderful."

Indeed, the cold salmon with cucumber and dill sauce, the vegetable casserole that Mrs. Laani served with it and the rich custard dessert were delicious. But part of Arden's satisfaction over the meal didn't come from the food but from the man who stared at her as intently as she at him.

Drew's eyes sparkled in the candlelight as he discussed

the match at her urging. He seemed reluctant to talk about it, self-conscious, humble, but she coaxed him to tell her his impressions of it. He seemed pleased that she had watched so closely and knew each stroke he referred to.

"You didn't mind losing it?"

"I always mind losing, Arden. I told you once, I like to win. But if I must lose, I want to lose with dignity in a fair fight. Today was a victory in spite of the score."

"Yes, it was."

His eyes looked into hers across the candlelit table. "I was afraid you weren't going to be at the club after you sneaked out of the hotel."

"I didn't *sneak*," she said evasively.

"I guess it was just a coincidence that I was in the shower when you returned to your room and an oversight that you didn't leave a message with either Mrs. Laani or the desk as to where you'd be."

She ran her thumb and forefinger up and down the slender taper in the candlestick. "That was inconsiderate of me, I suppose, since I was your guest. Jerry Arnold told me you were angry before the match." There was an unspoken question dangling at the end of the statement.

"I was. When I got to the club and he didn't have a ticket for you, I raised hell. I told him he'd better find a choice seat or else. As you know, he got hospitable real quick." His grin was just short of devilish.

She leaned across the table. "You know something? I think you like to shake people up, throw your weight around, be a bully."

He chuckled. "I do. Especially when something means a great deal to me." He was all seriousness when he said, "Your being at that match meant more than you'll ever know. I could feel your support and encouragement."

Her eyes went round with disbelief. "But you didn't even look at me."

"I didn't have to, to know you were there," he said in a tone that stirred her blood.

Mrs. Laani interrupted the intimate mood. "If you don't mind, I'm going to bed, Mr. McCasslin," she said from the doorway. "I'll clear these dishes in the morning. Ms. Gentry is in the room next to yours. Will that be satisfactory?"

"That will be fine. Thank you, Mrs. Laani. Good night."

"Good night." Arden's voice sounded like corn husks shifting against each other.

"Let's walk on the beach," Drew said, helping her out of her chair. He dropped a light kiss on her shoulder. "But you'd better change into something warmer. The wind can get cool after sundown."

He was waiting for her at the bottom of the stairs when she descended five minutes later wearing an apricot-colored velour warm-up suit. The pants were banded at her ankles, and she was barefoot. She had beautiful feet, with well-pedicured toes. He noticed the tantalizingly free swaying of her breasts beneath the sweatshirt and knew she didn't have a bra on. He had a strong desire to close his hands over her breasts, to feel their full softness under the velvety cloth. The pulses inside his head began to pound and were echoed in the lower part of his body.

"Sure you won't be too cold?" he asked as evenly as his unstable senses would let him. She nodded. He settled his arm over her shoulders and led her out into a moon-bathed night.

It seemed that speaking had become difficult for her, too, and he appreciated the fact that she didn't force conversation. He could see the emotion, the anticipation of what was about to happen, in her eyes. Words would be superfluous to what their bodies were communicating to each other.

They walked in silence down the gradual slope of the well-kept lawn, stepped over a low brick wall and onto the sand that led to the shore. Drew's beach was in a small semicircular cove. Waves rolled in to spend their force on the lava rocks before gently continuing forward to foam over the sand. The moon shone on the ocean in a silver band that stretched from the shore to the horizon. Its light shimmered in the curling crests of the waves. Wind soughed through the broad fronds of the palms. It was an enchanting setting.

As many times as he had sat on this beach alone and thought it a magical place, Drew now knew this scene would forever lack something if it didn't have Arden in it. She made the magic real, tangible, touchable. The moonlight paled her skin, but made her hair as dark as ebony. The stars had no brilliance compared to the emerald of her eyes.

He seated himself on the firmly packed sand and pulled her down with him. He sat with one knee raised behind her, the other leg tucked firmly against her derriere, her back against his chest. For a moment, he didn't make any move to touch her or to speak. After all, he didn't know how she would respond when he told her what he felt compelled to say. If he'd known fear that day as he faced Gonzales across the net, he was terrified now. The outcome of the tennis match wasn't nearly as important to him as the result of the conversation to follow.

"I love you, Arden."

There. A simple confession. A bold truth plainly stated.

Her hair swept his face when she turned her head. The moist lips he wanted to claim forever were parted in surprise. "What did you say?"

"I love you."

He looked out at the ocean and felt a kinship with it. It seemed so placid on the surface, yet was roiling beneath, just as he was. "I never thought I'd say that to another woman. I loved Ellie very much. I didn't think I'd ever love that way again. And I don't. I love you more."

All the air left Arden's body. She could feel her chest contracting and it was painful. He was going to kill her with softly spoken words. She couldn't let him. "You have me in residence. You don't have to say that."

He ran his finger down her cheek, smiling gently. "Don't say something ridiculous and get me mad all over again." His lips caressed her temple, but barely. "I'm not saying it for any reason except that it's true. I've given you ample reason not to trust me. I've behaved badly on occasion. But don't you see, Arden, that I was responding defensively? I felt guilty because I was coming to love you more than I ever loved Ellie. I couldn't cope with that. Today, when I thought you'd left me for good, I nearly went crazy."

"But during the match—"

"Not then, later. After the match, when you couldn't be found anywhere." He laughed. "Actually, during the match, I was still angry over the scene this morning. I don't think I would have played with such energy if you hadn't made me so furious."

She ducked her head in embarrassment. His fingers threaded through her wind-tossed hair. He loved the satiny feel of it as it slipped coolly along his skin. "You played it just right. You didn't coddle me. Nor did you try to talk me into or out of playing. You realized the decision had to be mine even though you knew I had no choice but to play."

"That's right. I knew you had to play. I knew you wanted to. But I couldn't tell you that. You had to figure it out for yourself."

"That's my point, Arden. You didn't tell me what I wanted to hear. As Ellie used to do."

"Drew, please don't."

"I want you to know."

"But I don't need to know."

"Yes, you do. I agreed that when we made love, it would be with no ghosts, no secrets between us."

She looked away quickly, but not for the reason he

thought. She still harbored a secret, a secret that might
cost her his love.

"Ellie backed anything I said or did even when she must
have known I was wrong. She wouldn't come to watch me
play because she was afraid I might suffer a defeat and she
couldn't stand to see me down."

Arden did look at him then, in amazement. "Strange,
isn't it?" Drew asked, seeing her incredulous expression.
"When she traveled with me, she stayed away from the
courts. And she couldn't be objective when I lost. If she
had been alive today, she'd have made excuses, apologies,
and commiserated with me over the loss. I'm not sure she
would have understood that it was a personal triumph.
You did."

He cupped the back of Arden's head and pressed it
down to the hollow between his throat and shoulder.
"Ellie could share victory with me. But I don't think she
could have ever shared defeat. Even after all we went
through to get Matt, I worried about what she'd do if our
bubble burst one day."

Arden closed her eyes at the mention of Matt. What
would have happened had he not been born perfect
and healthy? Would Ellie have rejected him? Ron would
never have reared another man's child. He might have
even had the infant terminated. The thought made
Arden shiver, and Drew's arms tightened around
her.

"I was almost more afraid of the future when I was
playing well and living with Ellie than I have been
recently. I don't think she could have faced a tragedy and
survived." His lips found her ear, and his breath filled it
warmly. "Arden, I feel that we could face anything
together. You make me feel strong and confident, at peace
with myself but always trying to be better. When someone
thinks you are perfect, as Ellie did me, there isn't much to
strive toward."

He captured her face between his hands and looked

down into her swimming eyes. "Do you realize what I'm telling you?"

"Comparisons are unfair, Drew. To everyone."

"I know. I just wanted you to know that I wasn't substituting you for her in my life. You're different. Better for me."

"Drew," she whispered, and laid her forehead against his chin, rolling it back and forth. She wasn't prepared for this. God, the last thing she'd ever expected was to have him fall in love with her. It was even more unheard of than her loving him. It was too much. She couldn't take that much goodness in her life. It frightened her. What price would she have to pay for it?

But with his hands warm and soothing, his words of love drifting into her ear, his heart pounding in tempo with hers, she didn't want to think of the future. She only wanted to revel in the fact that he was loving her. She should tell him about Matt now, while the mood was mellow and he was being honest with her. But . . .

"Arden, Arden." He uttered her name, only a heart-beat before his tongue filled her mouth. It plundered sweetly, rediscovering her taste, a miracle that happened each time he kissed her.

His hand slipped under the velour top. Her skin was warm velvet; he could feel her heart pulsing against his hand as he held her breast.

She sighed his name and moved against him in unspoken but undeniable need. "I don't want to usurp anyone's place in your heart, Drew."

He kissed her throat as he continued to fondle her breast. "You aren't. You're too rare. You hold a place uniquely your own because no one else has ever been able to fill it." His hands spoke as eloquently as his words as they touched her reverently. Then he withdrew them from her sweatshirt and wrapped his arms around her with unquestionable possession. Her head fell back against his raised knee as he kissed her.

Tongues swirled together in an erotic ballet. His lips clung to hers as though they never intended to let go. "I love tasting you," he said as his mouth moved back and forth over hers. His tongue flicked at the corners of her mouth maddeningly, until her hands came up to imprison his head.

She arched upward, flattening her breasts against the wall of his chest. Bravely, her tongue pushed past his, and she kissed him in a way she'd never dared kiss anyone before. Former inhibitions fell aside. Again and again, she kissed him, declaring her desire.

"My God," he rasped, when at last they fell apart, groping for oxygen. He clasped her head between his hands as he stared down into her eyes. "Inside?"

She nodded her consent, and they rose together. The house was quiet. Only night lights along the hallways had been left on. At the door to her room, he settled his hands on her shoulders.

"I've crowded you, Arden. Ever since I first met you, I've had things my way. I won't bully you again. I've told you I love you, and I do. But it's unconditional. It doesn't require anything of you. If you come to me, I'll show you how much I love you. If not, I'll understand."

He faded into the shadows of the hall and disappeared into the room next to hers. Moving automatically and purposefully, she went into the room where her things had already been unpacked. She didn't even notice the blue, avocado and beige décor that was somehow both elegant and informal. The adjoining bathroom was equally well decorated.

She peeled off the sweat suit and turned on the taps of the shower until it was steamy. Meticulously, she showered and shampooed, still caught in that trance that would not let her think beyond her senses, beyond her instincts. Certainly it wouldn't let her conscience become involved in her thoughts.

She dried her hair, splashed herself with a perfume too

expensive for such lavish usage and glossed her mouth with peachy gel. With an economy of movement, she wrapped herself in a silk kimono and left the room.

Her soft knock was answered immediately. He stood with a terry-cloth towel around his middle. His hair was only partially dry. The hair blanketing his chest curled damply. His eyes gleamed like sapphires in the dim light.

"Arden?" he questioned softly.

"I want you," she admitted huskily.

"In bed?"

"Yes."

"Naked?"

In answer, she stepped close to him and placed her hands flat on his chest. The springy hair teased her palms, her finger tips. She feathered it; she combed through it down the length of his torso. It became silky just above his navel and narrowed to a fine strip of gold. Her hands fumbled with the tuck he'd made in the towel; then it fell away.

The drumming of her heart drowned out every other sound, even that of her uneven breathing as her fingers drifted downward. They stirred in the thicker, coarser hair. Then courage deserted her, and she raised imploring eyes to him.

"I . . . can't . . . I'm . . ."

"Shhh," he said, pulling her against him. "You've come more than halfway. That wasn't a test. You'll never have to do anything just because you think I want it or expect it. Let's learn to love each other together."

His lips were suppliant as they met hers. They moved over her mouth with gentle persuasion until her momentary shyness vanished and she responded with the true sensuality that had lain dormant all her life. Her mouth flowered open beneath his. His tongue dipped repeatedly into it, giving, taking, enriching, ravishing.

His hands trembled with eagerness as he slipped them inside the kimono. He curbed an impulse to tear it from

her body and crush her against him. She wasn't one of his
fleeting, meaningless nighttime toys. They were in the
past. Arden was his present and future. And she was
precious, so precious. He wanted to go slow, to appreciate
every nuance of her and their lovemaking. He let his
hands rest at her waist, caressing softly. Only when he
heard her soft whine of longing did his hands lift the
garment from her body and let it float to the floor.

He stepped away from her and treated himself to the
sight of her perfect nakedness. His hands touched her
lightly, following the track of his eyes. Arden was dismayed to feel tears of gratitude flooding her eyes. Drew's
slow savoring of her body endeared him to her.

"I've never been worshiped before. Only devoured,"
she whispered.

His face looked incredibly sad, then incredibly happy.
"You're so beautiful," he said hoarsely. He swept her into
his arms and carried her to the bed. The spread had
already been folded down. He laid her on soft, fragrant
linens and followed her down, nestling himself close to
her. They smiled in pure enjoyment of the rough texture of
his body against the satiny texture of hers.

He caught her wrists in one gentle fist and raised them
above her head. His other hand massaged her breasts.
"You don't look like you ever had a baby." She caught
herself just in time from correcting him that she'd had two
children, not one. "Your breasts are firm and round." He
circled them with a talented finger. "Your nipples are light
and delicate." He touched them in turn, and they responded. "You have no stretch marks."

She arched her back when his finger trailed down the
straight column of her stomach and into the dark shadow
at the top of her thighs. "You're perfect," he whispered a
second before his mouth covered hers. When she had been
thoroughly kissed, his lips trailed down her throat. His
caresses had prepared her breasts for his mouth, and he

suckled them with infinite care. His tongue rolled over her nipples, lubricating them deliciously.

"Let go of my hands." When he complied, she tangled her fingers in his hair and pressed his head closer. "Oh, God, Drew. I've never been loved like this."

"I hope not. I want to be the only man you ever remember having touched you."

"No one has. Not like this."

His mouth practiced merciless torture on her navel, deflowering it with a nimble tongue, loving it with sipping lips. She twisted and writhed beneath him, a stranger to herself. A shudder rippled through her when his mouth nuzzled the dark delta of her femininity. She called his name half in panic, half in joy, when she felt his lips nibbling the inside of her thighs. Then he parted them gently, and the artistry of his touch told her she'd known nothing of intimacy before.

"Please, please, Drew."

He honored her hoarse request and the urgent clawing of her hands and climbed her body until he was poised over her. His eyes locked with hers as he introduced himself into her body. He didn't pause or hesitate but pressed deeply and slowly until she knew all of him. Then he did something her husband had never done during lovemaking; he smiled down into her face. When he began to move, he was still watching her, cataloguing her pleasure, memorizing her rapture, noting what movement made her eyes grow smoky with passion.

"You feel so good inside, Arden."

"I do?"

"Oh, God, yes," he ground out. "Move with me."

Conversation? Unheard of during lovemaking. The only sounds she'd ever heard in Ron's bed were meaningless grunts and groans.

"L . . . like that. Again," she stuttered when he stroked the portal, then sank into her completely. "Yes, yes, yes."

When the crisis came, it wrapped them both in a velvet glove of ecstasy, shook them, squeezed the breath from them and spun them about, lifted them, tossed them to the mercy of the heavens, then let them fall into a realm of glory to which each was alien.

Long minutes later, Drew raised his head from her shoulder and with his little finger lifted damp bangs from her eyes. When they opened in sleepy contentment, he dropped a kiss on her mouth and said, "Thank you, Arden, for making me new."

Chapter 9

THE SHEER DRAPES AT THE WALL OF WINDOWS OVERLOOKING the ocean billowed into the room. Arden's eyes opened languorously, and she sighed with the deepest pleasure she ever remembered feeling. The room, bathed with the ethereal lavender of dawn, encapsulated her like a sensuous cocoon of love. In it she had learned the meaning of life in its most splendored dimension.

Drew's breathing was deep and even. She could feel it on her naked back as he held her close to him, sharing the pillow, his arm lying along her thigh. She turned her head slightly, careful not to awaken him, as she looked about the room she had been too entranced to observe in detail the night before.

It was as tastefully decorated as the rest of the house. The walls were covered with grass cloth that contrasted in texture to the lambskin covering the bed. The thick carpet was ivory colored. Against that neutral background, there were accents of pumpkin and chocolate in two easy chairs arranged close to a small table near the windows, in numerous pillows that had been heedlessly tossed off the bed onto the floor, in subtle prints that hung in brass frames on the walls. The furniture had clean, uncluttered lines. The fireplace, in the wall opposite the windows, was a luxury that she found delicious in a tropical climate. It was bricked in the same ivory color and had a fan-shaped brass screen. She liked the room.

She loved the man.

A sliver of sunlight beamed across the carpet like a miniature spotlight. She ought to return to her room before anyone else began to stir. It was about time for Matt to wake up, and after that, no one slept, Arden thought, smiling.

She eased Drew's leaden arm off her thigh and inched to the edge of the bed. Gaining the floor, she pulled on her jade silk kimono and tiptoed over the carpet, which was lush and seductive against her bare feet. The doorknob was under her hand, and she was twisting it slowly when Drew's arms flattened against the door on either side of her.

She stifled a soft scream and collapsed against the wood.

"Where do you think you're going?" he growled into her neck. He pressed forward, trapping her against the door and his hard frame.

"To my room."

"Guess again." He kissed her neck, parting his lips and letting his tongue moisten a vulnerable spot. "You're not going anywhere except back to bed. With me."

She shivered as his mouth made a damp, treacherous path to the back of her ear. Playfully, his tongue batted at her ear lobe. "Ah . . . Drew . . . don't . . . I have to go back to my own room."

His hands slid down the smooth surface of the door to her waist. With a tiny yank, the tie of her kimono, which she'd carelessly looped but hadn't bothered to knot, fell away beneath his deft fingers. "Give me one good reason why."

"Uh . . ." He separated the folds of her kimono and ran his finger tips over her ribs. Moving closer, he settled his middle against her derriere. She knew he had come to her as he had slept—naked. And she couldn't think of one good reason why she had to leave him at that moment.

His arms crisscrossed her chest, and he closed a hand over each breast. "Your breasts are so pretty," he murmured as his hands formed gentle cones around them. "I like that line that marks your tan about here," he said, letting his index finger trace it. "Of course if you'd sunbathe on my beach, you wouldn't have a line. I could rub you with oil, and you could tan evenly all over while I watched."

His hands and provocative suggestions were lulling her into that same enchanted sphere she'd known the night before. Through no conscious thought, her body became malleable, conforming to the curves and bulges of his.

The tender caresses on her nipples had made them bead with desire. He whispered his praise of them in her ear, making her both exult and blush with the boldness of his language. "I love the feel of your skin against my tongue. You taste like all things maternal and all things erotic. Your taste epitomizes womanhood."

Drained of all energy and will to resist now, she laid her head against his shoulder. Moving slightly, she rubbed against him and felt his fierce passion nudging her hip.

His breath was like a storm in her ear as one hand surveyed the smooth plain of her stomach and abdomen. He paused not at all in finding his final destination. His palm settled over the gently swelling mound, while his fingers curved inward to seek the mysteries chastely hidden between her thighs. His thumb roved through the dusky nest.

"I love you here." Even as he spoke, he was moving his thumb in that lazy, hypnotic way that stole her breath, her reason. "Dark. And silky. So silky."

His exploring fingers discovered her dewy and ready for

his love, but he prolonged the rapture. Tenderly and carefully, he adored her with his finger tips, giving her untold pleasure and asking nothing in return. He stroked her to unbearable, mindless passion, finding and kneading the magic key that unlocked all that made her woman.

She shuddered against him, soundlessly and breathlessly and incoherently chanting his name. He turned her, and with his hands beneath her hips, lifted her and let her find his accommodating maleness. She sank upon him fully.

She sobbed her love as again and again he arched his back, driving himself higher and higher. The world fell away in one swift, sudden explosion. Her thighs clamped his, and her arms closed around his neck. Her breasts muffled his own ecstatic cries.

When Arden's consciousness returned, modesty prevented her from lifting her head to look at him. Sensing her shyness and knowing the reason for it, Drew carried her back to the bed and laid her down like a child. Still, she wouldn't look at him. He smiled in faint amusement and love, stroking her back.

"Arden," he whispered. "Was it so terrible?"

She rolled over to look up at him. Shaking her head, she closed her eyes. "It was beautiful."

"Then why can't you look at me?" He brought her hand to his lips and kissed the backs of her fingers. There was a tentative smile on her delicious lips.

"I'm embarrassed." The words were spoken so softly, he could barely hear them.

"I didn't mean to embarrass you."

"No!" Her eyes flew wide. "Not you. You don't embarrass me. I embarrass myself. I've never . . . been like this before." Her eyes stared at the forest of golden hair on his muscular chest. She longed to touch it, but was still timid, half-afraid of the changes taking place in her personality. "I've never done . . . well, things like this. I don't know myself when I behave with so little self-control."

She rested her cheek against his arm, speaking aloud the

thoughts that went through her mind. "It's like there's another woman inside me that I didn't know of before I met you. But that's not right, either, because it's not another woman; it's *me*. I didn't know that part of me existed. And I'm having a hard time getting acquainted with it."

"In other words," he said quietly, "you didn't know until you met me that you were a lusty wanton with an insatiable sex drive." Startled, she looked up at him, but laughed in relief when she saw the teasing light in his blue eyes. "Frankly, I'm delighted."

He clasped her to him, and they laughed softly, rolling together on the bed. His heart was soaring because they took such pleasure in each other and were able to laugh and love in the same minute. Since Ellie died, there had been no joy after sex for him, only a kind of frantic despair.

He couldn't stand the thought of that now, of how empty his life had been. He didn't want to even imagine a life without Arden in it. His arms held her prisoner as he kissed her, not with passion but with a telling need, a message of how vital she had become to him.

"Let's go wash," he said with a huskiness that came from a tangle of emotions.

The bathroom was hedonistically opulent. The sunken bath was enormous and had whirlpool jets placed at intervals along its deep sides. A picture window provided a view of the ocean. The oversized shower had a clear glass door. It was into this that Drew led Arden.

Whatever modesty she had left was swept down the shower drain, never to be regained. Drew's eyes and hands idolized every part of her. And instead of feeling sullied by his frank sexual interest, she felt purified because she knew it came not from lust but from love.

They kissed, licking droplets of water from each other's faces. Her hands slid down the muscled expanse of his back. The narrowness of his waist was briefly appreciated before her hands smoothed lower over his taut buttocks. Bravely, her eyes locked onto his as her hands familiarized themselves with each curve, each masculine line.

He watched with incredulous pleasure as she soaped her hands slowly, provocatively. His throat tightened, and he swallowed convulsively when she took his sex between her lathered hands. Her touch was timid at first but gained confidence and increased pressure as she watched his eyes grow dark and hot.

"Arden," he gasped, "do you know what you're doing to me?"

"I'm doing something wrong?" she asked in alarm, yanking her hands back.

"No, God, no." He caught her hand and replaced it and at the same time pulled her to him with his other arm. "You're perfect and so sexually innocent despite having been a wife and mother."

"One had nothing to do with the other." She was thinking not only of her private life with Ron but also of the sterile precision with which she'd conceived Matt.

"I'm a selfish bastard to say this, but I'm glad."

They rinsed and went back into the bedroom. "Lie down on your stomach," he instructed gently. Without a qualm, she obliged him. He stretched out beside her. "We really must do something about these strap lines," he murmured. Her back was marked by several pale stripes, and her bottom was noticeably white against her tan back and legs.

"What do you suggest we do now?" she asked sleepily, her head resting on her folded arms.

"Ummm, what do you think?" he said with a lascivious inflection.

"You're incorrigible."

"Where you're concerned I am."

His hands were massaging her shoulders and rubbing her back with a gifted touch.

"What will we do if Matt comes barging in?" she asked.

His hands slid down her ribs and back up again, lifting the plump sides of her breasts on their ascent. She sighed blissfully. "He won't. I locked the door." He leaned over her back and spoke directly into her ear. "I didn't want to be disturbed, even by my son."

His hand seesawed in the curve of her waist, then coasted over the slope of her derriere. She uttered a responsive moan when she felt his teeth nipping at her waist. As lifeless as a rag doll, she obeyed the urging of his hands to turn over. His lips continued their trail of kisses over her stomach and then lower.

Agilely, he positioned himself between her thighs and laid his head on her abdomen. His breath stirred the dark down. Idly her fingers trailed through his thick, tousled hair. She was astounded at her own acceptance of this new intimacy, her explicit trust in him, the now-familiar way her body began to warm and liquefy and swell with renewed longing.

Her bones melted beneath the warmth of his mouth when he kissed her stomach. "I want to love you again, Arden." His breath struck her skin in hot puffs that made her insides quiver.

"Then love me."

He levered himself up over her, nestling his sex against hers but not taking possession. "Your breasts are going to be sore," he said miserably, looking at their fullness and the tempting crowns. "Not to mention the rest of you."

She hooked a hand around the back of his head and pulled him down to her breast. "Kiss me here," she whispered. "Make them wet."

He groaned softly as he took her nipple into his mouth. He drew on it gently, ever mindful of hurting her. Lifting his head, he appraised his handiwork before painting the hardened tip again with delicate strokes of his tongue. He continued on each breast until they were glistening in the morning light. Arden writhed beneath him, loving the way he tugged on her so sweetly. She felt each contraction deep inside the heart of her femininity. She moved against his body, begging him to fill the void he had created.

With one sure thrust, he obliged her. He buried himself into her warmth, and she sheathed him tightly.

As before, it wasn't a culmination but a beginning. A rebirth. For as surely as Drew's life showered into her body, she filled him with her own essence. They lay together, breathing in the scent of their loving, feeling not depleted but filled with new life and energy.

"Arden," he said softly as he left her, only to gather her close to him.

"Hmm?"

"This illicit affair must come to an end."

She felt as though her heart plummeted to the floor and shattered into a million pieces. "End?"

"Yes," he said earnestly. "You must marry me."

"You haven't responded to my proposal, Arden."

It was hours since he'd made it. Arden knew no more now how she was going to respond than she had when he'd first astounded her with his proposal. They were on the beach, playing with Matt. The three of them comprised a family unit, and that as much as anything panicked Arden.

Lightly, she shrugged off his statement. "As I recall, it wasn't so much a proposal as an order."

"What else could you expect from a bully?" His retort was spoken lightheartedly, but she could see the underlying seriousness in his eyes.

He hadn't demanded an answer of her when he had first mentioned marriage. Instead, he had held her while he slept. She, however, couldn't go back to sleep. Her mind had been turbulent with thoughts of the night just past, the sensual discoveries of the new day and Drew's unheralded marriage proposal.

Her? Marry Drew McCasslin, world-famous tennis pro? Drew McCasslin marry Arden Gentry, a nobody, the hired surrogate mother of his child?

When Drew had awakened, they decided they'd been self-indulgent long enough. Matt was already at breakfast when they came down the stairs. He waved at them gleefully and sputtered corn flakes all over his highchair tray. Drew had dressed in tennis attire, Arden in a casual pair of shorts. He had tried to talk her into going with him while he practiced.

"Drew, my clothes have been packed in a suitcase in a musty closet for nearly a week. I need to sort them out for laundry and dry cleaning."

"I can do that for you," Mrs. Laani offered as she placed a plate of fresh fruit in front of Arden and poured her a cup of coffee.

"I appreciate that," Arden said, smiling at her. "But I'd feel better putting things away myself so I'll know where everything is."

No one seemed to doubt that she was staying indefinitely. Only Arden herself.

Drew had left for his tennis practice alone. After her clothes had been pressed and hung in the closet of the guest bedroom, Arden helped Mrs. Laani sort through the new clothes that had been bought for Matt in Honolulu.

"Oh, this is precious," Arden exclaimed, holding up a play suit with two tennis rackets appliquéd on the bib.

Mrs. Laani laughed. "I thought his daddy would appreciate that."

Matt was underfoot and in the way and meddlesome as they unwrapped his new clothes and put them either in the closet or the chest of drawers. Arden didn't mind even when he shredded tissue paper all over his bathroom floor. Periodically, she'd hug him to her, examining his face time and again and marveling over him.

How had Drew's seed, transfused into her body so clinically, without the loving emotion such a miracle warranted, produced this unblemished specimen? She thanked God she had had a part in bringing this life into the world.

Drew had returned just before lunch. He was crackling with excitement. "You should have seen the crowd watching Gary and me work out today. They gave me a standing ovation when I walked out on the court. UPI and the Associated Press picked up news of the match yesterday. The story's gone world-wide. Ham's beside himself. He called the resort while I was there and said phone calls have been pouring in, inviting me to play in tournaments both in the states and abroad. My sponsors called to congratulate him."

He referred to the companies whose clothes and shoes he wore, whose tennis racket he used, whose planes he flew when he traveled, whose toothpaste he hyped. These endorsements comprised as much—if not more—of his income as prize money. When his playing began to slide, so had the offers from these companies.

"I was scared that when my contracts came around for renewal, the sponsors would let them drop. Now they're talking bigger and better things. They're still wary, of course. It was only one match, and I didn't *win* it, but at least they haven't given me up for lost. I need to win one. Now I know I can."

His eyes sparkled as he clutched Arden's hand across the luncheon table top. "I only need one thing in my life to make me completely happy."

Arden knew what that something was. It had been haunting her all morning. Her heart was full to bursting with joy that Drew loved her enough to marry her. Why was she hesitating? Why hadn't she flung her arms around him the moment the words were out of his mouth and said, *Yes!* she'd marry him. Because she'd been immediately reminded of what had brought her to this man in the first place.

Matt.

What more could she ask for? She'd have her son, live with him, be his mother in every sense of the word, be able to watch him grow into boyhood, adolescence, manhood.

She'd be there, witnessing it all, helping him through the tough spots, loving him. Why couldn't she tell Drew that she wanted to marry him more than anything in the world?

Because he had been honest with her and she hadn't been with him. She couldn't enter into a marriage with that lie of omission between them. She'd been in a marriage like that, and it had bred contempt. Ron had married her for self-serving reasons, and she'd never forgiven him. She'd hated him for it. And he'd come to scorn her for her constant, meek submission.

What would happen if Drew found out who she was and the role she'd played in his past? He would think she'd married him solely because she wanted to be with her son. Would he ever believe that she loved him now as much . . . no, more . . . than she did the son she'd conceived of his seed? Knowing his pride, she doubted it.

So tell him now, she commanded herself. *Don't risk his finding out later. You can't have this secret between you, so tell him now. Today.* She shivered with dread. No matter who Matt's mother was, Drew wouldn't be happy to meet her. Each time he mentioned the trouble he and Ellie had had "getting" Matt, his eyes betrayed an uneasiness about it. No, he wouldn't be glad to meet Matt's mother. He certainly wouldn't be glad to learn that she was a woman he'd come to trust, to love, who had kept the secret far too long already.

When they had walked down to the beach after lunch, her mind had still been swirling in ever-changing patterns of indecision.

Now Drew was pinning her down for an answer. But Matt chose that moment to launch himself into her chest, knocking her backward. "Oh, you!" she cried, catching him around the waist. "I think you need to go on a diet."

Matt crowed with laughter as she tossed him down on the beach blanket beside her, wrestling him and tickling his fat stomach. When he'd worn her out, he pushed himself up and went jogging toward the surf. "Be careful,"

Arden called after him. He stopped, turned and then spontaneously came running back. He flung his arms around her neck and kissed her wetly and enthusiastically on the mouth.

Tears blurred his image as he tripped back toward the tide.

"He loves you, too, Arden." Drew's quiet voice compelled her to look at him. When he saw her tears, he smiled. "You love him, don't you?"

The truth couldn't be withheld. "Yes."

"And me? Am I seeing something that really isn't there?"

The tears rolled down her cheeks. She reached out to caress the wind-tousled strands of hair above his rolled bandanna sweatband. "I love you, too." Her fingers outlined his bottom lip. "I love you so much it hurts."

He caught her hand and pressed it to his cheek. "Then say you'll marry me. Ham wants me to go on tour in two weeks. I want you and Matt to go with me. I want you to go as my wife." The thought of going without her was too dismal to contemplate. On the other hand, he knew he had to go. The timing was right.

"Two weeks," she said mournfully.

"I know I'm not giving you much time. But why wait? If you love me—"

"I do."

"And you know I love you. Marry me now, Arden." He looked toward the boy who was chasing a shallow wave to shore. "I never thought I'd blackmail a woman into marrying me, but I'm going to play every ace." He sighed grimly and said, "Matt needs a mother, Arden."

"He has Mrs. Laani." It was a weak protest. Her heart seemed anchored to something in the bottom of her soul, and it was pulling her down, down, down, into a situation from which there was no easy escape. *Please don't use my son to talk me into doing something I know I shouldn't do.*

"I don't know what I would have done without her,"

Drew said of his housekeeper and friend. "She put up with my drunken abuse and my dark moods when a less charitable woman would have packed her bags and left. She's great with Matt. I consider her more family than employee, but she could never be a mother to him. She's too old for one thing."

He took Arden's hand and pressed it between his. "Arden, in a few years I'll have to move from here. When Matt's older and I'm too old to play the circuit, we won't be able to live in this partial isolation. Matt will need a mother, you, when he goes to school and sees that every other kid has one."

He could still see the indecision in her eyes. He had one more shot. It was a mean one, but he was a desperate man. "Be to my son what you couldn't be to Joey."

Her head whipped around, and she jerked her hand from his. "You're being unkind, Drew."

"I know that, dammit, but I can see I might lose you, and I can't let that happen. I'm fighting for my life, and I'm going to use all the ammunition I've got." His eyes were fierce, his jaw hard and stubborn.

"I told you, you weren't merely a replacement for Ellie, and that's the God's truth. Matt can't be a replacement for the son you lost either, but you've said you've grown to love him. Give him what you didn't have a chance to give Joey." He touched her lips with his. "We could even have a child of our own."

"Oh, God," she cried, covering her face with her hands and slumping against him as he pulled her forward. He cradled her in the shelter of his arms, stroking her head and whispering endearments.

"I know I'm bullying you again, but Arden, I want you in my life. More than tennis. More than anything. Still, I wouldn't ask you if I didn't think you needed Matt and me just as much."

Arden felt a clammy hand on her shoulder and raised her head to see Matt standing beside her. His lower lip was trembling, and his eyes, so like Drew's, were shimmering with silver tears. "Ah-den," he said on the brink of crying. "Ah-den."

"Oh, precious, no, don't cry." She wiped the tears from her eyes and forced a bright smile. "See, nothing's wrong." She remembered that Joey was never so upset as when he saw her crying. It shook a child's world to see an adult so visibly distressed. "I'm fine. See."

He looked doubtfully toward his father, but Drew's eyes remained on Arden. She pulled the boy to her and hugged him, distraught over causing him one moment of insecurity and pain.

"There, see, I'm happy," she said. "Where's your belly button? I see it, I see it," she said, poking it playfully. He giggled, and the tears began to recede.

Mrs. Laani called them from the wall separating the beach from the lawn. "Shame on you, letting that boy run naked like that," she scolded the two adults. "He'll grow up a pagan."

"This is the way God made him, Mrs. Laani," Drew said, casting a conspiratorial grin at Arden.

"Blasphemy," the older woman grumbled as she retrieved the boy and tried to pull bathing trunks up his thrashing, sandy legs. He squirmed and protested until she gave up with a resigned sigh. "See what I mean? He's half heathen now."

She labored up the hill carrying the boy, who repeated, "No nap," until they were out of sight.

"I didn't know he saw me crying. I shouldn't have upset him."

"If I start crying, will you say you'll marry me?" Drew's expression was so boyishly winning and his eyes so sad that she broke out laughing.

"Oh, Drew," she said, leaning over to kiss him. "I love you, but there are reasons why I shouldn't marry you."

"And so many more why you should."

She rested her head against his breast, letting the crinkly hair tickle her nose. She loved the salty, musky scent of his skin. "There's one profound reason why I shouldn't marry you. Something about me . . . my past. Something I did that . . ."

He tilted her head back to peer into her eyes. "Arden, there couldn't have been anything that shameful in your past. And even if there were, when compared to me, you've lived like a saint. I don't *care* about anything in your past. I care only for our future." His finger tips skimmed her cheek. "For that matter, there is something that I've been wavering about telling you, but I honestly can't think of what difference it makes. It doesn't concern or affect the love I have for you."

He kissed the corner of her mouth. "Does this secret have anything to do with me? What you feel for me? Do you love me less because of it?"

She could answer him honestly. "No. It takes nothing away from the love I have for you."

"Then forget it. Our lives started when we met each other. Our pasts we'll keep sacred and private. We'll close the book on them and begin to collect our own sacred and private memories." He kissed her. It was a deep and probing kiss, as though he wanted to erase physically her objections with his mouth. "Marry me, Arden."

"Drew, Drew," she said, meeting his mouth for another long kiss that made everything but the love she had for him seem unimportant.

He ground their mouths together, folding his arms around her possessively and symbolically sealing them off from the rest of the world. "Take off your top," he mumbled against her mouth.

She wriggled free of him in mock exasperation. "Is that the only reason you asked me to marry you? For unlimited carnal use of my body?"

"One of the reasons," he drawled, letting his eyes

descend in lecherous approval over the curves that the scant bikini did little to hide.

If he were going to keep Matt's origins from her, was her own secret so much worse? She suddenly felt free of shackles. She wanted to celebrate their love, to be happy, to shed the cloak of worry and guilt. "What if someone moseys by?" Her voice held a hint of mischievous promise.

"Mo and Mrs. Laani are the only ones allowed on the property without my prior approval. They both know that when I'm alone on my beach with a woman, they are to make themselves scarce."

"Oh? And just how many times have you been alone with a woman on your beach?"

"This is the first time. I circulated a memo this morning."

She bit her lip to keep from laughing. "What about boats? What if someone sails by and sees us . . . me . . . without any clothes on?"

"We'll see the boat first and duck for cover."

"I see you've thought of everything."

"Everything," he said, looking at her through a screen of thick, sun-gilded lashes. "By the way, did you ever say yes to my proposal? Or am I to assume by your kisses that the answer is yes?" His hands went around her. One untied the string at her neck; the other untied the one across her back.

"I didn't say yes . . ." The top of her bikini was caught by the wind. It fluttered against her body for a few seconds before being whisked away. "But since I'm going to be cavorting . . ." Drew stood up and peeled off his trunks. He was a modern rendition of Adam, perfect, golden and strong, a paragon of masculine beauty. The sweatband around his forehead lent him a savage aspect as he slowly lowered himself back to the blanket.

". . . cavorting on the beach with you . . ." As his

burning eyes watched, she peeled off her bikini panties. ". . . naked . . ." He came to her with sleek grace, and they reclined together on the blanket. ". . . I guess I'll have to become your wife."

His kisses were hot, almost as hot as the elements— sand, wind, sun—and just as primitive.

Chapter 10

"HELLUVA HONEYMOON," DREW MUTTERED. HE WAS DRIV-
ing toward the picturesque village of Lahaina.

"I think it's wonderful," Arden said, laughing and
straightening Matt's shirt under his overalls for the ump-
teenth time.

"My idea of a honeymoon is having you naked in my
bed engaging in all sorts of lewd physical acts."

"We'll get to that," she whispered. Drew's head swiveled around to look at her, branding her with a heated
gaze. "But for now, please keep your eyes on the road."

Once she had consented, he'd wasted no time in making
arrangements for their marriage, completing everything in
a few days' time. The ceremony that morning had been
private. They'd flown to Honolulu to be married by a
minister Drew knew well. Only Mrs. Laani and the
pastor's wife had been in attendance. And Matt. At
Arden's request, Drew hadn't notified the press.

"Please, Drew," she had pleaded. "I don't want to be in

172

the limelight. I'll go on tour with you. I'll be there cheering you on at every match, but I don't want to be photographed or interviewed."

She remembered the photographers swarming around him and Ellie as they left the hospital. How had they managed to keep the secret that Ellie wasn't the child's real mother? Arden had her own secret to keep. At least for a while. She had resolved to tell Drew she was Matt's mother, but not until he was secure in her love for him. For now, the fewer people who knew about their marriage, the better. She wanted to maintain a low profile.

"But I'm proud of you," he had objected. "Why would you want to hide the fact that we're married?"

"I don't want to *hide* it. I just don't want it publicized." She groped for a plausible excuse. "Because . . . because of Ellie. She was so beautiful, so much a part of your life. Until I learn the ropes of the touring life, I don't want people comparing me to her."

"There is no comparison," he had said tenderly, rubbing strands of her dark hair between his fingers.

"Others might think so, and that would make me terribly uncomfortable."

He'd conceded grudgingly, and they'd returned to Maui in the middle of the afternoon to put a cranky Matt down for a nap.

"You need to call Gary for a practice set or two."

"On my wedding day?" Drew had complained.

"Do you want to win on tour or not?"

He'd turned to Mrs. Laani and spread his hands wide. "Married only a few hours and already she's nagging." Beneath his teasing, Arden could tell he was pleased that she understood how demanding his career was. "You'll go with me and watch, won't you?"

"I wouldn't miss it."

Arm in arm, they went upstairs to the master suite. Mrs. Laani had already moved many of Arden's clothes into the spare closet. Her toilet articles and makeup were neatly arranged in the bathroom dressing area. "How'd she manage this so soon?" Arden asked Drew in dismay.

"She was under strict orders to move you in here as soon as possible. You made that ridiculous rule about not sleeping with me again until we were married." He came to her and wrapped his arms around her waist, nuzzling her breasts through the silk blouse she'd worn under her wedding suit. The evidence of his impatience pressed hard against her middle. "I'm hungry for you, Arden," he rasped against her breast, and it swelled with her own desire. "From now on, expect me to be merciless."

Their mouths met urgently, moving together with suppressed longing finally given vent. Keeping his mouth on hers, his hands fumbled with her clothes until she stood in an ivory charmeuse slip. He fondled her breasts, and when her nipples tightened in response, he ducked his head to touch them with his tongue through the shiny, slinky cloth.

She rid him of his shirt and worked feverishly on his belt buckle until he could kick his way free of the trousers. She slid her hands into his tight briefs and over his buttocks. The muscles she kneaded were taut with his forced control.

He caressed her back, her derriere, her thighs, smoothing his hands over the silky slip and her pale pantyhose. At the top of her thighs, his thumbs rotated arousingly over her hip bones. When he rubbed the triangular mound of her womanhood with his knuckles, she caught his hair in her fists and pulled his head away from hers.

"You've got to play tennis," she said with heaving breaths.

"To hell with it," he snarled, reaching for her again.

She was adamant. "That's exactly where your game will go if you don't practice."

He muttered a curse but stepped away from her to finish changing his clothes. She puttered with the things that had been left on her dressing table, placing them in drawers and trying not to be distracted by glimpses of Drew's body as he dressed. He wasn't in the least modest about his nakedness as he went back and forth from closet to bureau locating his tennis clothes. She'd never seen a man built finer than he.

He was stepping into a brief-style athletic supporter that he wore under his tennis shorts when he happened to catch her rapt gaze in the mirror. Insolently, he dragged the white stretchy garment up his thighs and adjusted himself within its tight confines. "See anything you like?" he asked, winking at her.

She blushed, rattling the contents of the drawer as she closed it. "I like everything I see," she admitted, risking another glance at him in the mirror. He came up behind her. "I'm glad." He lifted her hair to kiss the back of her neck.

When he had finished dressing and was stuffing a change of clothes into his tennis bag, she was still fiddling with things at the dressing table. "After spurning my romantic overtures for the sake of time, are you going to make me late by dawdling?"

She felt like a schoolgirl as she stood facing him in stocking feet and slip. "Why don't you wait for me downstairs? I . . . uh . . . I'll be ready in just a few minutes."

"What's the mat—" He caught himself. Walking to her, he placed understanding hands on her shoulders. "It's been a while since you've shared a room with a man, is that it?" She swallowed hard and nodded her head, feeling like a ninny, a fool. He kissed her cheek and squeezed her shoulders lightly. "I'll be downstairs. Take your time."

Before he was out the door, she halted him. "Drew?" When he turned around, she said, "Thank you."

He smiled and slapped the doorjamb with the palm of his hand. "I'll think of some way for you to repay me." After another hasty wink, he was gone.

Despite his objections to playing tennis on his wedding day, he played well. Another crowd had gathered to watch the practice match, and they applauded enthusiastically whenever Drew executed a particularly difficult return. He was in his element and loving every minute of it. He seemed oblivious to Arden, but she knew he was aware of her supportive presence.

He had planned to take her out for an elaborate celebration dinner, but Matt had set up a howl when they started to leave without him. "Couldn't we take him with us, Drew?" she had asked, clutching the tearful boy to her.

"Arden, since I kissed my bride this morning, I've been sharing her with other people. I want you to myself."

"And I want you, too. But I won't have a good time if we leave Matt crying this way."

Drew appealed to her intelligence. "He's only doing that to get your sympathy."

"I know. And I also know I'll have to start disciplining him. But not tonight."

Several colorful curses later, Drew gave in. "But don't get any ideas about him sleeping with us," he'd warned as he swung the car onto the highway.

"Where are you taking us tonight?" Arden asked now as the traffic on Lahaina's main thoroughfare slowed them down.

"Since you insisted on this family outing," Drew said dryly, "I'm going to let you cook my meal."

"What?" she asked, laughing in surprise.

"Just wait. You'll see."

He took them to the Pioneer Inn, a historic hotel that had accommodated seamen when Lahaina had been an important whaling port. The inn was built around an open-air central courtyard that was lit by lanterns and torches and filled with lush tropical plants.

"I love it," Arden exclaimed as the hostess led them to a table.

"I'm glad. But I wasn't kidding about cooking your own meal. See." He pointed to a large charcoal grill under a protective shed. A clock was mounted on the wall so one could monitor the cooking time according to preference. Condiments and bottled steak sauces lined the grill.

"I happen to be a terrific cook," she boasted. "When I was married and had Joey, I enjoyed planning meals and cooking. Then, after . . ." A spasm of sadness crossed her face. "I lost interest."

He squeezed her hand. "If you like to cook, you may cook for Matt and me whenever you want to. Starting tonight."

They gathered around the grill after they'd ordered Drew's New York steak, Matt's hamburger and Arden's *mahimahi*. The island fish was fileted and marinated, then wrapped in foil for broiling. There was much joking and advice giving as Arden wielded the long metal spatulas. Matt squealed every time a hissing flame shot up out of the charcoal pit. When the meat dishes were done, they carried them to their table and ate them with hefty salads and bowls of baked beans, the house specialty.

"Delicious," Drew said, rolling his eyes and smacking his lips over his steak. Matt comically imitated him.

Arden's heart was full to overflowing with love for the two men in her life. She cautioned herself about feeling smug. So much happiness terrified her.

Making travel arrangements for them all was an awesome responsibility. Mrs. Laani and Matt would share one room, Drew and Arden another, while Ham occupied a third. Fortunately the manager handled most of the details. With Mrs. Laani's help, Arden learned to pack with economy of space in mind, yet the job seemed endless.

Arden was nervous about meeting Ham Davis. He was a grizzled man well under six feet tall. He chomped a cigar that was foul and fat. His belly poured over pants he was constantly hiking up with hairy, beefy hands. But his charm was undeniable. Arden liked his brusque, candid manner immediately.

He was there to meet them when their plane landed at Los Angeles International. Taking her hands between his, he pressed them hard. His dark eyes probed into hers and apparently liked what they saw. "Whatever you're doing for Drew, keep it up" was all he said, but Arden knew she had earned his unqualified approval.

He was a little put out with Drew for insisting on two things. First, that he honor Arden's request for no publicity about herself. And second, that he leave them a few free days to visit Drew's mother in Oregon.

That was another hurdle Arden dreaded, and she was fidgety and nervous on the flight to Portland. She needn't have worried. Mrs. McCasslin was gracious and warm. After the flurry at the airport and the good-natured confusion of getting them settled into her home for their two-night stay, she and Arden had their first moments alone. They were in her sunny, immaculate and homey kitchen, waiting for the teakettle to come to a boil.

"You're not what I expected," Rose McCasslin said as she reached into the pantry for a tin of flavored tea bags.

"What did you expect?" The blue eyes were a family trait. Rose's were as bright as her son's and grandson's.

"I don't know exactly. Someone stridently efficient. Someone who would have taken over Matt's upbringing and either whipped Drew into shape or browbeaten him into alcoholism. Someone not nearly as beautiful or as . . . soft."

"Thank you," Arden said, moved. "Drew had whipped himself into shape before he married me."

"That's why I know you're good for him. You let him do it." She cocked her head to one side. "He's very much in love with you, you know."

"I think he is, yes."

"I'm glad. And relieved. I thought when we buried Ellie

and he moved to that tiny island, he'd rot there for the rest
of his life. He's happy again. I have only one request to
make of you."

"What?"

A familiar glint of humor lit the older woman's eyes.
"Make him bring you and my grandson to see me more
often."

They traveled first to Phoenix, then to Dallas, Houston,
New Orleans, St. Petersburg. Drew was making an impressive showing, winning steadily in the qualifying rounds
but losing in the finals. He wasn't discouraged, and neither
was Ham. He was giving the best in the business a run for
their money. Then he won in Memphis. And in Atlanta.
And in Cincinnati. His ranking began to climb.

Arden was tired of traveling but radiant over Drew's
success. Life on the tour was hard, especially with a child
as energetic and inquisitive as Matt. She had written all the
articles she'd been under contract to do before they left
Hawaii. Through long-distance telephone calls, she had
been pleased to learn they would all be printed without
revisions. For the time being, she had declined requests to
do more.

"What do you do all day while I'm working out?" Drew
had asked her one night as they lay wrapped together in
the aftermath of loving. "Are you getting bored?"

"Bored? With Matt to chase after? Hardly." She snuggled closer, loving the protective feel of him beside her. "I
look forward to your matches, and . . . I daydream . . .
about this." She swept her hand down his stomach to
touch him intimately. He gasped softly as her fingers
closed around him.

"Good God, Arden, are you trying to kill me for the
insurance money? I've played a hard match of tennis
today. Five of seven sets and . . . then made love . . .
Sweet heaven . . ."

"You don't feel as though you're on the verge of

collapse to me. On the contrary . . ." she whispered, stroking his hard length.

"When you're not thinking of ways to drive your husband into an early grave, what do you do?" he panted.

"I write."

"Write . . . ? No, don't stop . . . Yes, like that . . . Oh, damn . . . Write what?"

"Things. Notes for a novel. Poetry."

"Poetry? What you're doing to me now is poetry." Rolling her onto her back, he let her guide him into her receptive body. "Write a thousand verses of it."

They were glad to get home. Ham had been argumentative and badgering. He'd even tried to coerce Arden into lending him her support.

"He needs to play in every tournament he can," he said, punctuating each word with stabbing motions of his cigar.

"Drew wants to go home for a few weeks, Ham."

"You can convince him otherwise."

"Perhaps, but I won't."

"I figured that." He shoved the cigar in his mouth, cursed, and then said he'd drive them to the airport.

Mo had the house opened and aired and ready for them. They resumed a reasonably normal routine. Drew played every day with Gary at the club, working on the weak spots that he and Ham had discussed. Arden busied herself with Matt and made plans for their next tour, which would take them to Europe. Just thinking about it exhausted her. How could she convey to non-English-speaking waiters that Matt would prefer a peanut butter and jelly sandwich to anything on their overpriced menus? She hadn't been able to convince English-speaking ones.

One afternoon, she was relaxing in the master suite, curled in one of the chairs beside the wide windows, when Drew came in. He dropped his tennis bag just inside the door. They watched each other from across the room, silently telegraphing the love that had grown between them over the past few weeks.

"You look beautiful sitting there, Arden," he said quietly. "The setting sun's making your hair shine with red streaks."

"Thank you. I planned to be dressed by the time you got back, but I got busy on something." She closed a folder over a tablet and laid it on the table beside the chair.

He closed the door and locked it before proceeding into the room. She was wearing a dressing gown he was partial to. It fell on her shoulders in a wide scoop neckline. It was floor length, loosely covering her body like a filmy blue cloud. "You've just bathed," he commented.

She smelled of flowery bubble bath and woman. The sheer femininity of her seemed to beckon to his maleness. He knelt beside her chair and placed his finger tips on either side of her neck. He liked to think he felt her pulse accelerate when he touched her.

She symbolized peacefulness, home, love, all the things he'd given up hope of ever having again. Each time he saw her after brief little absences, he was surprised again at how much he loved her, how from the beginning there had been a oneness between them that he couldn't understand or explain.

"What something were you busy on?"

"Nothing really," she said in that offhanded way that he'd learned meant just the opposite. Who had convinced her that her opinion wasn't valuable? The husband she spoke so little of? Almost daily, Drew condemned the man to hell. She had been hurt. Terribly. And by more than Joey's death. The traces of abuse still lingered, though she never talked about her past. If it took a lifetime, Drew planned to teach her how valuable she was.

"You've written something, haven't you?"

Her eyes fluttered away from his. "It's terrible, I know, but it's something I've wanted to put on paper for a long time."

"May I read it?"

"It's not good enough for anyone to read."

"I don't believe that."

She licked her lips. "It's very personal."

"I won't insist if you don't want me to read it."

"I'd like your opinion," she said hurriedly.

He took the initiative of picking up the folder and opening it to the first page of the tablet. "Joey" was written on the top line. He lifted his eyes to hers, but she evaded them. She left the chair and went to stand silhouetted against the window and the vermilion western sky.

Drew read the four-page poem, his throat constricting tighter with each line. It was obvious that the words had seeped out of her soul and that it had been a painful process. They were poignant but not syrupy. They were spiritual but not pompous. They expressed the abysmal, impotent grief of a parent watching a child slowly die. But the last verses were a testimony to the blessings that had been drawn from that child. They expressed an enviable and rare joy.

Drew's eyes were wet when he stood, reverently replacing the folder on the table and going to her. His arms slid under her arms from behind and pulled her tightly against him, laying his forehead against her shoulder.

"It's beautiful, Arden."

"Do you truly think so, or are you just saying that?"

"It's beautiful. Is it too personal for you to share?"

"You mean submit for publication?"

"Yes."

"Is it good enough?"

"God, yes. I think parents, any parent, whether they've suffered the loss of a child or not, would empathize. I know I do. I think you should have it published. It may help someone who's going through what you did."

She turned to him and laid her head on his heart. She loved its steady, solid beat.

"I wish I'd been there when you needed someone. You were here for me to help me out of my crisis, but you had to go through your hell alone. I'm so sorry, my love." His fervently spoken words and the strong hands caressing her back told her of his sincerity. "Come here," he said, taking her hand and leading her to the bed.

He sat down on it and moved her to stand between his thighs. She looked into his loving face and smoothed the bushy slash of his eyebrows with her finger.

"I wish I could love away all the hurt inside you." He leaned forward and rested his head on her midriff.

"I wish I could love away yours, too. But it will always be a part of us. Maybe we love each other better because of past disappointments."

"I only know I love you more than I ever thought it possible to love." His breath, filtering through the gauzy gown onto her skin, was warm and moist. He nuzzled his nose against her breasts, loving their delicious weight on his face. "Arden, you're not using any contraceptives, are you?" He lifted his head and looked up at her.

She shook her head before answering in a strangled voice. "No."

"Good. Let's have a baby." His hands touched her breasts tenderly. He examined their shape, measured their fullness as though touching them for the first time. "Did you breast-feed Joey?"

"Until he got sick."

He nodded. His fingers caressed the nipples, and when they got hard, he rubbed his face against them, back and forth. "I want a baby with you." She clasped his head and pressed it into the softness of her abdomen. "A baby that's exclusively yours and mine. One we make together."

If only he knew what he was saying. She knew why he didn't feel that Matt had been exclusively his and Ellie's. Was this the time to tell him that they had a baby that was theirs, that they had made a beautiful baby together?

Could she tell him now? Would his lips continue to ravish her gently? Or would he stop loving her, accuse her of manipulating him unforgivably?

Her lips opened to voice the confession, but she had waited too long. His mood had passed from poignancy to passion. He was kissing the delta between her thighs, paying tribute to her womanhood with his loving mouth and adoring words. His hands gathered up the airy fabric of her dressing gown, raising it up her legs, over her thighs, until it was bunched at her waist. He buried his face in the frothy material, breathing in her scent.

When his lips touched her bare skin, she shivered with anticipation and clutched his shoulders with anxious hands. He pressed ardent kisses into her dark, silky down. "Let me give you a baby, Arden," he whispered. "Let me give you that most wonderful of gifts." His hands went around her, cupped her hips and tilted her forward to meet his mouth.

"Drew," she gasped. "You can't do this." He could. He did. Her whole body was caught up in a conflagration of passion. His seeking mouth sent columns of fire shooting upward, through her loins, through her heart, into her soul.

She responded mindlessly to his directing hands as he laid her down on the bed. He placed her legs over his thighs and knelt before her. "I love you, Arden. Let me heal your pain."

His mouth was masterful. He kissed her again and again with lips that were sure and possessive, yet conversely meek. His tongue was a bold, thrusting, pleasure-giving imp that brought her again and again to crashing climax, then soothed her afterward.

Hovering on the brink of oblivion once again, she tangled his hair around her fingers and drew his head up. "Inside me. Please, now," she gasped as another convulsion shook her.

Somehow he worked free the fastening of his shorts and

slipped them over his hips. He was a full, hard, warm pressure that filled her completely. He moved more adventurously than ever before, stroking the walls of her cleft, pausing, stroking again until she was senseless and knew only him and the rhythm of his loving. He plunged deeply time and again, touching her womb, making promises and then fulfilling them with one bursting rush of love so sublime that her tears flowed as freely.

When he withdrew, her body felt leaden, lethargic, yet seemed to defy gravity with a sensation of floating. He removed the rest of his clothing, pulled the twisted dressing gown from her perspiration-sheened body and lay down beside her.

Barely gathering the energy to form the words, she whispered, "Why did you do that?"

He let his finger trail down the center of her body to the dusky shadow of her sex. He followed with his eyes and then brought them back to marvel over her breasts. His eyes shone with the internal light of a fanatic worshiping his idol. "To show you there are no limits to how much I love you."

"I'm weak with love for you."

He smiled tenderly. "And you make me strong." Dipping his head, he plucked at her nipple lightly with his lips, then caressed it with his tongue. "And so very glad that I'm a man."

Her fingers wound through his blond hair. "Do you think we . . . made a baby?"

He chuckled softly. Laying his head next to hers on the pillow, he snuggled close. "We'll just keep doing it until it takes."

Then, wearing only the purple twilight for raiment, they slept.

"You two are bonkers," Arden called to the two tennis professionals.

Drew and Gary were batting the ball back and forth

across the net, lobbing it as high as they could. They were clowning to entertain Matt, who was standing beside the court, clapping his hands. When Drew bent over and hit the ball through his legs, Matt yelled happily and jumped up and down.

"Okay, showoff," Arden said, "before you hurt yourself and I have to be the unlucky one to inform Ham you're out of commission, I'm taking your audience home. Maybe then you'll get in some real practice time."

"Party pooper," Gary called congenially before trotting over to confer with his latest conquest, who was waiting for him with a towel and a thermos of cold water.

"Ditto," Drew said, wrapping a towel around his neck. He draped one over Matt, who beamed up at him. "Your mother is a slave driver and a spoilsport," he told the boy before kissing him on the forehead. He straightened up and dropped his voice to a whisper. "Except in bed, and then she's a regular party girl."

"And you're the life of the party," Arden said with a suggestive drawl, rubbing noses with him. "I'd love to kiss you, but I can't find a dry spot."

"Isn't that Bette Davis's line?"

"No, she said, 'I'd love to kiss you, but I just washed my hair.'"

"Oh. I knew it was something like that. Well, owe me a kiss. Do you have to go?"

"You know Matt's a monster if he doesn't get his nap. When you get home, maybe we can take him down to the beach."

"And play *nekkid.*"

"Don't you ever think of anything else?"

"Yes," he answered, acting offended. "Sometimes I think about making it with our clothes *on.*"

"You're terrible!" she cried, throwing a towel in his face. "Play well and we'll see you at home."

She hoisted Matt onto her hip, and settling her shoulder

bag on the other arm, headed toward the parking lot where she'd parked the Seville. She had more or less inherited it after Drew bought himself a jeep.

They had been in Europe for three months, hopping from country to country, tournament to tournament, and had only returned the week before. Drew was now ranked number five in world tennis. He was hoping that by the same time next year he'd be the number-one seed again.

"Then I'd retire."

"And do what?"

"How does a chain of sporting-goods stores sound? The emphasis would be on family participation. You know, jogging shoes for father and son, matching tennis dresses for mothers and daughters, yard games for the entire family. Things like that."

"It sounds terrific. And I like the concept."

"So do I. We're going to lead the pack."

"We?"

"Ham will retire, too. He says he's too old to start all over again with a cub tennis bum. He wants to go into the business with me. And *you*," he kissed her quickly, "of course."

Her poem "Joey" had been published by a ladies magazine and then by *Reader's Digest*. The ladies magazine had asked if she'd think about writing a short story or novelette. She was toying with several ideas.

"Did you enjoy watching daddy play?" she asked Matt, who had celebrated his second birthday in Paris. He was really too heavy for her to carry, but she never passed up an opportunity. He called her "mum," and each time she saw the name on his perpetually damp lips, she wanted to weep with happiness. "Isn't he terrific? But then you're biased in your opinion of him, just as I am."

Arden didn't see the man in the car parked next to hers until he got out. She glanced over her shoulder as she was unlocking the car door. And everything inside her froze.

She felt as though the blood were damming up in her veins, her lungs shutting down operation, her heart thudding to a standstill.

He was heavier by twenty pounds. His hair was thinner, grayer and badly cut. His skin looked pallid and contrasted garishly with the capillaries in his nose, which had reddened with too much drink. The jowls on either side of his face looked like empty, oversized pockets. His clothes were less natty and seemed uncomfortably hot and tight. His shoes were scuffed.

But that conniving look still lurked in his eyes. He still wore that familiar smirking grin, the grin that said he had something on someone and couldn't wait to use it to his advantage.

Arden needed very badly to vomit. She swallowed the hot bile that gushed into her throat and instinctively, with the fierce protectiveness of motherhood, clutched Matt to her.

"Hello, Mrs. McCasslin."

He made the name sound like an obscene insult. Revulsion swamped her, and she had an overwhelming impulse to run as far and as fast as she could. Instead, she stared back at him with eyes turned icy with hatred. "Hello, Ron."

Chapter 11

THE BLEARY EYES TOOK A TOUR DOWN HER BODY THAT MADE her feel as though she needed a scalding bath. She didn't want him to know how much he frightened her. That was the only thing that kept her from screaming.

"You're looking well," he said when his thorough appraisal brought his eyes back to hers.

"You look like hell," she said flatly, wondering where her new-found courage came from. But she knew. It was an outgrowth of Drew's love and the happiness she'd found with him.

Ron Lowery blinked, momentarily disconcerted by her uncharacteristic flippancy. When he grinned, it was with an evil curl to his mouth. "True. But then I didn't land on my feet the way you did, Mrs. McCasslin."

She set a squirming Matt down on the parking-lot pavement. He had long since lost interest in the conversation and was much more interested in the yellow metal button that marked the parking space in front of the automobile. Arden saw to it that he was well out of Ron's reach.

"Don't blame me or anyone else for whatever misfortunes have befallen you, Ron. You had all the makings of success handed to you on a silver platter. Or should I say through a golden wedding ring? If you failed to take advantage of those opportunities, then you've no one to blame but yourself."

His fists balled at his sides, and he took a threatening step forward. "Don't get all high and mighty with me. I can topple your little world with one fell swoop, *Mrs. McCasslin.* How'd you find him?"

She decided that her only defense was to admit nothing, to brazen it out. She tilted her chin up haughtily. "I don't know what you're talking about."

Steely fingers bit into her upper arm as Ron hauled her closer to him. "How did you find McCasslin? And don't think I'm stupid enough to believe you're his blushing bride by some wild coincidence."

She swallowed a lump of fear and blinked against waves of pain. She was seeing a side of Ron's nature that she had always known was there but didn't want to acknowledge. He would be ruthless, cruel, violent, if he had to be to get what he wanted.

"Deductive reasoning," she said with relief when his fingers uncurled from around her arm. "I had seen him and his wife the morning they left the hospital."

"Well, congratulations. You pulled off a clever one, didn't you?" He looked down at Matt in a way that made Arden's blood run cold. "He's a cute kid. I did a good job fathering him."

An ocean of nausea washed over Arden, and she thought she might very well faint. It came as a surprise to her to find herself still standing several seconds later. "You?" she wheezed.

He laughed. It was an ugly sound. "What's the matter, Mrs. McCasslin? Do you think you went to all that trouble for nothing? Do you think you're married to the wrong man? Hmm?"

His taunts sickened her further. "Is Matt Drew's child?" she asked desperately.

Ron eyed her slyly, enjoying to the fullest the tidal wave of despair he'd inflicted on her. "He provided the semen, yes. But as you'll recall, I did all the work."

Her relief was so vast that she slumped against the hot metal body of the car. It was several moments before the vertigo passed and the world righted itself. But the brassy taste in her mouth and the sickness in her stomach remained. This man was diabolical, capable of anything.

"Actually, you've done me a great service by marrying McCasslin," he was saying, idly picking his fingernails of imaginary dirt. Or maybe it wasn't imaginary.

She wouldn't humor him by inquiring how that might be. Instead, she met his cunning eyes levelly.

"I've fallen onto hard times, Arden. I know you'll be devastated to learn that the practice your sainted father worked so diligently to establish is no more."

"I divorced myself from it when I divorced myself from you," she said. "It was no longer my father's work but only your plaything. And I wanted nothing of yours."

"Well"—he shrugged—"it's gone, anyway, which brings us to the point of this pleasant visit." He leaned forward and whispered conspiratorially, "You're going to help me recoup some of my losses."

"You're insane. I wouldn't spit on you if you were on fire. And this pleasant little visit, as you call it, has just come to an end. Don't bother me again." She knelt down and picked up Matt, absently dusting off his knees. Yanking open the car door, she shoved him inside, ignoring his protests.

"Just a minute, bitch," Ron said, grabbing her arm before she could climb into the car. "How would you like it if I paid a visit to that new husband of yours?" Arden stopped struggling and held her breath as she stared wordlessly into Ron's feral eyes. "You hold a low opinion of me. But remember he and that insipid wife of his regarded me as just short of the Almighty. He'd be pleased to see me. Shall I go have a chat with him?"

Her panic surged to the surface, and she could only hope it was invisible to her ex-husband. But by the victorious gleam in his eyes, she knew that he'd seen it. "That's what I thought," he crooned. "Mr. McCasslin doesn't know who your former husband was, does he? He doesn't know what a high-priced whore he's married to. Fifty thousand dollars' worth of whoring. He doesn't know all that, does he? Well, isn't that interesting?" He pushed her into the seat of the car, where she landed with a jolt that stunned her. "I'll be in touch."

It was a vow, a threat that left her arms and legs rubbery as she drove home.

"You don't like the veal scallopini?"

Arden stopped stirring the food around her plate and smiled across the table into her husband's concerned, questioning eyes. "I'm sorry. I guess I wasn't up for a crowd tonight." They were having dinner alone in one of Lahaina's favorite nightspots.

"You should have said something. We could have gone somewhere else." He reached for her hand and squeezed it. His look was heart-meltingly intimate. "Or we could have stayed at home, had dinner in our room and had a *really* good time."

The insinuation behind his words, the recollection of just such evenings, the love so evident in his eyes, made Arden ache with the guilt she lived with.

All afternoon, she'd been as jumpy as a cat, afraid to look over her shoulder for fear of seeing Ron's leering, ominous presence. She loathed him. He was an odious person, and she despised his self-serving motives. Yet was she any better? Hadn't she manipulated Drew McCasslin in the most despicable way? Why hadn't she told him who she was in the beginning? And why was it so hard to tell him now?

The answer to both questions was the same. She loved him too much. The moment she had set eyes on Drew, her objectivity had flown. It had never returned. She could no more tell him now that she was Matt's mother than she could have that first day he'd walked up to her and said hello. But the guilt she lived with was becoming unbearable. It ate at her like a cancer. She didn't like to think of herself in league with someone like Ron Lowery.

"I'm sorry I'm ruining your evening." She sighed, wishing she could climb inside the security of his body and hide from all external dangers.

"No evening I've spent with you has been a ruin," he said softly. A grin slashed across his handsome face. "Well, maybe a few evenings before we married when I wanted to be in your bed and you did everything short of castration to keep me out of it."

She laughed in spite of her mood. "I was only being ladylike," she said with mock demureness.

"A curse on being ladylike. I'll bet you—"

His sentence hung unfinished as he spotted something across the room that rendered him speechless.

"Drew?"

It took a moment for his eyes to drift back to her, and then he seemed unable to focus. "I . . . what? Oh, I'm sorry. What were you saying?"

"You were saying something, not me." She laughed and turned to see what had captured his attention. Her laugh caught in her throat when she saw Ron Lowery sitting alone at a table across the room, casually studying a menu. His being there was no accident. Of that, Arden was positive.

She whipped her head back toward Drew to see if he had read her dismay, but he was still staring at Ron. "Do you know that man?" she asked hesitantly.

In that moment, she realized she'd chosen to perpetuate

her lie. She had been presented with an ideal opportunity to say, "Drew, I believe you know my former husband. You and Ellie went to him about three years ago. He found a surrogate mother for your child. I was the woman." Instead, she had taken the path of least resistance. She couldn't gamble with Drew's love now. It was still too new and fragile. Matt was too precious to her. She couldn't take the risk.

"Uh, yes," Drew said. He was watching Ron as he laughed with a waitress over the wine list. Was there a trace of bitterness in Drew's voice? His lips had narrowed in a way that Arden knew indicated he was displeased with something. Apparently, he didn't hold Ron in the esteem Ron thought.

"He . . . he . . . Ellie and I knew him on the mainland. At one time, he was a special friend to us."

"I see," Arden said, gulping at her ice water.

"He's a doctor. He did us a special service for which he was very well paid. Then he tried to wheedle more money out of me."

Arden could feel what little food she'd eaten churning in her stomach. Once she'd borne Matt, Ron had pressed the McCasslins for more money. Was the man totally without principles? "How could he expect you to pay more than he'd asked for?" She hoped the question sounded casual.

"He said he'd run into complications that he hadn't anticipated," Drew said absently, still staring piercingly in Ron's direction. Then, as though realizing he might have said more than he'd intended, he reverted his attention to Arden. His grin was forced. "We came to an understanding. I wonder what's brought him to Maui. Vacation, I suppose."

"No doubt." Arden wondered how her voice could sound so normal when she felt like screaming.

"If you're not going to mutilate that piece of veal anymore, we'll go."

"No. I'm done."

God, how was she going to live through this? she asked herself as she let Drew steer her through the maze of tables toward the door. They would have to pass Ron's table to reach the exit. She knew he'd followed them to the restaurant. It was his way of demonstrating to her just how serious his threats were. He wanted something from her, and he'd hang on with the tenacity of a bulldog until she capitulated. And she knew that to safeguard her life with Drew and Matt, she would.

He played the scene with the aplomb of a Barrymore. He actually let his eyes widen with surprised pleasure when he spotted Drew. Toward her, he exhibited not one sign of recognition. Her heart was hurling itself against her ribs like a caged animal gone mad as she heard him say, "Drew McCasslin! What a treat to see you after all this time."

Drew was coolly polite. "Hello, Dr. Lowery. How are you?"

They shook hands. "You're looking great, Drew," Ron said expansively. "Reports about you on the sports pages have been fantastic lately." His eyes clouded, and his voice lowered sympathetically. "I was sorry to hear about your wife. How is the little boy?"

Arden could feel Drew's muscles contracting with tension, but his voice was composed as he replied. "Thank you for your condolences. Matt is a strapping two-year-old now. He's terrific."

"Ah, that's good to hear."

"And"—Drew pulled her forward—"this is my wife, Arden. Darling, Dr. Ron Lowery."

It occurred to her that playwrights had often created comic scenes out of situations such as this, and she wondered how anyone could ever consider them funny. The irony was too cruel to be humorous. The hysteria that had threatened all day almost erupted. She didn't know if it would have taken the form of a high, deranged laugh or an imbecilic scream. She was able to stop it just in time. "Dr. Lowery," she said. Nothing could have compelled her to extend her hand.

"Mrs. McCasslin," Ron said kindly.

His sincere-looking smile infuriated her. She wanted nothing more than to expose him for the sham he was. But to expose him would be to expose herself.

The two men exchanged pleasantries, Ron saying that he was on the islands for several weeks' vacation and Drew wishing him a good time. Somehow she lived through it without going berserk. The smile on her lips was so brittle, she thought her face might crack like a china plate if she held it much longer.

"It was wonderful to see you again," Ron said silkily as Drew finally escorted her toward the door.

"Same here. Have a good trip," Drew said as they walked away.

Once in the car, he started the motor, but didn't engage the gears. He stared sightlessly over the hood ornament. "Is something wrong?" she asked.

"No, not really. There's just something about . . ." Drew's voice faded to nothingness while Arden sat stiffly beside him, only her rigid physical control managing to keep her hysteria at bay. "Dr. Lowery was important to Ellie and me. I told you that she had trouble conceiving. He . . . well, he made Matt possible. I have him to thank for my son. But . . . hell, I can't explain it, Arden."

He shook his head, as though by doing so, his random thoughts would rearrange themselves logically. "It's more than his demand for additional money. There's something about his mannerisms that bugs me, makes me wary of trusting him too far. I don't know why exactly, but for some reason, it disturbed me to see him tonight. On my turf, so to speak. I haven't seen him since Matt was born, and I didn't plan on seeing him ever again."

He chuckled in self-derision and shifted the car into drive. "I guess you think I'm crazy."

"No," she said, staring entranced at the lighted dials on the dashboard. "I don't think you're crazy. I don't trust him, either."

"Now that the lights are out, will you tell me what's been troubling you all day?"

Arden had already been in bed for several minutes when Drew snapped off the bedside lamp and joined her. He was naked, as was she. She had dispensed with wearing night clothes. "Saves time," Drew had said with a sexy grin the first week of their marriage. That night, Arden hadn't put on a nightgown, but she had wanted to. Her impulse had been to hide, to cover herself. She had curled up on her side of the bed, facing the edge, holding herself stiff.

"Nothing's troubling me," she mumbled into the pillow.

"Then you've undergone a personality change since you left the club this afternoon. You've been a bundle of nerves—you didn't eat your dinner, you were silent on the way home, and most unusual of all, you almost forgot to go into Matt's room to kiss him good night. Now dammit, something's wrong."

All her anxiety surfaced, and she lashed out at the nearest object, Drew. "Just because I don't want to make love tonight, you think something's wrong. Maybe I'm just not in the mood, okay? My God, you expect me to turn on and off like a light bulb. Can't I have one night's peace?" She pulled the covers up higher.

Several seconds of silence elapsed before Drew flung the covers off himself and shot out of bed. "Your memory is playing you false. I don't recall asking you to make love tonight."

He was three lunging strides across the room before she implored him to come back. "Drew!" she cried, sitting up and extending her arms. "I'm sorry, I'm sorry. Please come back. Hold me."

The moonlight filtering through the wide windows revealed the silver streams of tears on her cheeks. He was there instantly, gathering her to him tightly, smoothing her hair with loving hands, pressing her face into the curve of his shoulder. "What is it, Arden? What's wrong? Something I've done? Not done?"

"No, no," she said mournfully, rolling her head from side to side. "I shouldn't have been cross with you. I didn't mean it. I . . ."

"What? Tell me."

She searched her soul, looking for the courage to tell him about Ron, about Matt. She couldn't find it. At that moment, bravery was as elusive as the moonbeam that glinted on his hair.

She sniffed back her tears. "It's nothing, really. Just . . . I haven't felt 'with it' today. That's all."

"Lie down," he instructed softly, and reclined with her onto the soft linens. It was warm enough for them to lie uncovered, with the ocean breeze whispering across their flesh. He lay behind her, drawing her to him and wrapping his arms around her protectively. His breath sifted through her hair to caress her ear as he whispered, "I love you, Arden."

"I love you, too," she vowed, nestling her hips against him, feeling his manhood proud and warm.

He moved his hand up and down her front, trailing his finger tips in the shallow valley that divided her torso into left and right. "Are you worried because you haven't become pregnant?"

She had been concerned but hadn't spoken of it. Ever since that day he'd read her poem, they had been hoping she'd become pregnant soon. "It will happen," she said quietly.

"I think so, too. But whether it does or not doesn't matter all that much to me. I love you. *You.* I don't want you to think that if we don't have a child of our own, I'll love you any less."

She brought his hand to her lips and kissed it. "I'm selfish. I want to be everything to you."

"You are. I already feel like you're Matt's mother. To see you two together, no one would guess otherwise."

She stifled a sob and snuggled closer. She didn't deserve this blind trust. This love.

"When I make love to you, Arden, making a baby is the last thing on my mind. You are on my mind. I'm loving you. Exclusively."

Her dwindling sobs mingled with a sigh as his hand closed around her breast. His deep voice murmured a lullaby of love words in her ear.

"I think about your breasts, how perfectly they are shaped. I love their fullness. I like to caress them. Like this." His fingers grazed the dainty peaks and found them already aroused by his heated words. "You're so pretty," he whispered as his finger tips worked their magic on her flesh.

"You skin is creamy and smooth." His hand stroked down her stomach. "I love kissing it. It feels so good against my face and lips. And this . . ." His fingers brushed through the tuft at the top of her thighs. "This is what woman should be." The sweet exploration intensified. "I love you here."

Arden moaned in ecstasy at his bold touch and the tender invasion of his fingers. "It feels so good when you hold me here, buried inside you."

"Drew." She turned her head to meet his mouth. He kissed her deeply.

"Nothing you do could make me love you less. You can't win my love, Arden. You already have it. Free and unqualified and unconditionally and eternally."

She twisted in his arms and turned to face him. "I've changed my mind. I want to make love very much."

He smiled in pleasure and surprise when she flattened

her hands on his shoulders and pressed him onto his back. She positioned herself over him, and he groaned his ecstasy. Her breasts were a tantalizing display before his eyes. Not believing her own daring, she cupped one in each hand like an offering. "Can you . . . ?"

He levered himself up to replace her hands with his, accepting her gift gladly. He laved her tight, aching nipples with his tongue, rolling it over the dusky beads until she felt the swirling motion deep inside her. He took one breast into his mouth just as she sank onto his sex.

Against her breasts, he ground out curses that might have been prayers as she rocked upon him, sending him deeper into the well of her love to find its very source. "Ah, sweet . . ." he moaned, collapsing backward onto the pillows.

She rotated her hips, raised them, lowered them, wanting to take all of him inside herself so there could be no doubt of their belonging together, no question of the rightness of their marriage.

His breath was uneven and harsh, but his touch was tender. He fondled her breasts, then let one hand slip into the deep shadow where their bodies were fused. An exquisite thrill rocketed through her body at his knowing touch.

"Oh, Drew. Please, please." Whether she was pleading for him to stop or never to stop, she didn't know. But he knew. He continued that divine torment until he felt her body quaking with the coming tumult. His hands gripped her hips and anchored her to him as they experienced the final sensual assault together.

Exhausted, she collapsed onto him, their stomachs moving in and out together, panting for air. Their bodies were dewy with perspiration, their muscles limp and useless, but their hearts were full.

At last, Drew rolled them to their sides. He brushed damp strands of dark hair from her face as he held her close. "Our love represents all that is pure and good and honest in the world, Arden."

"Yes," she said huskily, smiling up at him. It was after he fell asleep that she began again to weep quietly.

"Is this the lady of the house?"

Arden's fingers gripped the telephone receiver tighter. She recognized the oily voice immediately. For days, she had dreaded hearing it. She had known Ron would call, she just hadn't known when. Now that he had finally contacted her, she could almost feel relieved. At least the suspense was over. Now she only had to dread what he wanted of her. "Yes," she replied curtly.

"The Orchid Lounge. Three o'clock."

The phone went dead in her hand. She replaced it with the care of one who has gone through physical therapy and wants to make sure his actions are precise and correct. Ron hadn't given her much time. It was past two now. Matt was taking his nap. Drew was in his office talking to Ham long distance on the other line. As soon as Matt awakened, they planned to go down to the beach.

"Mrs. Laani," Arden said, sticking her head around the corner of the kitchen door. "I don't want to disturb Drew while he's on the telephone. Would you tell him I've decided to do some shopping this afternoon. He and Matt should go to the beach without me. Maybe I can join them later."

"I'll be glad to do any household shopping for you tomorrow," the housekeeper offered.

"No, thank you. I need a few things for myself. I shouldn't be long."

She left the house a few minutes later, dressed in a poplin skirt and a polo shirt. She'd be damned before she'd dress up for Ron.

She knew the Orchid Lounge was in a ramshackle row of buildings on the outskirts of Lahaina. She had passed it many times on her way into the town. It was worse than she had expected. It was dim and smoky, the smell of stale beer permeating its gloomy atmosphere.

It took her several minutes to adjust her eyes to the darkness, and when she did, she noted she was the only female in the place. Pairs of leering eyes glowed at her from dark corners. Swallowing her trepidation, she walked straight to the nearest red vinyl booth and slid into the lumpy seat.

"Club soda, please," she said to the bartender, who came scurrying to the booth to serve her. His hair was thick with white grooming cream. The Hawaiian print shirt he wore was loud and baggy and none too clean.

"Yes, ma'am," he said in a lilting voice that made her flesh crawl. She trained her eyes on the neon clock on the opposite wall and left them there, even when the glass of soda was thumped down in front of her without benefit of napkin or coaster. She wouldn't have drunk out of it for all the gold in the world. She ignored the speculative glances thrown in her direction, the whispered comments followed by guffaws of laughter, the sinister stares.

Ron was over fifteen minutes late. *Damn him.* He was doing this on purpose to weaken her, frighten her, humiliate her. It was just the kind of psychological warfare he was capable of. Well, she wasn't going to stay in this sleazy tavern another moment.

Just as she was gathering up her purse to leave, Ron slid into the booth across from her. "Where are you going?" he asked belligerently.

"I don't like your choice of meeting places," she said tightly. The other patrons were smirking at her knowledgeably. She had been there to meet a lover. Or a client? She shivered in revulsion.

"You're not supposed to like it." Ron signaled to the bartender. "Double Scotch. Neat." Then he pinned her with those treacherous eyes that penetrated her wall of defenses like twin battering rams. "I need twenty thousand dollars."

The bartender asked if she wanted another drink when he set Ron's whiskey down on the greasy table top. It was a ludicrous question, since she hadn't touched the first. She shook her head, not deigning to look at him. He reminded her of a cockroach, the way he scuttled around in the dark.

Ron tossed down half the drink, winced, swallowed hard, then took a smaller sip. "You're going to get it for me."

"Go to hell. I'll do nothing of the sort."

His eyes slithered down her chest as a nasty curl deformed his heavy mouth. "Yes, you will." He took another pull on the drink. "I've got men after me, Arden. Hard men, butchers. I'm up to my ass in debt to them. They want their money."

"That's your problem, not mine."

"Oh, it's yours all right. I'm making it yours. You're married to a rich tennis player now. VIP. High roller. Big timer. You wouldn't ever have met him if it weren't for me. You owe me."

She did something she never thought she'd do in Ron Lowery's presence. She laughed. "You fool," she said with unveiled contempt. "After all you did to hurt me, even asking me to have a child for another man, you say that *I* owe *you.*"

He shrugged. "Whatever. You'll do as I say just as you always have. Because you're a spineless coward, Arden."

"I am not!" she hissed.

"No?" he asked with a sneer and another softly sinister laugh. He glanced over his shoulder at the dozen or so men watching them with keen interest. "Weren't you just a teeny-weeny bit afraid before I came in? You didn't like it in here, did you? All these guys were ogling you, thinking about what's under your skirt. Did that scare you a little? Huh? Weren't you just the least bit nervous? I'll bet there's a little river of sweat running between your breasts. Right? Are those nice big tits of yours damp with sweat?"

"Stop it."

"And there's probably a trickle of sweat between your thighs, too. Hmm? One word from me and I'll bet these guys would check that out."

"Ron, please."

He feigned surprise. "What? Did I actually hear a tremor in your voice? A plea for mercy?" He crossed his arms on the table and leaned forward. "That's where I want you, Arden. Compliant." He sat back after taking another sip of whiskey and signaled for more. "Now let's get down to business." When he had his fresh drink, he said, "I need five thousand immediately. The other fifteen, we can spread out over a few weeks."

"Ron," she exclaimed, struggling to hang onto her reason. "I don't have that kind of money."

"You have a goddam checking account, and I know it!" he shouted, his fist crashing down on the table.

She jumped in spite of her resolve not to show her fear. "Yes, I have a checking account," she said with forced composure. "But how am I supposed to account to Drew for that kind of spending?"

"That's up to you. If you're resourceful enough to con this guy into marrying you, you can think of a way to get that money."

"I didn't con him into marrying me," she said heatedly.

"But that's what he'd think, wouldn't he, if I went to him and told him who I had impregnated with his semen?" He shook his head pityingly. "No. I don't think he'd be quite the ardent groom if he found that out."

"I could deny it. I could admit that you were my husband, but that doesn't prove that I had Drew's child. I'd claim you were lying for the sake of blackmailing us."

He tsked. "Arden, Arden, are you still so naive?

Remember the lawyer, sweetheart? He's a buddy of mine. He's got the records sealed in a safe. All I'd have to do is show them to McCasslin. Besides, I told you he thinks I hung the moon because I got him that boy.''

It was her turn to look smug. "Don't count on that, Ron. He told me how you tried to get more money out of him because of the *complications* you ran into. He doesn't think nearly as well of you as you think.''

One corner of his mouth tilted. "Be that as it may, he wouldn't want me to tell the press what I know about that kid. It would make him look like a fool, not to mention besmirching the reputation of his dear departed wife.'' He lowered one calculating eyelid. "Tell me. Isn't it crowded with the three of you in bed? You, your tennis player and his wife's ghost?''

He had intended to hurt her, and he had. Whether he knew it or not, he had touched her one vulnerable point. "It's not that way," she said desperately.

"No? He was crazy in love with that woman. Even someone as jaded as I on the topic of love could see that. Do you expect me to believe you've replaced her? Remember, I was married to you, too, Arden. And you may be a helluva of a housekeeper, cook and mother, but as a lover, you're pathetic.''

Hatred, undiluted and pure, coursed through her. She wanted to flaunt her sex life with Drew, to tell this buffoon every glorious detail of their life together. Her fists were tightly clenched as she said, "He loves me. I love him. We want to have a baby. We—''

His rude laughter interrupted her. "Baby?" He laughed harder. *"You* have another baby? Where did you get the mistaken idea you could still have children?''

Chapter 12

"WHA . . . WHAT DO YOU MEAN?" HER LUNGS WERE squeezing closed. She had no air. She was going to die in the Orchid Lounge.

"I mean, Mrs. McCasslin, that when you had your last baby, you were fixed. Spayed. Sterilized."

"That's impossible," she whispered. "That's impossible."

"You were anesthetized, remember?"

"But . . . but there was no incision. For a tubal ligation—"

He waved off her arguments. "There are always new methods to try. Who is a better guinea pig than a gynecologist's wife? I was afraid you might regret giving up the baby later on, especially in light of Joey's health. Should your maternal instincts surface, I didn't want you to be able to have another child. I certainly didn't want another one. Joey cost me a fortune in medical expenses."

She uttered an anguished cry, as if he'd dealt her a

mortal blow. How could he speak that way of Joey, his own son? And now all hope of her having another child was banished by the base cruelty of this man. Feeling utterly defeated, she groped blindly for her purse. "How much do you need? Five thousand?" She wanted him out of her life. If buying him off would achieve that, she would give him any amount.

"For starters, yes. I need it tomorrow."

"Tomorrow?" How could she come up with that kind of money in that length of time? "I don't think I can get it that soon, but I'll try," she said as she stood. Dizzily, she swayed.

He caught her arm. "You'll deliver it tomorrow, or I'll pay a visit to that good-looking husband of yours. He and I have a lot to chat about."

Arden, still feeling poleaxed, worked her arm free and stumbled toward the door. The sunlight blinded her. Or was it her tears?

"Tomorrow?" Arden repeated. Drew had dropped his bomb just as she was bringing a bite of food to her mouth. Her fork was held suspended in midair. She lowered it to her plate. "We're leaving for California tomorrow?" Tomorrow, tomorrow, tomorrow. The word rolled around inside her head like a roulette ball. It seemed that she had echoed that word all day.

"I know it's a nuisance, but I only found out myself a few minutes ago." He had joined them in the dining room late. He'd been talking on the telephone to Ham again. Matt, as usual, was restless and eager for his dinner, so Arden had begun to feed him. "Mrs. Laani can pack for Matt tonight. We're catching a one o'clock plane to Honolulu tomorrow afternoon, then an overnighter to L.A."

"But why the rush?" Arden was dismayed. How was she going to pay off Ron? Ever since she'd left him, she had been trying to come up with an excuse to give Drew when she asked him for the five thousand dollars.

"Use your napkin like daddy, Matt," Drew said, demonstrating for his son. He smiled when the child did as instructed. "There are several reasons. First, there are three tournaments that Ham thinks I should play in. Few of the top seeds are going to play, so I might be able to rack up some wins. One's in San Diego, one's in Vegas and the other is in San Francisco, so the travel won't be extensive. There are only a few days between them. And Ham and I have other business to take care of."

She stared into her plate. It had been increasingly difficult to meet Drew's eyes ever since she had returned from her meeting with Ron. Now she had two secrets to hide—that she was Matt's mother and that she was barren. Should he find out either one, he'd have more than ample reason to despise her. Now she was trying to come up with a way to con him out of money to pay off her blackmailer. God, what had she sunk to?

Contrary to what Ron believed, she didn't have a limitless bank account. Drew had opened up an account in her name and kept a generous reserve in it. Into that account, too, went her checks for the articles or stories she sold. "It's yours to do with as you see fit," Drew had said when he made the initial deposit. "Just don't spend it on the household. There's another account for that. This is yours to play with."

She had checked the balance of it that day, and it was a far cry from twenty thousand. Currently, it was even short of five thousand. She knew Ron wouldn't hesitate to tell Drew about her should she not come up with the money. By tomorrow. And tomorrow they were leaving for the mainland.

She only nodded absently when Mrs. Laani came in to carry Matt upstairs so she and Drew could finish their dinner alone. She kissed the boy's cheek but later didn't even remember it. She felt like a mummy, swathed tightly in her problem, restricted and immobile, separated from life.

"You see," Drew went on once they were alone, "Ham and I have a chance to buy into an existing chain of sporting goods stores right now. It's a nationwide operation. We figure that in a few years we can buy out the other partners and then do with it as we want."

"That's wonderful, Drew."

"I've arranged a line of credit with a Honolulu bank. Cash may be tight for a few months until I chalk up a few wins and some of those renewed contracts start paying off. Can you stand living on a budget?"

His eyes were sparkling teasingly, but she could barely manufacture a smile. Even if she came up with a believable lie, Drew couldn't give her any money now. He would be using all the cash he had to buy into the sporting goods business so that their future would be secure. Arden could feel her spirit suffocating, could see her dreams leaking out of her heart, to be swallowed up by a black oppression.

Drew was startled by Arden's anxiety over their imminent departure. But then he'd been worried sick about her for days. He didn't know what to think of her sudden reversal of temperament. She'd never been nervous or high-strung before, but lately the slightest provocation set off either a crying jag or a fit of temper.

If he wasn't talking to her directly, she was gazing into space, totally unaware of what was going on around her. Even when they were engaged in conversation, her eyes would often glaze, and he knew that though she made the proper responses, she wasn't really listening to him. Even Matt, for whom she always had unlimited patience, had felt the brunt of her temper.

At first, he'd thought it was her monthly cycle throwing her off balance, but it had lasted too long. Then he'd thought with a surge of hope that she might be pregnant, but when he suggested that possibility with a teasing smile, she'd burst into tears and accused him of wanting her only as a brood mare. He'd stymied the impulse to curse and stamp from the room. Instead, he'd gone to her, taken her into his arms and comforted her with words that declared his boundless love. She'd cried all the harder.

Damned if he knew what was troubling her, but something was. Why wouldn't she open up to him, confide in him? He could help. He knew it. If only she'd tell him what was bothering her. He wanted his wife back, the one who laughed and loved as generously and as spontaneously as a young girl.

Her distress had been compounded by the news of their trip. Why? Was she dreading tour life? He had thought she'd adjusted to it so well. Nothing had seemed to ruffle her. *Dammit, what was wrong?* Was it he? Was she unhappy with their marriage? The thought brought an excruciating pain to his chest.

"I . . . I don't really have to go, do I?" He saw her tongue flash out to wet her lips nervously. "I mean it sounds to me as though you'd get along better without me . . . without all of us tagging along after you. Meetings and all . . ."

He studied her for a moment, his dinner forgotten. "I never think of you and Matt as 'tagging along.' I want you with me. As for the other, I was hoping that you'd attend the business meetings, too. I want you to be a visible and integral partner in any endeavor of my life. Since this venture is vital to our future, I would have thought you'd want to get involved."

His eyes bored into hers incisively. "There's another reason why you must go. More important than all the others. I want you to see a doctor."

To keep her hands from trembling, she clasped the seat of her chair until her knuckles turned white. "B . . . but that's ridiculous. A doctor? Why?"

"Because I think you need a thorough checkup. You

insist that nothing is wrong, but I want a professional opinion."

"What kind of doctor?" she asked testily. "A psychiatrist?"

"I think we'll start with a medical doctor." His gaze softened appreciably. "Arden, you're not Wonder Woman. You've taken on a new husband, child and climate. It's understandable if your psyche and your body are going through a period of readjustment. I think we'll both feel better once you see a doctor."

No doubt she'd feel very good when the doctor told her husband, "Your wife is in perfect health, but she's barren. I'm sorry, Mr. McCasslin. I hear you wanted another child."

What could she do? *What?* She really didn't have to do anything. Because when Ron didn't get his money the next day, he'd tell Drew about her, and then it would all be over, anyway. There would never be a doctor's appointment to worry about. For the time being, she wouldn't fight it. It was too energy consuming. The heartache and guilt plaguing her had depleted her strength. "All right, I'll see a doctor."

"Super. Ham's making an appointment for you."

Drew didn't make love to her that night. Instead, he showed his love by kissing her thoroughly and tucking her against his warmth. Even so, she shivered through the long hours of the night.

"What do you mean you can't get it?" Ron's voice was both threatening and desperate.

"Just what I told you," she whispered, fearing she'd wake the rest of the household. It was just past dawn. She'd slipped out of Drew's arms, wrapped a robe around her and crept downstairs to call the number Ron had given her. She didn't know where the telephone was. She didn't want to know. But he answered on the second ring. "I can give you a little over three thousand today. That's all I've got, and I can't get anymore."

"That's no good!" he shouted. "I've got to have five."

"I haven't got it," she hissed back.

"Get it."

"I can't. Ron, you gave me less than twenty-four hours. Be reasonable."

"The guys after me won't be reasonable."

"You should have thought of that before getting mixed up with them." She tried to push down the panic in her voice. "We're leaving for the mainland. Perhaps when we get back—"

"And when will that be?"

"About three weeks."

"Forget that, I'll be dead by then."

She couldn't say that that would be a relief, but that was what she was thinking. He sensed it. "Don't think my sudden demise would get you off the hook. Before I let them blow my brains out, I'd tell them where they could collect their money and give them the scoop on you and your new husband. If you think I'm a nuisance, honey, you haven't seen anything like these guys. You're far better off dealing with me."

"I'll get you the money," she said firmly. "You'll just have to put your creditors off for a while."

"No sale, Arden. You be at that bar at noon today with five thousand cash, or I'll make a lovely scene at the airport." He hung up.

She sat staring at the ocean for a long while before she climbed the stairs. It seemed as though she had a ball and chain around her ankles, making each step a dragging effort. Drew was right. Her mental anguish was like a physical ailment.

She heard sounds of laughter and scuffling coming from her bedroom the moment she reached the landing. Pushing the door open, she saw that Matt had joined his father in bed. They were wrestling, one as naked as the other.

Matt was shrieking with laughter as Drew tickled him, making growling sounds.

Arden went to the bed and sat down on the edge. Love flooded her heart, as tears did her eyes. These two were all she had in the world. They loved her. Until that afternoon. Then she would be exposed to them as a fraud. But her love wasn't fraudulent. She should tell Drew now, but she feared his wrath and misunderstanding. She had waited too long. And there was an outside chance she might be able to put Ron off. Perhaps if she went to the bar with what cash she had in hand, she could buy time. Each day with Drew and her son was valuable. She would collect as many as she could.

Drew winked at her as he stood Matt on his flat, hard stomach. "He's quite a boy, isn't he?"

"Yes." Her voice was husky with emotion.

Matt was toasty brown, but against his father's bronzed body, he was several shades lighter. His little buttocks were round and dimpled. Rolls of baby fat scalloped his thighs. Stubby, fat toes dug into his father's flesh. With unabashed vanity, he submitted to their adoring inspection. Taking his small penis in his hand, he declared, "Pee-pee."

Drew hooted with laughter. "Yeah, you know all the terminology; you just haven't learned the practical applications." He turned to Arden, smiling with paternal pride. When he saw her tear-clouded eyes, his smile faded. "Arden?"

She smiled a watery smile. "I love you both so much. So very much. You're my world, my life, everything."

Drew's own eyes became embarrassingly misty. "God, I've waited days for you to tell me that again. I was beginning to wonder if you felt you had made a bad bargain."

She reached out and touched his chest, combing her fingers through the luxuriant golden hair. "No. I got far more than I bargained for."

"More than two can join this orgy of the flesh," he suggested gruffly.

It wasn't fair to him for her to make love with lies weighing heavily on her heart, but it might be the last time she would ever know his touch, his kiss, his earth-moving lovemaking. Demurely, she lowered her lashes, drawing her fingernails over his flat brown nipples. "I've always thought more than two at an orgy was too many."

"You're absolutely right. One of us has to go." He sprung upright as though hinged at the waist and came nose to nose with his son. "Guess who, pal." He carried the boy to the door, set him on his feet, smacked him on the seat and said, "Go find Mrs. Laani. I think you're a fugitive from bath time, anyway."

Matt took off down the hall shouting, "Yawni, Yawni."

Drew locked the door behind him and hastened back to the bed. He wasted no time. He fell upon Arden, feasting hungrily on her mouth while his hands rid her of her robe and daringly explored.

Her fingers wound through his thick hair, holding his head still as she twisted her mouth under his for a better vantage point. She arched and writhed against his body, touching him in the places she'd learned he loved being touched, stroked, scratched. Her nipples beaded against his chest in their own caress. Her thighs parted to cradle his, and she strained toward him. He was full and throbbing with his need.

"God, I've missed you," he said frantically, as though she'd been away and had just come home. "I've wanted you like this, unbound by whatever it was that was upsetting you. Don't ever withdraw from me that way again, Arden. It scares the hell out of me. I can't lose you. I can't."

He rubbed her neck with his mouth, letting his teeth nip the delicate flesh. She moaned her consent to this gentle abuse, and when his lips closed over one flushed nipple, she told him in panted, disjointed phrases what heaven that was.

Her fingers glided down the ridges of his ribs, over his lean pelvic bones and into the dark golden thatch at the juncture of his thighs. She brushed him timidly, examined him, then ringed him with massaging fingers. She let him know her readiness, rubbing him against her body, moistening him.

"Sweet, sweet Arden." His sighs were music, love songs composed exclusively for her.

With one surging thrust, she arched up to drive him home. Hearts and bodies pulsed together. He stroked her long and leisurely, then quick and furiously, and she matched the pace he set, answering with responsive movements.

Despair was vanquished. He exorcised all of her devils and gave her his blessing, his love. This was her celebration of life before death, her swan song, the last wish granted to one doomed. She chanted his name and cried it softly when she felt his life stream bathing her womb.

She clung to him long after it was over, folding her legs across his back. She filed every sensation away in her mind for the time when she'd be without him. Greedy for his touch on her damp skin, his intoxicating smell in her nostrils, his hard fullness within her, she trapped him tighter in her velvet warmth.

His groan was one of pure animal pleasure. "Guess what?"

"What?"

He began to move again. "We're not finished yet."

"But . . . Drew . . . ahh . . . the time . . . ?"

"We'll make . . . Oh, my love, yes . . . we'll make time."

"I need to run a few errands," Arden said uneasily once she was showered and dressed and downstairs. Drew and

Matt were eating a breakfast of Mrs. Laani's macadamia-nut muffins.

"Now?" Drew asked, brushing crumbs from Matt's mouth. "Don't you want to eat something?"

"No, no," she said hastily. "There are a few things I need to pick up before the trip."

"Well, don't get too carried away shopping. Remember our flight time. Are you already packed?"

"Yes, except for last-minute things."

She was almost out of the room when Drew called her back. "I almost forgot. You have mail." Drew got up and left the informal dining room.

Arden sat down beside Matt and ate the bite of muffin he offered her even though she didn't think she could swallow anything. Drew's lovemaking had been the sweetest, most fervent, most dear, she'd ever known. In her silent way, she'd said her good-by to him. Now she scanned Matt's face, loving everything about him. Her fingers treasured each curl on his head. She touched him lovingly, wondering how she'd survive giving him up again.

"Here," Drew said, resuming his chair and pushing an envelope toward her. It was from the magazine that had published her first short story. Inside was a check for two thousand dollars.

"Oh!" she exclaimed, tears springing into her eyes. "I'd forgotten all about this." Unconsciously, she clutched the check to her breasts. Drew laughed.

"You sure look relieved to see it. Do you think I can't support you?"

"No, no," she stammered. Her heart was racing with exhilaration, but she couldn't let on too much. "Of course I know you can support me. But last night you said . . . your business . . ."

His smile was the wide, brilliant one she loved. "Darling, just because I said we'd be on a budget for a while, that doesn't mean you have to start living the life of a pauper. Did I give you that impression?" He patted her hand. "You spend that money in whatever way you see fit. It's yours. I'll handle the family finances."

On a sudden inspiration, she sat down and called for Mrs. Laani to bring her a cup of coffee. "I think I'll wait and do my shopping in L.A. or maybe San Francisco. I want to have breakfast with my husband and son."

Matt clapped his hands when his father leaned across the table and wrapped his mother in a warm embrace, sealing her mouth with a blazing kiss.

Arden left the house long enough to cash the check and make a withdrawal from her account. She sealed the five thousand dollars in a manila envelope and stopped at a pay telephone to call the Orchid Lounge. She asked to speak to Ron Lowery, purposefully leaving off any form of address.

"Where the hell are you? You're thirty minutes late."

"I'm not coming." She let him digest that for a moment before she continued. "The money will be in our mailbox when we leave. It's on the road that fronts the house and is plainly marked."

"What are you trying to pull? I said—"

"If you want your money, that's where you can find it. We're leaving for the airport about two-thirty. Good-by, Ron."

"Wait a minute!" he shouted. "When do I get the next installment?"

"When we get back from our trip." She hung up the phone before he could say anything more. She had no doubt that he'd be there to take the money out of the mailbox. He was more terrified of the loan sharks he owed money to than she was of him.

As she sped home, she was glad that she'd been able to pay him off with her own money instead of having to ask

Drew for it under false pretenses. That would mean one less lie. How she'd get the next five thousand, she didn't know. But she had bought another month of happiness.

Drew watched from the bed as his wife fumbled with the clasp on her strand of pearls. The slender, well-manicured fingers, usually so deft, were trembling. The body that he loved, the lithe form that became so malleable to his loving touch in bed, was drawn as tight as a piano wire. It seemed that all one had to do was touch her and she'd snap in two.

Mrs. Laani had left their suite of rooms earlier with Matt. Drew had instructed her to keep him entertained for several hours. Now Drew came up off the bed where he'd been lounging with the morning newspaper and crossed to Arden.

He extricated the delicate gold clasp from her fingers and latched it easily. He watched her in the mirror. He saw that hated wariness, that fear, clouding her green eyes just as he had dreaded he would. It had bewildered him several weeks before. It bewildered him more so now. For the last few weeks, they had been happier than ever before.

He'd won all three tournaments. He was now seeded third in world tennis. Few remembered and even fewer remarked on the months he'd been off the circuit or the reasons for his temporary retirement. He'd proved he could come back. He was a champion again. And Arden had been there to celebrate each victory with him. Now he could feel her withdrawing into that shell he couldn't penetrate.

By God, he wasn't going to let her slip back into it without a fight!

He caught her shoulders so she couldn't evade him. "You're making far too much fuss over a medical examination, Arden."

"You are making too much of it," she snapped back.

"That's the prerogative of a worried husband. If the shoe were on the other foot, you'd feel the same."

"I wouldn't badger you."

"Yes, you would."

Yes, she would, Arden admitted. But there was nothing wrong with her! Nothing except that in a few hours Drew would learn they could never have another child.

She put on her earrings. "I'm fine, Drew. Have I seemed sick to you?"

"No," he answered honestly. Since the day they left Hawaii, she'd been all a man could hope for in a wife, a woman, a lover. Only in the last few days, when he'd insisted that she see the doctor—two appointments in Los Angeles had already been canceled—had she started behaving in that guarded way again. And each mention of home dropped a veil of discontent over her features. Drew felt a sudden wrenching in his gut. Did she suspect that something terrible was wrong with her? Lumps? Pains? *My God, no.* Was there something she hadn't told him to keep him from worrying?

"Arden," he said, turning her to face him. His blue eyes searched hers as though looking for signs of suffering. "You're not . . . I mean, you don't hurt anywhere or anything, do you? Darling, if you suspect something is wrong, it's better to have it seen to. It's what you don't—"

She covered his mouth with her finger tips. "Shhh." Her heart turned over when she realized the unnecessary worry she had caused him. "No. No, darling, no. I'm in perfect health."

His relief was visible. One arm slid around her waist and pulled her close. The other hand smoothed the glossy length of her hair. "You like our home on Maui, don't you, Arden?"

"Of course," she said earnestly, seeing the concerned furrow between his thick brows and hating herself for etching it there.

"Because each time we mention going home, you seem upset by the idea. If you don't like it there, we can leave. I bought that place as a refuge. I don't need it anymore. All I need is you. And Matt. With the two of you, I can live anywhere. It's difficult for some people to live in so remote a place—"

"But I'm not one of them. I loved your home the first time you took me there, and now it's *my* home. I could live there forever with you and Matt."

He crushed her to him, loving the feel of her compact body against his. He knew each curve, each hollow, each dainty bone intimately. He loved them all. Every time he touched her, naked or clothed, he was filled with strength. She had made him happier than he'd had any right to expect, and he couldn't bear to think that she wasn't completely happy with him.

"I love you, Arden. Have I told you that today?"

"I can't remember," she mumbled into his shirt front. *Oh, God, he would feel so betrayed if he ever found out about Matt. It would kill him.* "Just in case, tell me again."

His lips said it all as they came down on hers tenderly. His tongue roamed her mouth lazily as the pressure of his lips increased. The knuckles of his right hand lightly rubbed her nipple until he felt it flower beneath the ecru georgette blouse. The tip of his tongue touched hers suggestively, and he smiled when he heard her throaty purr. His other hand found the firm curve of her derriere and squeezed it gently, urging her forward and upward.

She pulled back in alarm. "Drew, you're getting—"

"Um-huh." He grinned wolfishly and started to pull her back.

"We can't. I'm not supposed to right before going to the doctor."

"Oh, hell," he ground out, burying his face in the fragrant hollow of her neck. "I forgot about that."

Then a brilliant idea occurred to her. She pressed close again and let her hand trail down his stomach to the fly of his trousers. "It probably wouldn't matter," she cooed, outlining his shape with a bold caress.

"No, you don't," he said, pushing her away. "I know what you're thinking, and it won't work." He made an agonized face as he turned away from her to pick up his sport jacket. "Get your purse. Let's go before I change my mind. Or lose it."

"Are you sure?" Arden stared at the doctor with wide, disbelieving eyes. Thank God Drew had agreed to let her see this doctor in San Francisco. The one Ham had made an appointment with would have known her as the ex-Mrs. Ron Lowery. This doctor was a stranger to her, but after what he'd just told her, she thought she might forever think of him as a friend. "Are you absolutely positive?"

The doctor chuckled. "I'm absolutely positive that there's no medical or physical reason why you can't have another baby. If you're asking for a guarantee that you'll get pregnant, I'm afraid that's something I can't give you." He noted Arden's astonishment. "Where did you ever get the idea that you'd been sterilized?"

She licked her lips, trying at one and the same time to absorb the fact that she wasn't sterile and to tamp down a killing rage at Ron Lowery. This had been just another of his psychopathically cruel tricks. "I . . . I . . . uh . . . had an infection, and the doctor I was seeing at the time thought it had made me infertile."

The doctor looked puzzled. "I saw no remnants of any infection. You're a wonderfully healthy woman with a normal set of reproductive organs." Linking his fingers together on his desk top, he leaned toward her. "Are you happy with your husband? Do you love him?"

"Yes," she said fervently. She could actually feel the burden she had carried with her for over a month being lifted from her shoulders. "Yes," she repeated, breaking out in laughter.

"Then let's go tell him that you're as fine as a fiddle." At the door, he caught her arm. "Relax, Mrs. McCasslin. You'll have that other baby."

Arden was as impulsive and playful as a child as they drove the rented Lincoln back to the hotel. She virtually sat in Drew's lap, her left arm around his neck. Every chance she got, she stole a kiss from his lips. While he negotiated the hilly streets of San Francisco, she contented herself with nibbling his neck, his ear.

"For god sakes, Arden, did that doctor give you a tonic, an aphrodisiac? You're driving me crazy."

"How crazy?" she breathed as her hand slid between his thighs. There she felt a good indication of how near he was to losing control.

"What did you and that doctor do to turn you on like this?"

"That's crude." She punished him with a gentle squeeze that almost made him swerve the car into another lane. "I'm turned on because I have the handsomest, smartest, sexiest . . ." She placed her lips against his ear. "And hardest husband in the whole world."

His curse testified to his agitation. "Okay, two can play this lusty game. Did you know that every time I look at your breasts, I'm ready to make love right then? Remember that cocktail party in San Diego after the tournament? You were wearing that yellow halter dress, and I knew you didn't have a bra under it. All the time I was making small talk to everyone, I was thinking about how I'd love to slide my hand inside your dress and touch your breasts."

"Drew," she groaned. Moving slightly closer, she pressed her breast against his arm. His sensual monologue was producing the desired effect.

"The other day when we met Ham for lunch on Fisherman's Wharf, you wore that peasant skirt with sandals and no stockings. I had watched you dress that morning. All you had on under your skirt was that pair of lilac panties with the lace panel in front. I couldn't think about anything else but the last time you'd worn them and I kissed you through that lace—"

"Stop," she cried, laying her head on his shoulder. "This is insane. We won't be able to walk through the lobby."

That was close to the truth. They were breathless with excitement by the time Drew latched the hotel door behind them with a DO NOT DISTURB sign dangling from the knob. He had already stripped off his coat and tie, his shoes and socks, before Arden stopped him.

"Wait. I want to." First, she eased out of her own clothes with the practiced, sinuous moves of a courtesan. The georgette blouse had an interminable number of tiny pearl buttons, and Drew's eyes were glazed with passion by the time she peeled it off her shoulders and down her arms. Her breasts thrust proudly beneath the lacy confinement of her brassiere. It came off with deliberate slowness. His eyes ravaged the warm mounds and coral nipples. She peeled off her half slip and pantyhose with one graceful movement, then stood before him wearing the panties he'd mentioned earlier.

His mouth curved with humor as he reached for his top shirt button. Staying his hand, she led him to the bed. She sat down on its edge and ran her fingers up his chest to the top button. Each one was released with meticulous precision. Her fingers took leisurely detours over the crinkly mat of hair, the firm bunched muscles, the smooth flesh, the masculine nipples.

"Arden, please," he begged on a shuddering breath. She took off his shirt, then met the fiery gaze he turned on her upraised face. "Let me love you."

"Let me love *you*." She worked free his belt buckle, the snap of his trousers, the zippered fly. Her eyes were still locked with his as she slid her hands beneath the tight briefs and cupped his taut buttocks. She smoothed her hands down, taking the garments with them. When he was free of them, she laid her cheek on him.

"I love you," she vowed in a soft whisper. Then her lips took him beyond paradise.

Chapter 13

THE ORCHID LOUNGE WAS AS MURKY, THE CLIENTELE AS unsavory, as before. A dozen or so men were grouped in pairs and trios. Their conversations were low and indistinct to the only woman in the place. The air was thick with the odor of beer and tobacco smoke.

Arden had never been more composed in her life.

The trip home from San Francisco had been nothing short of a party for them all. Drew was still euphoric over his success at the tournaments. He was no less glad over Arden's frame of mind since her visit to the doctor. Whatever had been worrying her seemed to have been resolved in that hour. His heart still flip-flopped, and his breath grew short each time he remembered the unselfish way she had loved him afterward. That whole afternoon had been given over to sexual indulgence. He would recommend such an afternoon to any married couple.

Arden, after having dreaded it, was now anxious to return home. She was basking in the glow of Drew's success and his love. During the long flight over the

225

Pacific, she could barely keep her hands off him. She took advantage of every occasion to touch him, and he responded in kind.

Matt sensed their lightheartedness and was at his most good-natured. He charmed all the flight attendants until Mrs. Laani pulled him into her lap and he fell asleep on her generous bosom. Arden could have been jealous, but Drew pulled her into his own arms for a little "nap." Numerous times, she had to covertly swat his hand when it crept into compromising territory.

The morning after their return, Ron telephoned.

"It's about time you answered. The first two times I called, I got your housekeeper and had to hang up."

"I'm sorry to have inconvenienced you."

"Cocky all of a sudden, aren't you?" He chuckled unpleasantly. "Don't forget your bills are due."

"Where and when?"

"The same place. Two o'clock."

She had hung up without another word. Now she was sitting in the same booth, and he was as late as before. She had disdained the bartender's ingratiating invitation to have a drink on the house. Instead, she sat with her back straight, her hands folded in her lap. And rather than ignore the stares this time, she met them with enough condescension to turn them away.

"Glad to be back?" Ron asked as he slid into the booth opposite her. "Good trip?"

"Yes, on both accounts."

"Your husband's making a name for himself. Does it make you proud to have such a famous hubby?"

"I'd be proud of him whether he was famous or not."

He placed his hand over his heart. "Such wifely devotion makes me thirsty." He called his order to the bartender, then turned back to her. "Wonder how proud he'd be of you if he knew you'd sold your body for fifty thousand dollars?"

"I don't know. But I intend to find out. I'm going to tell him everything."

Ron's eyes glittered in reptilian fashion as he stared at her. Even when his drink was set before him, he didn't move.

"You bastard," Arden said in a calm, emotionless voice. That tone conveyed her contempt more than shouting at him would have. He wasn't worth wasting the energy shouting would require. "I didn't know that any man, even one as low as you, could play a trick as dirty as the one you played on me."

His grin was insolent and obnoxious. "You found out I'd lied about sterilizing you." He began to laugh a low, rumbling laugh that could have passed for the devil's. "Scared you, didn't I?"

"Why did you tell me that?"

"Because you were getting too self-assured. You seemed to think you could shake me off like a bad dream. I wanted you to know that I meant business. I still do."

"Well, I'm terribly sorry to disappoint you, Ron, but our *business* dealings are over. Your threats are empty ones. If they weren't, you wouldn't be skulking around in dives like this and hanging up when I don't answer the telephone. You accused me of being a coward, but you are the coward. It takes a man to make it in the real world. And you never could. Even when you had all the advantages handed to you, you couldn't hack it as a doctor, as a husband, as a father, as a man."

She stood up with proud dignity. "You don't frighten me anymore. You've browbeaten and used me for the last time. There's nothing you can do to hurt me any longer. Go to hell."

She turned on her heel and walked out. Her knees were weak and her mouth dry by the time she reached the car. But she had done it! She had rid herself of Dr. Ron Lowery forever. That night, she'd tell Drew the entire story. She was no longer afraid that their love couldn't withstand the truth. Their lives were grafted together too securely to be torn apart now. She would make the setting perfect. She'd tell him everything. And then, at last, she'd be free.

The bottle of wine almost slipped from under her arm as she maneuvered her way through the wide front door. "Mrs. Laani," she called, laughing. She clutched the bouquet of flowers, trying to keep them from being crushed against the box that contained her new negligee.

Mrs. Laani came rushing out from the back of the house, but the moment Arden saw her, she knew it wasn't her call that had brought the housekeeper running. "Mrs. McCasslin, I'm so glad you're home."

"Is something wrong?"

The housekeeper darted her eyes toward Drew's office. The door was closed. "Mr. McCasslin wants to see you right away. He said the moment you got back." The normally self-contained woman was wringing her hands.

"Why? What's—" Arden gripped Mrs. Laani's arm. "Matt? Has something happened to Matt?"

"No, he's with me in the kitchen. You'd better go to your husband." She wouldn't meet Arden's questioning eyes.

Arden's reflexes took over. She operated mechanically, acting as though nothing were wrong when indeed she knew something was terribly wrong. Mrs. Laani wasn't the kind to panic. "Chill the wine and arrange the flowers in a vase for our bedroom, please. We'll eat the steaks tonight. Please see that Matt's dinner is ready beforehand. And put this box in my closet."

"Yes, Mrs. McCasslin," Mrs. Laani said, relieving Arden of her packages and backing away from her. Arden was alarmed by the commiserating look on the woman's face.

She smoothed her hands over her skirt and was amazed

to note that the palms were damp. Stifling her panic, she turned the knob and pushed her way through the door into Drew's office.

"Darling, I'm—" The first thing that caught her eye was the bottle of Scotch on the polished surface of Drew's desk. She stared at it for several seconds before her eyes wandered to the highball glass next to it. A white-knuckled hand was wrapped around the glass. Drew's hand. It wasn't until then that the incongruity of that struck her.

Her eyes flew up to meet his, and she flinched at the hatred she saw smoldering there. His hair was a wild blond tangle, and it wasn't simply wind-blown. It had been torn at with maniacal hands. The muscles of his jaw were working as he ground his teeth, and in his temple beat a furious pulse.

"Come in, Mrs. McCasslin," he said in a voice Arden had never heard. It dripped with sarcasm and repugnance. "I believe you know our guest."

For the first time, Arden noticed the man ensconced in the deep easy chair facing Drew's desk. He turned, and she met Ronald Lowery's mocking face. Her knees collapsing, she slumped against the door, clutching at it for support.

Drew laughed harshly. "You act surprised to see your ex-husband when in fact Ron's told me that the two of you have been seeing a great deal of each other."

Bile rose into her throat, but she forced it back down. She must make Drew see the true situation. "Drew," she said, reaching out a beseeching hand. "Drew, what has he told you?"

"Quite a tale, quite a tale," he said with that same sneering laugh. "I thought I was the king of sinners. I certainly didn't think any form of human treachery would surprise me. I congratulate you on your ingeniousness."

"Drew, please," Arden said, advancing into the room. "Listen to me. I don't know what he's told you, but—"

"*Did* you let your husband impregnate you with my sperm, and *did* you carry my child for nine months, and then *did* you give him . . . or should I say *sell* him . . . for half the one hundred thousand dollars your husband charged me? *Did* you do all that?"

Tears streamed down her face. "Yes, but—"

"And then *did* you have a change of heart and come to Hawaii to worm your way into my confidence, into my life? *Did* you?"

"It wasn't—"

"Godammit, what a fool I've been." The chair went flying backward when he lunged out of it. He drained the glass of Scotch and then slammed it back onto the desk top. He turned his back on them as if they were too disgusting to look at.

"It wasn't like that," Arden said. "It *wasn't.*"

Ignoring her plea for understanding, he whirled around. "How much were you planning to bleed me for, huh?"

He was demanding that of her, not Ron. "Nothing."

"Nothing! Nothing? My money, my son? When was it going to be enough? You already had my life sewn up with your deceit."

She swallowed, trying to capture the thoughts that were darting through her head. She couldn't think with Drew scowling at her, his eyes as hard and cold as diamonds. "He contacted me several weeks ago. He said he'd tell you who I was if . . ." She quailed at his snarl but doggedly continued. "If I didn't give him twenty thousand dollars. He's a gambler and indebted to loan sharks. That's why he needed the money before, the money you paid him for Matt. I needed that money too, for Joey. And I wanted to be free of Ron." Distressed, she rubbed her forehead when Drew righted the chair and dropped down into it. His whole bearing reflected indifference to her dilemma. She must make him understand!

"I paid him five thousand dollars before we went to the

mainland. It was my money, Drew, not yours. Mine. And I would have given him twice that to spare you this scene."

"So you would have gone on giving this scum money indefinitely to keep me from finding out what a deceitful bitch I'm married to. Your concern for my welfare overwhelms me."

She sobbed and shook her head. "No, Drew, no. I was going to tell you myself."

"When? When, Arden? I'd be interested to know. When Matt went off to grade school? When he graduated from college? Or when he was marching down the aisle with his bride, were you planning to tap me on the arm and say, 'Oh, by the way, I'm the woman who gave him birth.' Is that when you planned to tell me?"

The scornful words pounded against her skull like tiny mallets. "I couldn't live with the secret any longer. I love you and Matt. I was going to tell you . . . tonight."

He bellowed with laughter then, ugly, ridiculing laughter. *"Tonight!* Isn't that touching?" He stared up at her from under glowering brows. "Do you really think I'll believe that now, when you've lied to me from the very beginning?"

"I didn't lie!"

"This whole goddamned affair has been a lie!" he roared. Once again, he came out of the chair like a bullet. "When I think of how you duped me." He shook his head, laughing mirthlessly. "So prim and proper, so polite, so sympathetic, so—" He waved a hand toward her and then dropped it at his side in a gesture that stated how pathetic a creature he found her.

His attention returned to Ron, who was sitting like a vulture anticipating the bleeding carcass that would be left for him to finish off. "Get out," Drew said succinctly. The gloating smirk on Ron's face disappeared.

"Wait a minute. We haven't talked about how we're going to handle this."

"If you think I'll give you one goddam cent, you're crazy as well as criminal. And if you don't get out of here now, I'm going to beat the bloody hell out of you, and then I'm going to turn you over to the police."

Ron stood, trembling with rage. "You'll sing a different tune when I tell the newspapers my titillating story about you and your pale wife and how you came to me asking to find a mother for your baby. That would make the son you hold so dear little more than a freak in a sideshow. To top that off, you're now married to the natural mother. Maybe I won't tell them that I artificially inseminated Arden. Maybe I'll let them think Matt came about in the natural way. That would make the kid a bastard."

Arden shivered, but Drew shrugged theatrically. "Who do you think is going to believe such a farfetched story? Especially from a doctor who has lost his practice, the respect of his peers, who is in debt to everyone in the world, including the Mafia, and is now living the life of a bum. Who do you think they'll believe? Me or you? Celebrities of my status are constantly the victims of crackpots out to make a quick buck, and the press knows that. They'll laugh in your face, Lowery."

Arden could see the confidence leaking out of Ron as freely as his sweat. "That lawyer. He's got papers. He'll back me up."

"Will he? If you were he, who would you back up? A world-famous tennis player who's on the rise or a derelict out for revenge on the wife who left him? Even your caliber of friend wouldn't be that stupid. If he were, I could pay him more to keep quiet than you could to talk."

Ron's face had gone the color of putty. Drew came around the desk. "I say once again, get out. And if you so much as show your face to any member of my family or household again, I'll have you locked up so tight that only your Mafia buddies can get to you. And you know what they'll do when they find you."

"You can't get rid of me so easy, McCasslin."

"Yes, I can, and you know it. That's why you stink of fear."

Ron looked at Arden, his gaze filled with hate. "At least I ruined you, too. He despises you, just as I always did." He left the room. Moments later, she heard the front door opening and closing.

Minutes passed. There was no movement in the study. A deathlike pall hung over them. Drew stared out the window at the incessant motion of the ocean. Arden stared at his back, wondering how she could ever make him understand enough to forgive her. Why hadn't she told him? *Why?* If only she had it all to live over, she would tell him everything. She could imagine him taking her in his arms and whispering his understanding. "You did what you had to do at the time," he would say. "I can't fault you for that. I know you married me because you love me, not because you wanted to be with Matt. I know. I understand."

Instead, he was brittle with fury and wounded pride. She didn't recognize the face that turned to her now. "Are you still here? I thought maybe you would leave with your first husband to see what new adventure the two of you could embark upon."

She bowed her head. "It was never an adventure. I did it for Joey."

"So there really was a Joey? I was beginning to wonder."

Her head snapped up a moment before she lurched toward him angrily. "I did it to prolong his life. I did it because it was the only way I had to get out of an intolerable marriage with a man I loathed more every day. When you stop feeling sorry for yourself, maybe you can see your way clear to understand what it was like for me."

"Feeling sorry for myself!" he shouted. "I feel nothing but contempt for my blind stupidity. Every time I think about the callow way I watched you, how I carefully planned my approach like a jerk asking for his first dance, how I sat there talking to you with my pants near to bursting, I could retch. How did you manage to keep a straight face? I don't know why you didn't collapse with laughter."

"It wasn't like that, Drew," she protested urgently. "Initially, yes, I wanted to meet you because of Matt. *I wanted to see my son!*" she shouted. "Was that so wrong? But once I met you, I wanted you, too. Even more than I wanted Matt." That admission cost her dearly, but she knew it to be the truth.

"You wanted nothing but to seduce me."

"Seduce . . . ?" she began incredulously. "Have you lost your memory as well as your reason? If that's all it had taken, I'd have done that the first night."

"Oh, no, not you. You're too smart a schemer. If you'd taken me to bed right away, I might never have come back. No, you baited me with all that well-thought-out resistance. To a man who has women clustered around him all the time, that's the strongest turn-on of all."

"Yes, you could have had your pick of girls. They follow you in packs. So don't make me out as a temptress who snared you into a trap with the promise of sex that couldn't be had anywhere else." Her impatience with his bullheadedness was increasing and with it her volume. "You were a bonus I hadn't counted on. My objective was to become a trusted friend, not a lover. Then I fell in love with you and couldn't find the courage to tell you who I was for fear you'd act exactly as you're acting. Your pride, your fierce temper, makes you unreasonable, Drew."

Her breasts heaved with agitation beneath her silk sweater He found himself staring at them and tore his eyes away, sending blistering curses toward the ceiling.

Even now, knowing what he did about her, she appealed to him as no other woman ever had. She was so damned beautiful. He still wanted her. Vivid in his memory was the first time he'd seen her sitting under the umbrella of that patio table. Her serenity seemed to lure him. He'd wanted to be near her, to absorb that peace she seemed to exude. How could she have fooled him? Why hadn't he been able to see the calculation in her eyes? It must have been there no matter how much she denied it now. She'd plotted the whole thing long before he'd ever seen her. All right, yes, part of his anger was out of pride. But what man likes to find out that he's been manipulated like a puppet into loving and marrying a woman? What man with any pride could tolerate that?

He kept telling himself he hated her. Why then did he want to kiss her mindless, to empty his frustration, which was only a hair away from being desire, into her? Why did he still crave the succor of her body and the joy of her laugh and the balm of her love? He hated her most for the weakness she induced in him.

"I tried to tell you once," she said barely above a whisper. "And you said that any secrets about our pasts were better kept to ourselves. That if they didn't affect the way we loved each other, they were better left unspoken."

"I didn't know your little secret was of such magnitude, Arden." It was his superior tone, that arrogant drawl, that went down her spine like fingernails on a blackboard and brought her own temper to the surface.

"And what about *your* secret, Drew? You never told me that Matt was born not of Ellie, your beloved wife, but of a woman you wouldn't recognize if you met her on the street. You were willing to let me marry you without knowing that, weren't you?"

"What difference did it make?"

"None!" she yelled. "That's my point. I would love you and Matt just the same if I weren't his mother."

"Would you, Arden?"

The question had the impact of an explosion in the room. For seconds after it had been detonated, there was an intense silence.

"Yes, Drew," she said with soft intensity. "Yes."

He impaled her with his startling blue gaze. "But I'll

never know for sure, will I? You sold your body to me
once for the sake of a son. Isn't that what you've done
again?"

She watched in helpless desperation as he went to the
desk and picked up the bottle of Scotch. Going to the open
window, he leaned forward and shattered the bottle on the
outside wall of the house. He tossed the jagged bottle neck
into the shrubbery.

"I sure as hell won't let you drive me back to *that*," he
said. "I'm a winner again, and I won't let you or anyone
take that away from me."

"You're making a mistake."

Arden turned from folding a blouse into her suitcase to
see Mrs. Laani standing in the door of the master suite.
She looked comfortingly domestic and normal with a dish
towel slung over her shoulder. Arden longed to go to her,
to lay her head on that maternal breast and let loose the
tears that she thought should have been spent by now.
She'd been crying for a week, ever since Drew left.

Without a word of good-by to her, he'd left his office
and packed quickly. The next thing she knew, he was
striding across the lawn calling to Mo. "Drive me to the
airport, please." He'd called three times since to check on
Matt. He spoke with Mrs. Laani, never to her. He was in
Los Angeles, ostensibly working with Ham on his serve
and closing the final negotiations of their business deal.

"I don't think it's a mistake," Arden now said quietly,
and turned back to the suitcase that lay opened on the bed.

She heard Mrs. Laani's shuffling footsteps as she came
into the room. "He's a stubborn man, Mrs. McCasslin.
Proud. I would have had to be deaf not to hear the
argument the two of you had after that horrible man left.
You're Matt's mother. I should have guessed."

Arden smiled. "It was easy to slip into the active role.
Sometimes I thought my love would be so transparent that

you . . . or Drew . . . would guess, but . . ." Her voice trailed off on a tremulous sigh.

"It was a shock to Mr. McCasslin, but when he thinks about it, he'll realize how irrational he's been."

"He's had a week to think about it. I don't know what he plans to do about us, but I can't just sit here like a convict awaiting execution. I'm the intruder. He was already playing competitive tennis before he met me. He and Matt have a close relationship. They don't need me interfering in their lives any more than I already have."

Mrs. Laani pulled herself erect and crossed her arms over her stomach. "So you're going to play the martyr and sneak away like a coward."

Arden sat down on the bed and looked up at the woman's reproachful expression. "Try to understand this, Mrs. Laani. All my life I've been a coward. I did what my husband wanted me to do even when I knew it was wrong. Before that, my father took care of me, made my decisions for me."

She sighed and fiddled with the lacy hem of a slip she'd been folding. Drew liked its peachy color. He'd remarked on it every time she wore it. Once, jokingly, he'd pretended to take a bite out of her breast, chewing lustily. "The ripest fruit on the tree," he'd said, and they'd laughed together at his clowning. Would memories like that haunt her in the lonely years to come?

"The cowardly thing to do would be to stay and submit to Drew's scorn, to live with it, just like I lived with my former husband's. He actually hated me for the doormat I became. I can see that now. He contrived ways to humiliate me, perhaps in the hope that I'd show some backbone and say no to him just once."

"But Mr. McCasslin would never be like that," Mrs. Laani protested vehemently.

"No, he wouldn't be cruel. But year after year, I'd see his respect dwindling. Because I'd be so afraid of offending him again, I'd want to do everything he asked. I'd be tempted to cater to him for fear he'd throw my one major mistake in my face again and again. I'd feel forced to prove my love by never disagreeing with him. And very soon, he'd hate me. And I'd hate myself worse."

She looked back up at the housekeeper, whom she considered a friend. "I can't live like that again. If Drew doesn't know by now how much I love him, then no amount of demonstration will convince him. I won't spend my life trying."

"But Matt." Mrs. Laani's eyes were filled with tears.

"Yes, Matt." Arden smiled gently with remembrance of the week they'd had together. She'd spent every waking hour with him. At night, she'd go into his room, sit in the bentwood rocker beside his baby bed and watch him as he slept. Her heart ached for what she must do. "Hopefully, Drew will let me see him periodically. I wouldn't be so unreasonable as to fight him for custody. This is the only life Matt knows. I couldn't uproot him from it." A tear rolled down her cheek. "It's just that he changes every day. Months will go by, and I won't see him, and I'll miss so many of those wonderful changes."

"Please change your mind." Mrs. Laani was weeping unashamedly now. Arden envied her the freedom to do so. "You love them both too much to leave."

"I love them too much not to," Arden responded quietly.

She explained the same thing to Matt later that night. He had long since fallen into the innocent sleep of a child.

"I don't know what your daddy will tell you about me. I hope someday you'll know who I am and that you'll forgive me for giving you up. I was trying to save your brother's life, Matt." A poignant smile flickered over her lips. "I wish you had known Joey. You would have liked each other." She wiped her cheeks of flowing tears.

"Your father is a competitor, Matt. He can't bear to lose without having fought an honest fight." She remembered the match against Gonzales. It had been a defeat, but a defeat Drew hadn't minded because he'd played hard and fair. Arden hadn't allowed him to play fair. She'd cheated him of an honest game, because the victory had been certain. He'd been a pawn and not a participant. That was what he couldn't forgive.

"I love your father, Matt. And I don't want to leave either of you. But it would be an unhealthy family environment for you to grow up in with him holding me in contempt and me hating him for his intolerance. Someday you may learn that love can't exist if one's self-esteem is sacrificed to it. I can't be an object for any man again, something that goes with the house, something with no will, no opinion worth considering. Please understand why I must leave."

She fingered the soft, butter-colored curls. She traced his pudgy cheek to the drooling mouth. She touched the dimpled knuckles of his fist.

"I had to give you up before, Matt. Then as now, it wasn't because I didn't love you." She stood, groped her way to the door and fumbled for the light switch. She didn't look back before she plunged the room into darkness, a darkness not nearly as absolute as the one in her soul.

Chapter 14

THE MOTEL ROOM WAS LIKE AN EFFICIENCY APARTMENT. IT was on the wrong side of Kalakaua Avenue if one wanted a view of Waikiki. The complex had seen better days. Now it was only an insignificant, inexpensive motel dwarfed and humbled by progress and modern architecture. It suited Arden's budget and needs, as good a place as any to idle away the long, lonely days.

She wasn't completely without occupation. She took long walks along the beach. She thought about Matt, wondered what he was doing, if he was missing her. And she thought about Drew, what he was doing, if he was missing her. She wrote. Thoughts and impressions that had no form filled tablet after tablet. She was seized by a compulsion to put her feelings on paper.

She was doing just that on the fourth day after leaving Maui. The muses had taken leave, for she had stared at the blank page for fifteen minutes. A shadow crossed the sheet of paper, and she looked up at the window to see Drew standing there.

For a small eternity, they stared at each other through the smudged window screen. Her mental faculties failed her. Stunned fingers let go of the pen. It dropped to the table top and rolled onto the cheaply carpeted floor. He didn't speak before he moved toward the door.

She had to persuade her muscles to move. Wobbly knees brought her to her feet. Self-consciously, she smoothed her hair and ran her palms over the old jeans covering her thighs. It was ridiculous, but she wished she had put on a bra that morning under the T-shirt she wore. Unreasonably, she felt vulnerable, unprotected; she would have felt more confident behind that lacy armor. She stepped to the door. He hadn't knocked, but she pulled it open.

His face looked so ravaged that at first she feared he'd been drinking abusively again. But despite the lines around them, his eyes were clear, and his marvelous athletic body was agile and lithe as he walked into the room. His hair was longer and shaggier than usual. He had on a pair of white shorts and a yellow polo shirt. To her, he'd never looked better. She ached with the need to touch him.

After one cursory glance around the stark room, he turned to her. "Hi."

"Hi."

"Are you all right?"

She looked down at the floor, then as quickly back up into his eyes, unable to keep from looking at him. "Yes." She could sense a tension about him as powerful as that which gripped her. He seemed to radiate a heat that her body responded to. Her breast filled with emotion. "You? Are you well? Matt?"

"I only returned to Maui this morning."

"Oh."

"I wasn't home long, but Matt seemed fine. Healthwise, that is. Mrs. Laani said he's been crying a lot lately." He seemed to find the palm tree outside the screened window captivating. He stared at it as he said, "He misses you."

She ducked her head. "I miss him, too." A pain like a laser beam shot through her heart. *And I miss you!*

"I . . . uh . . . I didn't know you had left until I got home." He coughed unnecessarily and cleared his throat. It sounded loud in the cramped room. "I flew back to Honolulu immediately."

She turned toward the window and gazed out. Her pulse was pounding so hard she could count each beat, and her hand trembled as she toyed with the draw cord of the tacky drapes. "How did you find me?"

"With a bag of quarters."

She turned her head. "Pardon?"

"I got a bag of quarters from the bank, found a pay phone and started dialing."

"Oh." She turned back to the window before allowing herself to smile. "I decided to stay in Hawaii until arrangements were made in Los Angeles. Since . . . since my trip over here was left deliberately open-ended, I gave up my apartment before I left. I'm waiting to hear from a friend. She's looking for a place for me."

"You're going back, then? Back to L.A., I mean?"

Was there anxiety underlying the question? She didn't dare look at him. What if that tremor in his voice indicated relief? "I suppose so, yes," she mumbled.

She heard him coming nearer. He stood in front of the table where she'd been working. The sheets of paper she'd discarded rustled under his hand. "You're writing?"

"Yes," she said huskily. He wasn't going to argue with her about the separation. He was going to let her go. He was condemning her to a sterile existence without color, without life. "I write when the mood strikes me," she said with forced casualness.

She heard more paper crackling in the brief pause that followed. "What mood were you in when you wrote this?"

In her peripheral vision, she saw a wrinkled piece of paper floating to the table top. Turning slowly, puzzled, she looked first at Drew. His eyes seared into hers, and she rapidly shifted her gaze to the sheet of paper he referred to.

She recognized her handwriting instantly. After reading the first line, she realized it was a poem she'd penned more than a month before. Like everything she wrote, she had dated it at the top of the page. They'd been in San Francisco. Mrs. Laani had taken Matt downstairs to the hotel's restaurant for his breakfast. They'd ordered theirs up from room service. After a leisurely breakfast in bed, they'd made even more leisurely love. When Drew left for his practice session, Arden had reached for a tablet and pen and, still languorous from their sweet lovemaking, she'd composed the poem.

It was a tribute to him, to what he meant to her. The last two lines were, "Where once your life transformed my body, / Your love now shapes my soul."

Tears blinded her and made the edited lines bleed together. "I think the mood is self-explanatory." She hazarded a glance up at him to find his own eyes shiny and wet.

"I found it crumpled in the corner of the suitcase yesterday."

"I'd forgotten what I did with it."

"I had decided days ago that I was the biggest heel in history. You had every right to hate me for the things I'd said, not to mention my goddamned stubborn pride and short temper. I was going to beg for your forgiveness, promise that I'd never consider you an opponent again. Finding this gave me the courage to come home and face you. I figured that if you felt this for me once, you might find it in your heart to feel it again."

"*You* were going to ask *my* forgiveness?"

"Yes. For behaving like a moron, a sore loser, a spoiled brat."

"But darling, your anger was justified. I tricked you into marrying me."

They had been inclining toward each other. Now he pulled her into his arms and crushed her against his body. He buried his face in the glossy mass of her hair. "You did no such thing. I married you because I love you. I wanted you for my wife. I still do. God, I almost died when Mrs. Laani told me you had left. Don't leave me, Arden."

"I didn't want to," she cried. "I only left because I thought you couldn't bear the sight of me." She pushed him away and peered up into his eyes. "But I can't live with judgment every day. I have to know you understand why I did what I did. Given the same set of circumstances, I'd make the same choice, Drew. I won't live the rest of my life being censured for it."

"Come here," he said gently, leading her to the bed. They sat down on the faded spread, and he took both her hands in his. "What you did wasn't wrong, Arden. Unorthodox, maybe, but not wrong. When Lowery told Ellie and me he had found a healthy young woman who was willing to have our child, in our minds, we placed her on a pedestal. The day Matt was born, we thought she was the most wonderful woman on the face of the earth."

Lovingly, he touched her face, her hair, as he talked. "Why I acted the way I did when I learned you were that woman, I can't explain. I guess I felt betrayed because you hadn't told me in the beginning that you were Matt's mother. It hurt that you hadn't trusted my love enough to tell me. What I should have done when I found out was what I'd felt like doing the first time I saw my son. I should have dropped to my knees and thanked you from the bottom of my heart."

"You don't think less of me because I sold my baby?"

He lifted tears from her cheeks with his finger tip. "I didn't think badly of you before I knew who you were. Why would I now? I know you did it to try to save Joey's life. If I thought I could save Matt such a fate, I'd make a bargain with the devil."

"I did."

He smiled wryly. "Having come to know your former husband better, I couldn't agree with you more. I can't believe that at one time I actually considered him a miracle worker."

"You're not afraid he'll make more trouble?"

"I don't think he will. He's a gutless bastard running scared."

"I should have realized that the first time he approached me on Maui. I was so afraid of what he might do. Kidnap Matt. Anything was possible."

"He's got more than us to worry about. But if he does bring on a crisis, I know I can face anything as long as I have you and Matt with me." He planted a tender kiss in her palm. "You will come home with me, won't you? And never leave?"

"Is that what you want?"

"It's what I wanted from the first time I saw you, touched you, kissed you." His mouth blended with hers as they fell back onto the bed. It was a sweet kiss, but rife with hunger. He sampled the texture and taste of her lips before breaching them with his tongue. He reclaimed her mouth with the gentle thrusts and lazy strokes that characterized his kisses. They sent desire curling around her breasts and weaving between her thighs. But the time wasn't right for them to give way to their physical needs, and Arden was gratified that Drew was sensitive enough to realize it, too.

Pushing her away gently, he sat up. His eyes darted around the room. "God, this is a depressing place. Let's go home."

Matt was elated over having such an appreciative audience. His parents sat on the living-room floor on the oriental rug and applauded his playful antics, which became wilder by the minute. He somersaulted and jigged and ran in circles until he toppled over backward and bumped his head on the leg of the grand piano and set up a howl.

"You'd better put him to bed before he gets any more wound up," Mrs. Laani cautioned. She'd been dabbing copious tears of happiness out of her eyes ever since Drew and Arden came through the front door, arm in arm, looking grubby but radiant.

"Okay, Bozo, you heard the voice of authority." To quell Matt's tears, Drew lifted him up to straddle his neck. His hands caught in his father's thick blond hair. Arden placed her arm around Drew's waist as they ascended the stairs.

Arden decided that they had waited too late to calm Matt down. He was uncontrollable, bucking their attempts to snap him into pajamas. "Pee-pee," he kept repeating.

"Maybe it's not a false alarm," she said. Drew looked highly skeptical. He was wondering how many more delays were going to keep Arden and him from their own bed. His body was raging. He made his decision quickly.

Off came the pajamas, off came the bulky overnight diaper. Matt was carried into his bathroom and placed in front of the training potty. He did the deed, to his mother's overwhelming praise and his father's astonishment. Matt beamed up at them and submitted to their hugs and kisses of congratulations. Even Mrs. Laani was summoned to join the celebration. Such adoration was tiring. As soon as he was redressed for bed, Matt curled up into a ball and fell asleep, one chubby arm strangling Pooh Bear.

"We made a great kid," Drew whispered, his arm keeping Arden close.

"We certainly did," she concurred, snuggling against him. "Before I gave Ron the five thousand dollars, he told me he had sterilized me after I had Matt."

Drew's curse was vivid. "No wonder you walked around here like a zombie during those weeks."

She shivered, and he placed his other arm around her as well. "That's why I protested so much over seeing a doctor. I didn't want you to find that out. I was already keeping one secret from you."

"It doesn't matter, Arden. We don't need any other child—"

"No," she cried softly, not wanting to disturb their sleeping son. "He was lying. He only told me that to terrorize me."

"That sonofabitch," he said viciously.

"That's why I was so relieved and happy after we left the doctor's office. Remember?"

His hand found her breast and fondled it lovingly. "I remember," he rasped.

"The doctor said there was no reason why I couldn't have as many children as we want."

He branded a kiss on her forehead. "I'll love them if we do. But it won't bother me if we don't. I'm going to be the top-seeded professional tennis player next year." She squeezed his waist to show him she fully agreed. "Then I can gracefully retire. I have a wonderful son. And I have a wife whom I love with all that I am. What more could I ask for?"

They gave the sleeping boy one final good-night kiss and left the room. The hallway yawned before them, and they were both suddenly self-conscious and nervous.

Drew looked down at her. "I can't help wanting to rush you into my bed again, but I know you like to be courted."

Her eyes took on a dreamy glow. "That was before I was married."

"And now?"

"Now I want to make love with my husband."

"I need to clean up."

"So do I."

"I'll use the bathroom downstairs. Fifteen minutes?"

She smiled, glad that he was going to leave her alone to prepare for him. "Or less."

She bathed and shampooed quickly, blew her hair dry, scented herself with perfume and moisturized her skin with lotion. The negligee she had brought home the day her world fell apart was still in its long, flat box. She shook out the transparent violet folds and slipped into it. Its sheer covering only enhanced her nakedness beneath.

She was reclining against the pillows when he came in, wearing only a terry-cloth wrapper around his loins. It rode low, just below his navel with its whorl of dark golden hair. She tracked the intriguing pattern of hair up a silky narrow strip to the spot where it fanned out over the broad expanse of his chest.

Locking his eyes with hers, he walked to the bed, unsnapped the wrapper and let it fall. Unashamed, she looked at him.

"That's pretty," he said of the new nightgown. His eyes traveled down the slender column of her throat to the curves of her breasts. Beneath the gossamer fabric, he could see her nipples. The material clung to her thighs and legs, outlining their shape. Her slender, high-arched feet were chastely crossed.

"Thank you," she answered.

"I like you in that color."

"I'll remember that. I like you in that color, too."

He flashed her a wide grin. "I need to work on my tan. It has paled in the last week." Leaning down, he slipped one finger into the V at her bosom and peeped inside. "Yours needs work, too."

The tantalizing touch of his finger near her nipple made her breath falter. Her breasts rose and fell against his finger, and her eyes took on that slumberous quality that made desire concentrate in his loins.

"Arden," he whispered. He lay down beside her facing the opposite way, resting his head on her thigh. "I love you. I've hated being separated from you. Let's never be apart again."

"Never," she vowed, running her fingers through his hair.

He parted the folds of her nightgown and laid his hard cheek against her silky skin. "You smell so good," he murmured. He kissed her navel, consummating his love for it with his tongue. "You had my son. Carried him . . . here." His lips glided over her abdomen as he flicked the responsive flesh with his tongue.

"Yes," she breathed. She turned her head into his warmth, pulled his scent into her body by taking deep breaths of it. His body hair felt good against her face, her lips. Her mouth encountered the deep dimple of his navel and explored it inquisitively.

"Oh, God, Arden." His fingers dug into her hair, pressing her head nearer.

"Each time I felt the baby move, I'd think about you." Her arm slid around his hip. "I wondered what you looked like, prayed that you'd be a good father to my child, imagined what I'd say to you if we ever met."

"I thought about you, too. I knew you were healthy, so I couldn't see you as overweight or too thin. But I was curious about what you looked like, your personality, your motivation for having a stranger's child. I wondered if you ever thought about me."

She smiled against the golden nest that surrounded his manhood. "Yes. I did." His whole body convulsed when first her lips, then the tip of his tongue, touched him. "Drew," she murmured, "when you . . . collected the . . . the . . ." She couldn't bring herself to ask, and she didn't want to speak of Ellie now. Not now. Not when his hand was closing over the curve of her derriere and drawing her toward his mouth.

"I was alone," he said, divining her thought. His breath stirred the dark down that sheltered her feminine mystery.

"And had I met you before then, seen you, thoughts of you might have conflicted with thoughts of my wife." He planted an ardent, intimate kiss at the point of the triangle, using all his mouth.

The love play went on and on until desire was flowing through them like warm, thick honey. He turned to her, kneeling between her thighs and parting them lovingly and slowly. Just as tenderly, he draped her thighs over his and slid his hands under her hips, lifting her to him. His gaze fused with hers just as he sheathed himself in her.

Working his hands up her back in a sensuous massage, he brought her upward to face him. He sealed her mouth with his in a kiss that declared his eternal need for her. His hands stroked up her rib cage to her breasts. Touching them, he marveled over their lushness, their womanly heaviness. Then his thumbs lightly circled the love-swollen nipples.

"Drew, do what I never felt Matt do."

He understood. Lowering his head, he lifted her breast to his mouth. Her nipple was drawn between his lips with sweet tugging pressure. He suckled her gently, but with an urgency that continued to build. Responding to it, her body milked him, contracting and releasing until their passions reached a summit. When the crisis was imminent, he gently lowered her to her back and followed her down. With one final surge, he imbedded himself deep within her and gave her all his love.

The earth swirled around them, timelessly, direction-less, in uncharted chaos. They didn't mind. They had created their own private universe in each other. Jealous-ly, they guarded it. It was a long time before they returned to a world more mundane and less splendored.

"Arden, I love you." He braced himself above her and gazed down at her replete body with unqualified love.

"I love you. From the first. Irrevocably."

"Tell me everything. From the beginning. Fill me in on all the details I don't know, no matter how insignificant. I want to know how you felt when you learned you had conceived. What did you think and feel when you discovered I was the man who had fathered your child? How did you find out about me? Let me experience it all with you."

Painstakingly, she began, leaving out nothing, neither the heartache nor the joy. Her quiet voice drifted on the cool ocean breeze that wafted through the open windows and caressed their entwined naked bodies.

Loving lips frequently got in the way and promised that the best chapters of their life together were yet to unfold.

Books by Erin St. Claire

Silhouette Desire

Not Even for Love #7
Seduction by Design #41
A Kiss Remembered #73
Words of Silk #139

Silhouette Intimate Moments

A Secret Splendor #29
Bittersweet Rain #76
Sweet Anger #93
Tiger Prince #112
Led Astray #120
Above and Beyond #133
Honor Bound #144
The Devil's Own #180
Two Alone #213

ERIN ST. CLAIRE

has pursued several careers, but there is no occupation she enjoys more than writing. When asked why she writes romances, she replies, ''I believe in happy endings and I love a love story!'' Erin St. Claire is a pseudonym for Sandra Brown, who also writes as Rachel Ryan.

COMING
NEXT MONTH

#13 SEIZE THE MOMENT by Ann Major

Someone had tried to kill top model Andrea Ford, and she
fled to Mexico in a search for safety and peace. Her trip
was a dismal failure until she met Race Jordan. He was a
dream come true—exciting, courageous and determined to
have Andrea for his very own. But time was running out
for them, and her past threatened to destroy all their hopes
for the future.

#14 DEEP WATERS by Laurey Bright

From the moment Dallas Thorne met Nick Kane, she knew
she was in over her head. He was irresistible, exciting,
dangerous—and very much a man. She had every reason
to fight the attraction and she did—from the steaming
jungles of Enigma Island to its silvery beaches. But finally
the floodgates broke, and they were both swept into a
future neither could, or would, deny.

AVAILABLE THIS MONTH:

 *Silhouette Intimate Moments*

Rx: One Dose of

DODD MEMORIAL HOSPITAL

In sickness and in health the employees of Dodd Memorial Hospital stick together, sharing triumphs and defeats, and sometimes their hearts as well. Revisit these special people next month in the newest book in Lucy Hamilton's Dodd Memorial Hospital Trilogy, *After Midnight*—IM #237, the time when romance begins.

Thea Stevens knew there was no room for a man in her life—she had a young daughter to care for and a demanding new job as the hospital's media coordinator. But then Luke Adams walked through the door, and everything changed. She had never met a man like him before—handsome enough to be the movie star he was, yet thoughtful, considerate and absolutely determined to get the one thing he wanted—Thea.

Finish the trilogy in July with *Heartbeats*—IM #245.

Silhouette Special Edition

**In May, Silhouette SPECIAL EDITION
shoots for the stars with six heavenly romances
by a stellar cast of Silhouette favorites....**

Nora Roberts
celebrates a golden anniversary—her 50th Silhouette
novel—and launches a delightful new family series, THE
O'HURLEYS! with *THE LAST HONEST WOMAN* (#451)

Linda Howard
weaves a delicious web of FBI deceit—and slightly embellished
"home truths"—in *WHITE LIES** (#452)

Tracy Sinclair
whisks us to Rome, where the jet set is rocked by a cat
burglar—and a woman is shocked by a thief of hearts—in
MORE PRECIOUS THAN JEWELS (#453)

Curtiss Ann Matlock
plumbs the very depths of love as an errant husband attempts
to mend his tattered marriage, in *WELLSPRING* (#454)

Jo Ann Algermissen
gives new meaning to "labor of love" and "Special Delivery"
in her modern medical marvel *BLUE EMERALDS* (#455)

Emilie Richards
sets pulses racing as a traditional Southern widow tries to run
from romance California-style, in *A CLASSIC ENCOUNTER*
(#456)

**Don't miss this dazzling constellation of romance stars in
May—Only in Silhouette SPECIAL EDITION!**

*previously advertised as *MIRRORS*